GOLD CLASH

Praise for

GOLD CLASH

"Steve Westover has written a fast-paced, thought-provoking story of action, intrigue, and even a spot of romance. He takes historical facts and weaves them into a compelling tale that's hard to put down."

—Gregg Luke, author of *Deadly Undertakings*

"*Gold Clash* is a gritty thriller that delivers a powerful dose of action combined with the perfect measure of historical significance for the LDS reader. Westover instantly draws the reader in and takes them on a non-stop ride. This hunt for gold and power will not let go until the final page."

—K.C. Grant, author of *Venom*

GOLD CLASH

STEVE WESTOVER

BONNEVILLE BOOKS
AN IMPRINT OF CEDAR FORT, INC.
SPRINGVILLE, UTAH

ISBN 13: 978-1-4621-1097-1

Published by Bonneville Books, an imprint of Cedar Fort, Inc.
2373 W. 700 S., Springville, UT 84663
Distributed by Cedar Fort, Inc., www.cedarfort.com

LIBRARY OF CONGRESS CATALOGING-IN-PUBLICATION DATA

Westover, Steve, 1974-
Gold clash / Steve Westover.
p. cm.
ISBN 978-1-4621-1097-1
1. Mormons--Fiction. 2. Historical reenactments--Fiction. 3. Teenagers--Fiction. 4. Treasure troves--Missouri--Fiction. 5. Gangsters--Fiction. 6. Missouri--Fiction. I. Title.
PS3623.E876G65 2012
813'.6--dc23

2012035230

Cover design by Erica Dixon
Cover design © 2012 by Lyle Mortimer
Edited and typeset by Melissa J. Caldwell

Printed in the United States of America

10 9 8 7 6 5 4 3 2 1

*Dedicated to the youth and leaders of the Hamilton Branch,
the Far West Ward, and my friends and neighbors
in Caldwell County, Missouri*

Also by Steve Westover

Defensive Tactics

Crater Lake: Battle for Wizard Island

(1)

THE STENCH FROM THE PILED bags of garbage in the entryway assaulted Ace's nostrils as he stepped over the threshold from the cluttered front porch into the filthy bungalow-style home. Draping a heavy duffel bag over his shoulder, Ace rubbed his nose with the back of his hand.

"Uncle," he called, finding a light switch near the front door. He flipped it on and called again. "UNCLE!"

Ace looked through the doorway into the living room but didn't dare step in further for fear of stepping on a half-eaten tuna sandwich or twisting an ankle on scattered beer bottles. He checked his watch and prepared to yell louder when he heard a muffled voice coming from upstairs. His eyes scanned the staircase, and his nose twitched with disgust. He examined the banister then placed one hand on the rail and stepped over a moldy donut.

"Uncle, where are you?" At the top of the stairs, Ace peeked through a door on the left and saw a brown blur scurry past a full-size mattress on the floor. He set his bag inside the doorway with a clank and then continued down the dingy hallway.

"I'm in here," a voice called.

Ace stepped forward and eyed a closed door. He looked from side to side and then knocked quietly. "Uncle Alex, are you in there?"

The door creaked open and Ace's eyes widened. "Uncle Alex—" he started, but his gaze wandered from his uncle. The room's sterile environment opposed the filth that defined the rest of the house. Fluorescent lights brightened walls that were sheeted in white plastic, giving the room the anesthetic feel of a makeshift hospital. "Interesting place."

Alex Nicas's puckered lips flattened in an attempted grin. His suit coat was unbuttoned and his collar loose, absent the usual silk tie. Alex held his arms wide and then hugged his nephew in a stiff embrace. "Acacio, it is pleasing to see you. Have you finished making the arrangements?"

"Yes, the plan's in motion. Today's the day."

Alex Nicas removed the round glasses from his rodent-shaped face. His shoulders loosened with a visible sigh, and he stepped behind a desk at the center of the room to sit. His small body looked like it would be devoured by the oversized chair.

"That is good, Acacio. And my former associates, have they been agreeable?"

Ace smiled as he rubbed the soul patch dangling from his lower lip. "I think I have everyone in line. They needed some prodding at first, but I can be very persuasive."

Alex laughed. "I'm sure you can. You have done very well, and you've been far more useful to me than your father ever was. I plan to reward you handsomely."

"Thank you."

"Instead of living the peasant life like your father did, you'll be wealthy beyond your wildest dreams. You'll possess power and prestige second only to mine."

Ace smirked and bowed his head in deference to his uncle. "I like the sound of that."

"Once we obtain the resources, I'll use my contacts and infrastructure to grip the syndicate by the throat."

Ace smiled at his uncle's attempted grin because it made him look like a constipated rat.

"It will all be mine . . . again," Alex Nicas said.

"The men want leadership. They are loyal to you, Uncle," Ace said.

Alex Nicas shook his head as he scoffed. "No. They are loyal to themselves. Make no mistake, if we fail to deliver all that we promised, they will not be forgiving."

"Yes, Uncle. Of course you're right."

"After our success today, I'll come out of hiding and no one will dare contest me." Alex leaned forward and placed his wrists on the edge of his desk. He put his spectacles on his nose, looked at the monitor, and began typing.

"Uncle, one last thing," Ace said, standing in front of the large desk with his hands held behind his back.

"What is it?"

Ace smiled. "I brought something for you. I left it in the other room. Come look."

The older man glared at Ace and exhaled an exasperated breath.

"It will only take a minute. Please."

Alex nodded and slowly stood.

"I'm going to show you something that will change our lives. It's monumental. I promise," Ace said as he prodded his uncle toward the door.

Alex stood at the edge of the clean room, eyeing the filth on the other side of the doorway.

"It's worth it. Come," Ace said, motioning forward.

Ace watched his uncle take a pained step into the dingy hallway as if avoiding cracks in a sidewalk. Motioning with his hand, Ace ushered his uncle into the next room. Ace followed him in and closed the door.

"Check this out." Bending over, Ace picked up the duffel bag. With his back turned to his uncle, he unzipped the bag and pulled out an item, letting the bag fall to the floor. Turning slowly, Ace hid the item behind his back.

"What is it, Acacio?" Alex checked his watch. "We have much to do and little time for games."

Ace took a deep, cleansing breath. "I've told you, Uncle, my name is 'Ace.'"

Brushing the comment aside, Alex turned back to the door. He reached for the knob but stopped to look over his shoulder.

Ace stood with a stiletto clenched in his outstretched hand.

The dull yellow light from the overhead fixture glimmered off the blade. "Thank you, Uncle Alex. You have given me everything I need to step into your old role in the syndicate . . . but I no longer need *you*."

Alex faced his nephew and stood as tall as his small frame would allow. His jaw hardened and his eyes glistened with anger. He removed his glasses, tucked them into his shirt pocket, and then glared into his nephew's eyes. "Do you honestly think my men will follow you?" Alex spat.

Ace stared at his uncle, his expression flat. "Like you said, they are loyal only to themselves . . . and those who provide the paycheck. That will be me."

Wrinkles formed at Alex's eyes as he studied his nephew. His lips puckered. "Do your best and do it quick, or I will make you pay."

Ace nodded. With his fingers folded tight around the hilt of his knife, he lunged at his uncle. Alex stepped to the side and landed his elbow between Ace's shoulder blades. Ace fell to his knees and then jolted as his uncle kicked him in the gut with his pointy Italian shoes. He moaned and looked at his uncle standing above him. Moving the blade to the other hand, Ace swiped and connected with Alex's calf. Alex slumped over to grab his injured leg. Ace angled the blade upward and stabbed his uncle's chest. The blade penetrated deep. Ace jammed it in further, and his uncle's eyes widened with pain and surprise.

Staring at his uncle, Ace twisted the stiletto, then pulled it out and stabbed twice into his uncle's abdomen. He pushed his uncle to the right and leaned out of the way, causing Alex Nicas to collapse onto his side on the wood floor.

Ace glared at his dying mentor. He removed the gold cuff links from his uncle's wrists and tucked them into his pocket, claiming them as his own. He then rummaged through his duffel bag and removed rubber rain pants and a poncho. After dressing in the rain gear, he pulled the hood over his head and placed goggles over his eyes. Reaching back into his bag, he took out a machete.

Ace swallowed the bile rising in his throat as the coppery smell of blood filled his nostrils. His shoulders rose, and he shivered in disgust. Shaking his arms, he hopped up and down softly like an athlete psyching himself up before a game.

Ace's mouth tightened and his forehead creased as he raised the machete over his head and then hammered down onto his uncle.

After a few minutes, Ace studied his gory work and set the machete on the floor. He raised the blood-spattered goggles onto his forehead and then removed three new items from his duffel bag: a butcher knife, some pruning shears, and a hacksaw.

(2)

CLAY HEARD SNICKERS AS HE slid next to the window on the front row of the fifteen-passenger van. A boy whispered, "Nice Mohawk." Clay turned in his seat and rubbed the sides of his shaved head, staring down the two young boys in the row behind him. Instant silence.

"Hey, don't worry about it. I like your hair," one girl said from the third row. The left corner of Clay's mouth twitched.

Clay turned around, stuffed his earbuds into each ear, and stared into the early morning darkness. He rubbed the back of his neck and wondered how he had ended up in a place like this.

Clay glanced at the girl who claimed the seat beside him. He raised his chin in appreciation of her cute but unusual Mormon punk appearance. Her dark bangs hung low across her moderately shadowed eyes, and two red-streaked pigtails stuck straight out above each ear. She wore long lime-green shorts with black and white striped socks pulled to her knees, and a black T-shirt with a name emblazoned on the front. Clay didn't recognize the name. *A local band?* he wondered but didn't care enough to ask. The van door slammed shut, and the lights went out.

"Hi," the girl said, glancing at Clay. "I'm Liz."

Clay gave a half nod, but it was too early to be friendly. He gazed out the window, but there was nothing to see. Even in the daylight, there wasn't much except cornfields and cows. He couldn't care less about either. His eyes glazed over.

Time passed, and the blacktop roads turned to gravel. The van jolted as it hit a large pothole, and Liz jostled against Clay, her head bobbing, lurching her back into consciousness.

Liz rubbed the corner of her eyes with her fingers. "Are we getting close?" she asked, clearing her throat. Clay didn't respond. Nudging his elbow with her hand, Liz waited for Clay to remove his earbuds. "Are we close?" she repeated.

"No idea. I don't even know where we're going," he said in a low, gravelly tone. "Or what I'm doing here," he mumbled.

"Well, why are you here?" Liz asked.

"Mom thinks I need to make some church friends," Clay said with a mellow chuckle. "So here I am."

Liz smiled. "I saw you at church Sunday, but that's different," she said, pointing to his Mohawk. "Are you moving in or just visiting?"

Clay grunted.

"Welcome to Missourah," Liz said with a thick hillbilly accent.

Clay's eyes drooped, but he managed a crooked grin. "Thanks. It's a little different here."

"A little?" Liz laughed. "So, what's with the hair?"

"Football starts next week. It's tradition."

Liz nodded. "Yeah . . . cool. It would look great with a little red."

Clay winced as he looked at Liz's appearance, unsure if he wanted to accept her fashion advice. "Thanks. I think I like it the way it is."

Liz shrugged and turned away. Clay faced the window, reinserting the earbuds. On the horizon, he noticed the first shaving of daylight peek in between the rows of corn.

After three turns and five more minutes of boredom, the van pulled through a cattle gate and stopped at the edge of a pasture.

The door slid open and the interior lights brightened, but the young passengers remained lumped in their seats. "Up and at 'em, kids! Come on. Out of the van!" a man hollered. Another van pulled up alongside.

Clay climbed out after Liz and stood near the back of the van while the rest of the kids followed, moaning and shuffling their feet. The two boys who had teased him about his Mohawk engaged in a playful shoving match while a group of girls stood close by, whispering and giggling. Clay spotted a couple of athletic-looking boys and moved toward them but stopped when they scooted away to join their friends. Clay stood alone at the rear of the group.

"Hello, kids. I'm David W. Patten."

The man was dressed in a Joseph Smith–styled cream shirt and trousers held up with brown suspenders. Clay looked at the other kids in confusion. He tapped the shoulder of a boy in front of him, "Isn't that Bishop Taylor?"

"Yeah. Shhh."

"Well, why did he say his name was—?"

"Shhh."

Clay scowled and his eyebrows furrowed as he inhaled the fresh morning air. At least it was as fresh as air can be standing in a cow pasture.

Sliding along the van behind the rest of the group, Clay scooted next to Liz and touched her elbow. "Liz, what's going on?"

"We're about to find out," she whispered.

Bishop Taylor beamed from ear to ear as he looked at the groggy expressions on the assembled youth's faces, but then his face became somber, and he spoke earnestly. "Brothers and sisters, we are here today because a grave injustice has been committed. Just last night, three of our brothers were abducted by mobbers and taken across the county line into Ray County. We're here to rescue them."

The gathering group jolted visibly as their sleepy minds attempted to make sense of what was being said.

"I am David W. Patten. In 1838 I was an apostle of the Lord and captain of the militia at Far West. This is Charles C. Rich," Bishop Taylor said, pointing to a younger man in the group.

Without further explanation, C. C. Rich opened the back of the van and removed a shotgun. He handed it to one of the other adults, along with some ammunition. He continued until five shotguns were in the hands of leaders. "We've tracked our brothers and their abductors to a location nearby. They need our help. As a legally organized militia at Far West, in Caldwell County Missouri, called to action by Judge Elias Higbee, we are going to free our brothers. Are you with me?"

No one answered. A cow mooed.

"I said, ARE YOU WITH ME?" A few confused mumbles rose to meet the sun that was poking up from behind a thicket of trees. C. C. smiled. "Follow me! Oh, and stay close. I don't want anyone to get captured or shot during this rescue." Sliding the pump action on the shotgun, C. C. placed the gun on his shoulder and started jogging at a modest pace.

Clay chuckled and met Liz's gaze. "Is this for real?"

"Yeah, Clay, we're really going to free our kidnapped friends," Liz said with a grin. She blew the hair out of her eyes, watching him, but Clay's expression remained even. "Clay, it's a reenactment."

"A reenactment of what?"

"The Battle of Crooked River."

Clay smiled and his head bobbed. *Sweet!* "Uh, what's the Battle of Crooked River?"

*****

Following the rest of the group, Clay jogged through the hovering fog along the rugged cow path. As the trail entered a wooded ravine, one leader slowed, raising his hand in a fist. The group stopped and waited in silence. Clay watched as C. C. Rich wandered a short distance into the woods and then halted. The brush rustled, and the loud mooing of cows interrupted the silence as a small herd of cattle rambled down the ravine in front of the group. C. C. Rich turned to look at the group, his eyes excited and bright.

"We're getting close." He lifted a finger to his mouth to quiet the energized chatter and then motioned forward.

Clay walked slowly, watching each step to avoid any land mines left by the cows. Morning rays snuck through the leaves, lighting the path. The humid smell of grass and cow pies filled Clay's nose, and the chirping of early birds in the trees filled his ears. Behind him, a man walked with his shotgun ready, peering into the woods and occasionally stopping to take aim. The man never fired his weapon, but he was ready.

Around a bend in the trail, the grove of trees lowered into a grassy clearing. A covered wagon and four simple tents camped in the center of the grove. Horses were tethered to a nearby tree. White smoke rose from a breakfast campfire and mingled with the thin layer of fog. Clay strained his eyes to see. Three men, their wrists shackled, sat at the front of the wagon, while four men sat near the fire, laughing and eating their meal.

Clay studied the shackled prisoners but was distracted by the smell of bacon. *Mmmm.*

David Patten moved alongside C. C. at the front of the group, whispering before heading farther down the trail. C. C. raised his fisted hand, and the company halted. He knelt on one knee, and the company crouched quietly in place. Pointing with two fingers to his eyes, C. C. then motioned for the other armed men to spread out and take cover behind trees. The men crept into position.

Clay couldn't help but smile at the primitive military operation taking shape in front of him.

"No one fires until Captain Patten gives the order," C. C. ordered quietly. "'God and Liberty' will be the signal." Clay found himself nodding. "O'Bannion, get close to their camp and report what you see."

A man Clay assumed was O'Bannion descended from the path, hiking cautiously through the trees. Each step was deliberate as he crept down the gentle slope toward the camp, the rising sun lighting his back.

A loud burst of gunfire killed the morning silence. O'Bannion reeled backward and fell to the ground holding his face.

Clay flinched at the sound, but there was a momentary silence.

"GOD AND LIBERTY!" David W. Patten yelled into the morning air.

Steam wafted from the shotgun barrels as a flurry of gunfire erupted. The Far West militia attacked, slinking closer to the wagon with each reload of their weapons.

Clay watched as the shackled prisoners tried climbing beneath the wagon for safety. After a brief moment, they were dragged from their hiding place and held out as human shields by two of the captors.

From the flank position on the other side of the wagon, David W. Patten emerged from the woods with his gun drawn, firing. He paused behind a thick oak.

The captors abandoned their prisoners and fled as the entire camp was caught in the chaos of a full retreat. Shots fired on both sides as men scrambled for cover.

When the volley stopped, Patten stepped from behind the tree to watch the enemy retreat but was met instantly by a barrage of fire. The gun fell from his hands, and Patten collapsed, twenty yards from the wagon.

Clay blinked, unsure of the scene he had just witnessed. Gunshots rang out and an abductor fell to the ground. The skirmish only lasted a few moments before the pasture fell silent once again. The only sound was the gentle lowing of cattle, and the only smells were grass, bacon, and gunpowder.

The youth remained crouched on the trail when the first calls rang out.

"Durphee!" came the call.

"I'm okay."

"Emmett—Higbee—Phelps."

"I'm fine." "Here." "Yeah, I'm okay."

"Patten."

There was no response.

"Patten!" C. C. Rich repeated.

Clay looked to the location where he had seen David W. Patten fall. Bishop Taylor played the role, lying on the ground, curled up and holding his stomach. "Here," he muttered feebly. "I'm here."

The men from the company raced to Patten's side. They hovered around him, tended his wounds, then carried him into the camp and laid him inside the wagon box.

Kids filtered into the grassy valley near the wagon. Some checked out the wagon, while others stood next to the campfire. One boy picked up a plate and finished eating the captor's eggs and bacon. Clay absorbed the scene: trampled grass, shafts of light filtering through the leaves and haze, moaning from the injured warriors. Still on the trail, Clay turned to the left and then the right, but the path was clear—except for Liz. Still crouching, she appeared to be watching the wagon box and David W. Patten.

"Pretty intense, huh?" Clay said, but Liz didn't respond. "I said, pretty intense, wasn't it?" Clay repeated with greater emphasis.

Liz's body flinched, and her head swiveled to look at Clay. "Yeah . . . intense." She watched in silence for a moment longer and then stood, the indifference replacing the concern on her face. She chuckled softly. "Dad's kind of overselling it."

"Dad?"

"Yeah, Bishop Taylor . . . I mean, David W. Patten. Dad."

"Your dad is Bishop Taylor?" Clay asked.

Liz nodded.

Clay nodded in return and grinned. "Got it. The whole wild child look makes perfect sense. Of course. You're the bishop's daughter."

Liz scowled. "What's that supposed to mean, Mr. Mohawk-man?"

Clay held up his hands to block himself from Liz's fiery eyes. "Hey, no worries. I figure hair is pretty harmless as far as rebellion goes. At least it's all my mom will let me get away with."

Liz's eyes softened, and her head tilted. "So what are you rebelling against?"

"Me?" Clay dressed his face with his most innocent look and then smirked. "Nothing. Mohawks are just tough." He winked and then looked back to where Patten lay in the wagon. "Oh, and by the way, I'm sure Patten . . . uh . . . your dad . . . will be fine."

Liz looked unsure.

"He's an apostle. He probably has some kind of special spiritually protective force field around him or something. Or the others will just give him a blessing or something," Clay responded. "No worries."

Liz nodded. "Hey, everyone's gathering at the wagon. It looks like Brother Younger's going to say something."

"Brother Younger?" Clay asked.

"Yeah, sorry. I forget you don't know anybody yet. Brother Younger is playing Charles C. Rich."

"Oh. Okay."

Liz motioned Clay to come closer. "Come on. Let's find out what's going on."

(3)

C. C. Rich stepped onto a stump and waved the kids over. He wore blue jeans and a beige, short-sleeved collared shirt, with a red bandanna tied around his neck and a cowboy hat topping his head.

"Nice outfit," Liz mumbled.

Clay took another look at Liz's green shorts, knee-length socks, pigtails, and black shirt. He smirked at the irony of her mockery.

"Hardly authentic for pioneer apparel, but a decent effort," Clay suggested.

The entire company of adults and kids huddled around C. C.

"Brothers and sisters, I have good news." He paused for dramatic effect. "We have rescued our friends. They appear to be unhurt, and they are grateful for our efforts in the rescue. And the mobbers have retreated."

"Woo-hoo!" one of the kids hollered. A couple of kids clapped as they began congratulating themselves.

C. C. waited for the excitement to die down. He raised his arms and motioned downward. "Hey, brothers and sisters, I have something else to say."

Some of the kids quieted, but others continued in their mock celebration.

"I also have bad news."

The group slowly became quiet.

"Our success has come at a heavy cost. Seven brothers have been wounded. Our friend and guide, Patrick O'Bannion, has been killed. Without him, we would not have found our brothers and we could not have staged this rescue. We mourn his loss. And his family, who are not members of our church, will be deeply saddened. Please remember them in your prayers." C. C. stood on the stump, reflecting quietly. "We have also lost Gideon Carter."

Even though C. C. was still putting on a show, Clay felt a strange stab in his chest. He looked at Liz and could tell by her somber expression that she was also feeling something. Even though the men had died nearly 175 years ago, it felt fresh, like it had just happened.

"What about Elder Patten?" Liz asked.

C. C.'s shoulders hunched. "We don't know yet," he said quietly. He straightened, standing tall once again as he addressed the group. "Our leader has been seriously wounded."

"Will he make it?" one of the kids shouted.

C. C. shook and lowered his head. "I don't know, but it doesn't look good."

"Did you give him a blessing?" another kid asked.

"We did. The faith of our brethren is united, and our prayers are raised to the heavens. I know our Heavenly Father has heard our plea, but I don't know if it's the Lord's will that Elder Patten be healed. Time will tell."

Liz's lower lip stuck out, and she looked at Clay. "What are you grinning about? Two men died and another is seriously wounded. They don't know if he'll make it."

Clay scratched his Mohawk with his fingertips, trying to subdue his smile. "Sorry, Liz. I'm just impressed. That's all."

"Impressed with what?"

Clay whispered in Liz's ear. "Everything! The gunfight, C. C. looking so sad, pretending Patten won't make it."

"Pretending?" Liz asked. "You realize Patten might actually die."

"Yeah, whatever."

Liz shrugged and moved to stand next to another friend, leaving Clay alone again at the back of the group.

"Here's the rest of the bad news," C. C. continued. "One of the mobbers has been killed."

The kids cheered.

"No. That's nothing to be happy about. We had hoped it wouldn't come to this. We are a militia from Far West, in Caldwell County. We have crossed the county line to free our friends and have killed a citizen of Ray County."

The kids looked at each other. *So what*?

"It's like crossing the border and killing a person in another country. Some people could say we've just declared war," C. C. said, grave concern showing on his face. "We need to get out of here . . . fast. Gather your things. We'll hitch the wagon. Be ready to move out in five minutes. We have a long hike ahead of us."

"A hike?"

"It's a long way back to Far West—nearly thirteen miles," C. C. explained.

"What about Patten? Will he make it that far?" Liz asked.

C. C. scrunched his eyes. "I hope so." C. C. nodded to one of the other men.

"All right. Let's move out."

(4)

HITCHED TO A WHITE PICKUP truck, the covered wagon came to a stop at the pasture gate. Tents, sleeping bags, pillows, and even some backpacks were transferred from the vans to the wagon.

"I hope you brought good sneakers or hiking boots. We've got a long walk ahead of us today," Jimmy Younger said, lifting the cowboy hat from his head.

Clay glanced at his tennis shoes. He lifted one foot to look at the worn sole and then looked at Liz's thick combat boots. "Nice."

Jimmy waved his hat high over his head. "Oh, and one last thing before we go . . . electronics please." Grumbles filled the morning air, and Jimmy laughed. "That's right, bring them on over. I want iPods, PSPs, anything with Nintendo on it, and of course . . . dun-dun-dun . . . cell phones." Angry youth surrounded Jimmy, sniping and murmuring. Jimmy shifted in place, looking as if a convict was ready to stab him with a shiv.

"Hey, easy, kids!" Sister Nichole Blair said as she moved next to Jimmy to offer reinforcement. "Lindsay Brooke, you be nice," she scolded a girl playfully.

Jimmy watched the woman and smiled. Her brown hair was held back by a thick elastic headband, and her faded, well fit jeans and boots made her look like a cowgirl. His curious stare lingered a little bit long.

Liz brushed by Jimmy, handed him her cell phone, and mumbled under her breath. "Creeper."

Jimmy grinned. "Huh?" He thought for a moment and then turned his gaze away from Nicki and whispered at Liz. "But she's cute . . . and single."

"Ooh, gross! That's Sister Blair!"

Jimmy laughed. "Yeah, I know."

Nicki held a backpack open as the kids placed their contraband electronics inside. "Yes, you'll get them back. No, you don't need the cell phone for emergencies. Yes, your mom can get mad at me if she wants. No, it's not a violation of your constitutional rights," she said, responding to the myriad complaints.

"Thanks, Nicki. Man, those kids are tough," Jimmy said with a crooked grin. "I was never like that."

Nicki laughed. "Right, Jimmy. Whatever you say."

Jimmy took the bag of electronics and placed it in the front passenger seat of the van. "Take good care of this stuff, or we'll have a riot on our hands," Jimmy told the driver.

When the vans were empty and the wagon was full, the vans pulled away, spitting up a cloud of dust as the kids looked on, shocked that they were trapped in the middle of nowhere without music or texting.

Standing on the back lip of the wagon, Jimmy called out, "Okay, gather up! We'll be hiking mostly along gravel roads, but there will be a couple of blacktops along the way as well. We'll stay on the left side of the road so we can see oncoming traffic. For safety, please walk two by two or single file. We don't want to stick out into the roads. Our number-one rule is that no one is allowed to get smashed by passing traffic." Jimmy watched as the kids found buddies to walk beside and formed into a long line. "Ah, Bishop Taylor, nice of you to join us. How are you feeling?" Jimmy asked.

Bishop Taylor had changed out of his pioneer clothing and now wore blue jeans, hiking boots, a gardening hat, and a plaid shirt that looked like a picnic blanket. He held a long, carved walking stick. "I'm doing great," he said with a smile. "But David W. Patten is getting worse," he announced to the group. "Patten is badly injured. We'll transport him in the wagon while I hike with you guys."

"All right then. Bishop, will you lead the way?"

"Absolutely. Jimmy—I mean, Brother Younger, you bring up the rear. Everyone else, fall in."

"Lead on, Bishop."

Bishop Taylor looked both ways on the gravel road and then turned left, planting his walking stick, pulling himself forward like a gondola captain.

Jimmy shepherded the long line of kids and leaders through the gate and then solicited Clay's help. Together they closed and chained the cattle gates. Removing his cowboy hat, Jimmy wiped the sweat from his brow with his bandanna and then looked at his Velcro watch. At 7:00 a.m., beads of perspiration already lined his forehead.

"Ready for a scorcher?" Jimmy asked.

Clay paused for a moment and then smirked. "Why not? Bring it on."

(5)

IDIOT! HURRY UP!" SCUD WHISPERED. He was crouched on all fours, looking into the freshly dug hole. He wiped a dirty hand on his white ribbed tank top and then cleaned the other on his jeans.

"Would you shut up already? Here, take the shovel," Jack said, passing the handle to his partner. Jack stood atop a black casket with his shoulders rising above the moist cemetery grass. His head swiveled and his eyes roved. Even though the grave was hidden in shadow, the sunshine brightened nearby tombstones as the morning fog burned off.

"Come on. Get that thing open and let's get out of here," Scud ordered. "Wait, hold on. I hear something."

The man in the hole stooped over, hiding himself below ground. "What is it?" he whispered.

"I don't know . . ." Scud said but then became silent and dove behind the base of a neighboring obelisk monument. Taking quick breaths, he peered around the base to see a groundskeeper driving a golf cart. Scud jerked his head back. The sounds of the humming motor from the cart and the jostling of tools came closer. He held his breath and then sighed with relief as the cart continued down a trail, through a patch of trees, and out of sight.

"Get the truck. I've almost got it," Jack whispered from inside the hole. Kneeling on top of the casket, he wiped a thin layer of dirt away and ran his finger along the side of the lid. "Gotcha," he muttered.

Scud rushed to the side of the hole and peered at his partner inside. Jack slid a latch, and a portion of the casket lid loosened. He lifted the viewing lid and peered inside, his eyes tight, half closed. A thin grin brightened his expression, and his gaze relaxed. Propping the lid open with his free arm, Jack reached to the spot where a head would lay, but in its place a brick rested on a satin pillow next to a scroll. He carefully scooped the scroll into his hand and grabbed the brick. Removing his arm from the casket, he let the lid fall shut.

Scud hurried to the truck and climbed in. Looking through his side mirror, he slowly backed up, watching as Jack placed the items on the grass and prepared to pull himself out of the grave. A grin suddenly crossed Scud's face and he hit the gas and the truck accelerated backward. Then he slammed on the brakes and skidded to a stop over the opened grave. A loud snort escaped his lips when he saw Jack fall back into the hole with a shriek. Scud hopped out from the driver's seat and walked around to the grave. Jack lay with his back on the casket, his arms lifted protectively.

"Scud, you moron," Jack complained. Scud snorted with laughter, walking back to the driver's side. Jack climbed out of the hole, picked up the scroll and the brick, and hopped in the passenger seat, slamming the door. "Go already."

The tires spun in the dewy grass and then caught traction, and the truck sped down a gravel path and onto the main road. The tires squealed as the rusty beige-and-red truck raced away from the Richmond cemetery.

*****

Sitting in his golf cart near the cemetery fence, the groundskeeper scrambled for a pen and a scrap of paper. Then he scribbled down a partial license plate number and a description of the truck.

(6)

CLAY FELT EACH ROCK PRESS through the worn soles of his shoes. Moving to the shoulder of the gravel road, he walked along the soft grass for relief. Jimmy whistled beside him as he walked, but Clay trudged along in silence.

"So comc on, you'vc got to talk to mc at somc point. I'm bored out of my mind over here," Jimmy said, exaggerating the whine in his voice. He snuck a sideways peek at his hiking partner.

Clay smirked but didn't speak.

"Hmmm. Try this on for size." Jimmy began to sing—loudly and opera-style. "I'm hiking by my friend, but I don't know his na-ame. He won't say a word, and this hike is so la-ame."

"Dude, seriously? What are you—twelve?" Clay mumbled as he noticed kids turning around to stare. "You're embarrassing."

"Oh, really? I'm so sorry. I had no idea," Jimmy said, his brow furrowing with concern. He then broke into a broad smile. "Hah, I'm just kidding. I know I'm embarrassing. That's the fun part of being me. You should give it a try sometime. Besides, I finally got you to spcak, didn't I?"

"You're not like other people are you?" Clay commented. He stepped on another sharp rock and winced.

"No, he's not," someone called from a cluster of hikers five yards ahead.

"Who said that?" Jimmy hollered.

Nicki raised her hand.

"Oh." Jimmy chuckled. "Sweet of you to notice."

Clay's face twisted like he had just sucked on a lemon. "I think that lady's flirting with you."

"With me? No. Well . . . maybe," Jimmy admitted with a smile. He turned back to Clay. "So, are you going to tell me a little bit about yourself, or am I going to have to make something up—and sing about it?"

"No!" Clay responded, more forcefully than he intended.

Jimmy's eyebrows rose. "Well?"

"Yeah, come on, Clay. I'd like to hear this," Liz said as she slowed her pace to join them. "So, you've been in Missouri for like a week now. It's a little different than California, huh? What do you think?"

"Well, I'm hiking in the middle of nowhere, and it is stinking HOT out here. I've already got some kind of bug bites on my legs—lots of them—and it feels like I'm breathing water." Clay paused but didn't wait for a response. "So in other words, Missouri is lovely."

"Those are chigger bites," Jimmy said, glancing at Clay's legs. "When Adam and Eve were cast out of the Garden of Eden, they entered the lone and dreary world. 'Misery!'"

"You mean Missouri, right?"

"Yeah, sure. Whatever," Jimmy said with a grin. "Tonight, when you really start feeling those bites, you'll be in misery."

Liz laughed. "Don't worry, Clay. I've got something you can put on them."

"Chiggers are like Satan," Jimmy said.

Liz rolled her eyes.

Jimmy continued. "A chigger bites you and you don't think much of it because it's just a mild irritation. I mean, one bite really isn't the end of the world. But before you know it you'll have hundreds of tiny little bites, all enticing you to scratch. At first you think you can resist. Then you'll scratch one, but as soon as you do, you'll have to scratch another, until finally, you're going crazy scratching them all. They'll turn red and fill with pus—pure torture."

"Uh . . . gross," Liz said.

"So what's your point?" Clay asked.

"Easy—don't scratch that first chigger bite, because it just gets easier to give in after that."

Liz stopped on the path and folded her arms, staring at Jimmy. "You just snuck in a spiritual thought," she accused.

Jimmy chuckled. "Now that's just silly. Man, I hate chiggers."

"Brother . . . ," Clay started.

"Younger," Liz reminded.

"Jimmy," Jimmy corrected.

"Brother Jimmy?"

"No, just Jimmy," he said.

Clay shook his head. "Okay, Jimmy. What's the deal with the whole running-with-guns-through-the-woods thing this morning?"

"Pretty awesome, huh?" Jimmy said, his head bobbing.

"Actually, yeah. But there's got to be a point. Usually there's some kind of a lesson. Don't get me wrong, the gunfight was pretty cool—just not what I expected. And, why all this walking? You're killing me here."

Jimmy thought for a moment and then shrugged his shoulders. "What do you think, Liz?"

"Are you asking me because you don't know? Or are you testing me?" Liz asked.

Jimmy nodded. "Yes."

Liz smiled. "Sometimes it's important to remember history. You know, to learn from mistakes."

"Yeah, I guess that's true," Jimmy agreed. "History is full of surprises. Anything else?"

"Not that I can think of," Liz said.

"Don't look at me. I'm the one asking," Clay said. "Clearly I don't know squat."

"Well, good. If we don't know squat, we're bound to learn something, right?" Jimmy asked.

Liz looked up ahead to see the group gathering in the grass beneath a pair of tall walnut trees. "Hey, it looks like they're stopping for a rest up ahead."

"Finally," Clay moaned. "My feet are killing me."

"So what do you hate the most: the chiggers or the rocks?" Jimmy asked, noticing Clay wincing again at the pain in his feet.

Clay thought for a moment and wiped the sweat from his temples with the sleeves of his shirt. "Being here at all," he said.

"The hike or Missouri?"

Clay nodded. "Yes."

*****

Leaning against the walnut trunk, Clay removed his shoes and socks. He massaged the bottoms of his feet and then set them flat, allowing the meadow grass to tickle his toes. A few roving adults sprayed a mist over the grumbling group and passed out bottles of water. Clay snatched one up and gulped, replenishing the sweaty moisture that dampened his shirt. Setting the water bottle at his side, Clay glanced at his feet, wondering how many chigger bites he was inviting. He closed his eyes, unconcerned. The grass felt good.

Bishop Taylor stood at the front of the group and waited a moment until all eyes were on him. "My friends, I regret to inform you that David W. Patten has died." Clay's eyes opened with surprise. He looked at Liz, but her expression was blank, as though she had expected the bad news. Bishop Taylor continued. "It is sad to lose a man as noble as Elder Patten. He is the first martyr of the Restoration."

The group was silent. Maybe it was because they were all so tired, but Clay didn't think so.

"Fortunately, before he passed away, his wife was able to visit him beside his deathbed. Even with his life hanging by a thread, Elder Patten's thoughts focused on the gospel of Jesus Christ. Before he died, he begged his wife, no matter what happened, to never lose the faith." Bishop Taylor paused. "The most important thing to Elder Patten before he died was bearing testimony of Jesus Christ."

Clay listened to Bishop Taylor, but his thoughts drifted to the image of a dying man and his wife. He closed his eyes and scowled. His lips tightened and the muscles in his jaw bulged as he thought about the injustice of the man's death.

"Hey, buddy, mind if I sit here?" Jimmy asked, plopping to the ground next to Clay. Clay remained silent with his eyes shut tight.

"Sad, isn't it? David Patten died a hero," Jimmy whispered.

Clay's eyes reopened, and he examined his feet closely and then pulled on his socks. With a weary sigh, he placed his shoes back on his feet. The warm breeze rustled the leaves and blew across Clay's body like a desert wind. He wiped the sweat from his reddened face and stood as Bishop Taylor concluded his remarks.

"All right, kids. We've hiked about four and a half miles so far. We've got about another six before we make camp for the night." The kids, and even a few adults, moaned in chorus. "Everyone doing okay?" Bishop Taylor asked. There were a few responses, but mostly just nodding heads. "Drink lots of water and let's keep moving. If the mobbers are following us, we don't want to make it easy for them to catch us."

The kids filed back into line, and Clay resumed his position at the back. He limped for the first two steps, but his feet quickly remembered their purpose, and he strode evenly, wincing only when the occasional sharp rock stabbed his sole.

(7)

"I DON'T GET IT. IT'S A BRICK."

Scud laughed at his stupid partner.

"Why go through all this trouble for something I can get from a dozen different buildings in town? Why steal a brick from a grave?" Jack asked.

Scud considered the question as he flipped his blinker and turned onto a rural state route. The crusty beige pickup belched down the road, the missing muffler amplifying the roar of its engine.

"And what about the scroll? Why can't we open it? What does it say?" Jack asked.

Brushing aside the questions, Scud focused on the curving road. "Shut up. Your job is to help me dig, not badger me with questions."

"Seems reasonable to me," Jack whined, picking up the heavy brick. He turned it over in his hands. It was smooth on every side.

Scud grimaced when Jack tossed the brick to the floor. He slammed his fist into the side of Jack's chest.

"Awhhh. Hey, what was that for?" Jack asked, rubbing his chest.

"Show some respect," Scud growled.

"It's a stinking brick, man. Relax." Jack rubbed his chest again and scowled at his partner. "Ouch."

He picked up the scroll from the crease in the middle of the seat and held it close to his eyes. "It's like a little fortune cookie." He held the scroll to his eye, as if he were peering through a spyglass. Then twisting the ribbon in place, Jack slid the ribbon from the center of the scroll, leaving a thin red mark where the ribbon had been. He looked at the ribbon more closely. It had once been red but now was a dark, rusted black.

"I'm just going to take a little peek," he said, sliding the tied ribbon further down the scroll.

"Put it down, you idiot. It's not yours to mess around with," Scud reminded him.

"Come on. What's the harm? I can slide the ribbon back into place. No one will ever know the difference."

Scud tapped on the brakes. "Fine, but hold on for a minute until I can stop."

Scud turned the old pickup from the blacktop highway onto a thin dirt road. Dust and gravel spat from behind the monster tires as he raced farther into rural desolation. After a few minutes of driving, he spotted what appeared to be a deserted property. To the left, high grass sprung up in front of a rusted green cattle gate. The truck stopped.

Jack threw his door open and jumped out of the truck to unwind the short chain that held the gate closed. The gate swung open and Jack climbed back in the passenger side.

Scud drove across a meadow and down a rolling hill toward a line of trees. He stopped just short of the trees and killed the engine. He grabbed the scroll and got out of the truck, stepping toward the front. Jack joined him. Carefully he removed the blackened ribbon. The scroll creaked as the torn edges unrolled.

"Well, turn it over," Jack said. "Let's see what that baby says."

Sliding one hand between the hood of the truck and the scroll, Scud flipped it over, careful to keep the fragile document in one piece. He hovered over the scroll, squinting as the sun reflected from the yellow page.

"What is it?"

Scud's eyes narrowed, but he didn't respond. "Here, take a closer look," he prompted. Moving to the side, Scud allowed his partner a better view of the page. "I'm going to grab the brick," he said, moving toward the passenger-side door.

Jack nodded, but he seemed more focused on the document in front of him.

Returning to the front of the truck, Scud placed the brick on the hood with a buckling thud. Removing a slender pocketknife from his pants, he extended the blade and then shaved a corner off the brick like he was whittling a stick. The top layer of brick scraped away easily, revealing a golden shimmer. Jack's eyes brightened with greed.

"Here. Check this out," Scud said, handing the brick to his partner. "It's gold." He laughed. "This is a golden brick, and that," he said, pointing to the scroll, "is a piece to a map." He cackled some more.

Jack held the gold brick and scraped more of the thin façade away while Scud gingerly picked up the scroll and rolled it, returning the ribbon to its proper place at the center.

"That don't look like any map I've ever seen," Jack said.

Scud grinned from ear to ear and placed the scroll back on the front seat. Removing a handgun from the back of his pants, he approached his partner, the gun held down, tight against his leg.

Scud watched as Jack admired the weight of the heavy brick and the gold gleaming from its hiding place underneath the baked mud. Jack looked up in time to recoil at the gun aimed at the center of his chest.

The crack of gunfire invaded the silent morning, and birds evacuated nearby trees and lofted into the air. Jack fell to the ground, holding his chest and sputtering for air, blood gurgling in his mouth. Scud bent over his dying partner, picked up the brick, and spat. Pulling a phone from his pocket, he speed dialed and waited. After three rings, Scud heard light breathing on the other end, but no one spoke.

Though he was in complete isolation with no living soul within earshot, Scud covered the receiver with his hand and whispered into the phone with a deep, confident tone. "I've got it."

(8)

Agent Emily Mathews pulled the black SUV through the gate to the Richmond City Cemetery. The gravel beneath the tires crunched as she pulled up next to a man standing beside his tool-packed golf cart. Removing a notepad and a pen from the glove box, she grinned at her partner. "Are you ready for your first official day outside of the bean counter department?" she asked.

"Absolutely," Agent Paul Stephens said. "And for the record, Emily, it's the Financial Analysis and Cyber-Crimes Unit."

"Of course it is, Paul," she said with a crooked grin.

They opened the doors in concert.

The humidity assaulted Agent Mathews the instant she stepped out of the air-conditioned SUV. Her blonde hair was pulled back in a tight ponytail that hung to the nape of her neck, and she wore her usual FBI uniform: black slacks and jacket with a pale purple dress shirt. Feeling the instant barrage of heat, she removed her jacket and threw it into the backseat.

The forty-something groundskeeper leaned against his cart, lifting up his sunglasses to get a better look. He spit a stream of brown tobacco juice onto the ground as he leered at Agent Mathews's every movement.

Agent Stephens cleared his throat and glared at the man with warning. "Hello, I'm Special Agent Paul Stephens, and this is Agent Mathews," he said, tilting his head toward Emily but keeping his gaze locked on the man.

"FBI agents?" he asked with a chuckle. "Wait 'til I tell my girl about this. I thought I'd get Joe from the Richmond PD or one of those freckle-faced boys from the sheriff's department." He looked at both agents, nodded, stood up straight, and adjusted his clothing as if trying to act official. "Um, what exactly does the FBI care about vandalism at a cemetery?"

"We're just here to gather some information," Paul said.

Emily inched forward, placed her hands on her hips, and met the man's gaze. She smiled. "You called the police this morning about a truck speeding away from the cemetery. You gave a partial Missouri license plate ATG 36. Is that correct?" she asked.

The man looked at the two agents and shrugged. "Yeah, that's right. It was an old farm truck . . . 1990s pickup . . . big tires . . . kind of rusty. We got lots of those around here. Mostly tan with a reddish stripe down the side."

"Were you able to see the driver?"

"No."

"Were there any passengers?"

The groundskeeper thought for a moment. "Yeah. One I think."

"Can you give us any description all? Male or female? Fat? Bald? White? Asian? Anything you tell us could be helpful," Agent Stephens said.

"Well, can't tell you much," the man said, staring at the ground. He scratched his belly, causing it to bounce lightly. "They must have been here a while though."

Agent Mathews scrunched her eyes. "Why do you say that?"

The grounds man chuckled and then spit, hitting a spot near his foot. He rubbed the brown juice into the gravel. "Because that's a big hole."

Mathews cocked her head. "What hole?"

The man looked at the agents again and tilted his shades up to stare them directly in the eye. He grunted, hopped in his cart, and motioned them to follow.

Paul looked at Emily. "So I guess we follow him. What do you say, boss?"

Emily glared playfully. "Really? I asked you not to do that."

"Do what?" Paul asked innocently as he climbed into the passenger seat of the SUV.

Emily closed the door and faced Paul. "I already feel awkward. I shouldn't be your 'trainer,'" she said, making quotation marks with her fingers. "I'm sure Agent Stark thinks he's pretty funny. The big jerk."

Paul smiled. "Yep. Stark's getting a kick out of it. Give the guy a little power and this is what you get. Big surprise."

Emily laughed.

Reaching over, Paul grabbed Emily's hand and squeezed. "Don't worry about it. You can be my boss for the next two weeks. You're definitely the cutest boss I've ever had," Paul said, leaning over and kissing his girlfriend on the cheek. "Besides, that's what I get for transferring units. One suggestion though."

"Sure, what?"

"You might want to get a move on. It'd be a little embarrassing for my 'trainer' to lose a witness driving a golf cart," Paul teased.

Emily looked ahead to see the golf cart disappearing around a stand of mature trees.

After catching up, Emily and Paul climbed out of the SUV and stood next to their witness, who was staring into a hole at the top of a casket. "That's the hole. I suspect that's what they was doing here."

Emily nudged Paul with her elbow. "Casket looks pretty new for an old grave," she said, nodding to the ancient limestone grave marker.

"Was anything disturbed inside the casket?" Paul asked.

"Don't know. I was told to wait for the police."

"Good."

"Here, hold my jacket," Paul said, removing his black suit coat and handing it to Emily.

"Yes, sir," Emily said.

Paul lowered himself into the hole and then snapped on blue latex gloves. Standing atop the casket, he bent over and lifted the viewing lid. He peered into the vacant casket. "Nothing. It's empty," Paul said.

Emily considered the implications. "Was the body moved? Is

there any organic matter left inside—jewelry, clothing, anything?"

"I don't think there ever was a body here. It's clean." Paul stood. "Why would someone bury an empty casket?"

"What do you care?" the groundskeeper asked. "Doesn't the FBI have anything better to do?"

Emily focused on Paul atop the casket as she responded to the man. "We care about the people who were here, and we want to know what they're up to."

"If you know who they are, why are you asking me about them?" the man questioned.

His gruff manner sounded hostile, but Emily could tell he was just curious. Still, his questions distracted her from focusing on the puzzling scene. *Is this how people feel when I ask them questions*? Emily took a breath, plastered a cheerful expression on her face, and refocused on the man. "We don't know the people. We know the truck," she answered.

"Wait a second. It looks like there *was* something in here," Paul said from inside the hole.

"What do you see?"

"Whatever was in here was rectangular . . . heavy. A box of rocks, maybe."

"A box of rocks, huh?" Emily asked with a chuckle.

Paul shrugged. "Yeah, probably not. I'm just spitballing here."

Emily looked into the trees and then into the sky, sighing as Paul climbed out of the grave. The warm breeze blew her blonde ponytail onto her shoulder. "Well, Paul, it looks like we may actually have a little investigating to do here." She rubbed her hands together with excitement.

"Good. I didn't want to go back to the office anyway."

(9)

THE PROVIDED LUNCH WAS ONLY a peanut butter and jelly sandwich, an apple, and a piece of beef jerky, but Clay was happy to eat it. Finishing his sandwich, he drank a second bottle of water and looked around the shaded grass at the other kids, hoping to find someone he could convince to share half an apple or a bite of sandwich. The small lunch only seemed to awaken Clay's appetite.

Clay's stomach grumbled as he searched the group, who mostly lay in the grass. Many were on their backs, blocking the sun from their eyes, while others were sprawled on their bellies. Clay chuckled at the scene and wondered about the possible chigger repercussions. The group reminded him of a kindergarten class lying down for their afternoon nap. But instead of whiny little five-year-olds, these were teenagers and adults.

Clay's bare feet throbbed, and the muscle above his right knee twitched. The smell of warm grass, pollen, and sweat filled his nose, and the quiet buzz of cicadas in the trees enticed him to sleep. Fighting the urge to close his eyes, Clay stood and spotted Bishop Taylor. Even the Bishop was lying on his back with his hat over his face—sweat darkening his shirt around the neck and armpits.

Clay walked around the carefully strewn bodies as he foraged for leftovers.

"Hey, Clay."

Clay looked around for the whisperer.

"Clay. Over here."

He turned to see Jimmy sitting up.

"How are those feet?" Jimmy asked.

"Fine," Clay lied.

"You still hungry?" Jimmy asked. Clay moved closer but didn't respond. "I've got something for you." Jimmy held out a Snickers bar and smiled. Clay's eyes lit up.

"Where'd you get that? And how is it not a puddle of chocolate?" Clay asked, again wiping the sweat from his face with the sleeve of his shirt.

"I've got my ways," Jimmy said. His weary words lacked his usual joviality and charm. "I'll split it with you."

Clay sat next to him, gladly accepting the halved candy bar. He took a bite, savoring the feel and sweetness of the cool chocolate.

"Do you have a mini-freezer in your pocket or something?" Clay asked. "This candy bar is awesome. It's still cold."

Jimmy grinned. "We all have our little secrets, don't we? I'd love to tell you mine, but it's classified . . . sorry."

Clay took another small bite and looked at the resting hikers. Then he stopped as his eyes fell on Liz. She was staring back at him. He looked away quickly, pretending he didn't see her, but as his eyes wandered back to where she rested, he noticed her eyes locked on him. *Dang it!*

Clay motioned Liz to join him, and she quickly took a seat between him and Jimmy. Her face was red, but she looked otherwise unbothered by the heat. Her boots were still laced high and her black shirt appeared fresh, though Clay supposed that had to be an illusion.

Clay prepared to put the last bite of Snickers into his mouth but stopped. Though she wasn't bold enough to ask for his last bite, Clay noticed Liz lick her lips, as if savoring an imagined taste. He held out the remainder of his candy bar, and Liz took the morsel, popping it into her mouth.

"Thanks, Clay," she said. "That is soooo gooood."

Jimmy smiled at Clay's kind gesture and then turned away from the kids as he shoved his last bite into his mouth. He turned back toward them, chewing stealthily.

"I've been thinking about the question Clay asked. You know . . . why reenact the battle of Crooked River? And why do all this hiking when it's a thousand degrees out here?" Liz said.

"Oh yeah?" Jimmy said. "Did you come up with some profound answers?"

Liz thought but then hesitated. "Well, it's not really profound," she admitted sheepishly.

Jimmy winced. "That's okay. Most answers are simple."

"What you got, Liz?" Clay asked.

"I was just thinking that maybe the point of this whole thing is to test us like our ancestors were tested. Even when Patten was dying, he told his wife to keep the faith. Maybe we're supposed to remember to keep the faith, even when things are hard," Liz suggested.

Clay nodded.

"Sounds good to me," Jimmy admitted.

"Well, is that it? Is that the answer?" Liz asked.

Jimmy thought for a moment and smiled. "Sure."

Liz looked at him. Her eyes narrowed as she studied his expression.

Jimmy glanced at his watch and sighed. Taking a deep breath, he rose to his feet, cupped his hands to his mouth, and bellowed his best Tarzan yell. The resting dead began to stir.

Liz laughed at Jimmy's wake-up alarm, but Clay cowered away with embarrassment. "Dude, you really are a freak," Clay said, turning away from Jimmy.

"Yes I am. But even freaks need hiking partners."

Liz and Clay looked at each other, but neither volunteered to walk with Jimmy.

(10)

EMILY HELD THE PHONE TO her ear as she adjusted the air conditioner vent to blow directly onto her face.

"Yeah?" Agent Thrasher said, grunting on the other end of the line.

Emily imagined the pudgy black agent sitting at his desk in the field office, more focused on his doughnuts and coffee than on her phone call.

"Thrasher, are you listening to me?" Emily asked.

"Yeah, yeah."

Emily turned to Paul, covered the mouthpiece, and shook her head. "He's not listening." She uncovered the phone. "Thrasher, if you're paying attention, your next word should be anything other than 'yeah.' Can you do that?"

There was silence for a moment before Thrasher responded, "Yeah."

Holding the phone next to the stereo speaker, Emily turned on the car radio and cranked it up, blasting sound into the mouthpiece. She turned it off quickly, returned the phone to her ear, and listened as an expletive flew from Thrasher's mouth. "Thrasher—buddy—paying attention now?" she asked with a smile in her voice.

Thrasher grumbled. "What do you need? I'm busy."

"We confirmed the truck at the cemetery is the one we're looking for. The driver dug up a grave and removed something from a casket."

Thrasher's voice sounded like a tuba. "Our guy's a grave robber?"

"Looks like it. But it doesn't make any sense. We need to know what was inside that casket. We need to know what he's up to."

"I'll send a team," Thrasher said.

"Perfect. I'll have the local PD stay with the evidence until the forensics team arrives. Paul and I are going to check things out in town. See if anything unusual's been going on."

"Oh . . ." Thrasher paused. "Stark's looking for you. He's grumpy today."

Emily laughed. "Stark's grumpy? Who'd have guessed? Thanks, Thrasher." She thought for a moment, lamenting Agent Stark's new supervisory position. "Well . . ." Emily paused, "he knows how to find me if it's important."

"Yeah."

"Oh, and Thrasher, please put a rush on that forensics team."

(11)

SITTING IN FRONT OF THE Red Rooster Inn on Polo's Main Street, Scud held the mud-caked gold brick in his hands. His eyes gleamed like the sliver of gold peeking from underneath the crusty coating.

Noticing his once-white tank top was splattered with his ex-partner's blood, Scud set the brick beside him on the vinyl car seat, yanked the shirt over his head, and tossed it on top of the gold. An old woman walking with her grandson passed by, glancing with disapproval at Scud's lack of clothing. "What are you looking at?" Scud growled and pounded the glass with the side of his fist. The woman kept walking, her hand placed protectively around the child's shoulder.

Scud laughed as he hopped down from his truck and moved to the tailgate. Lowering it, he leaned inside, rummaging around shovels and buckets, sundry tools, and a pile of rocks until he located a threadbare maroon sweatshirt with the sleeves torn off and a V ripped near the collarbone. The shirt looked like it had been used as the official dipstick cleaner. Lines of black oil covered it, but that didn't matter. Scud put it on.

Entering the Red Rooster for a late lunch, Scud nearly took the doorknob off as he turned it. The walls were covered with folksy Americana art of tractors, cows, and, of course, roosters. The white textured ceiling was discolored by age and cigarette smoke. Except for a small group of farmers in overalls and camouflage caps sitting in the corner, the diner was nearly empty. Cigarette smoke billowed from the farmers' mouths between sips of coffee and daily gossip.

Scud sat in a red booth along the wall midway between the door and the counter. In the booth directly behind him sat another man with his back to Scud. Sitting back to back, the two men looked like strangers who would have little interaction in the real world. Scud's filthy clothes, foul odor, and greasy, straggly hair contrasted with the man's rich Italian suit and accented yellow pocket square that matched his socks and shirt. His dark hair was brushed smoothly across his forehead, and his olive skin glistened in the light. His round spectacles gave the illusion of filling out his thin, opossum-like face.

The man's gold cuff links caught a glimmer of afternoon sun through the side window as he sat with his hands folded in front of him. An errant thread poked out from a button on his jacket sleeve, and the cuff of the expensive shirt appeared worn. A cup of black coffee lay to his right.

Scud accepted a glass of water from the waitress, drank, and then motioned for a refill. He faced forward without even a hint at turning or leaning toward the gray-suited man behind him. Scud spoke as though speaking to someone directly in front of him. "That's a new look. Where's Mr. Nicas?"

Ace's knuckles popped as he clenched both hands into fists, and then he relaxed, placing them palm down on the table. "Mr. Nicas had a bad morning. I'm Mr. Nicas now."

Scud lowered his voice and stared at the top of his cup. "Nice suit. You've come a long ways, *Ace*. Poor boy makes good. I'm inspired."

Ace spoke through clenched teeth. "Are we going to have a problem?"

Scud started to speak but then paused as the waitress set down a fresh glass of water. When she was gone, he seethed through clenched teeth. "I brought you in because I needed your uncle's connections. I need nothing from *you*."

Ace stood, his back to Scud. "I think we need to have a more private conversation. Perhaps I can express my value in a way you will understand. *I* am Mr. Nicas, now. Got it?"

Scud shook his head, reaching to feel the gun tucked into the back of his pants. "Fine, junior."

"What did you say?"

Scud paused for a long moment. "Do you want to hear my report or not?"

Ace sat back down in his seat.

"We're on schedule. I have two more quick stops this afternoon, and by tonight, the final piece of our puzzle will be in place," Scud said with confidence.

"Will we be ready to make the delivery tomorrow?" Ace asked.

"Tomorrow? I wouldn't make any promises until we have the goods in hand. These aren't the kind of guys we want to disappoint." Scud scoffed, "Tomorrow?"

Ace pulled his phone from his jacket pocket and pressed some buttons. He waited for a moment. "Check your phone."

Scud patted his pockets, searching for his phone, and then pulled it out. He flinched as he saw the gruesome text photo of Alex Nicas.

"I'm not the kind of guy you want to disappoint," Ace said.

Scud's mouth hung open. He enlarged the photo with his fingers and swallowed. "Is that. . . ?"

Ace grinned. "Like I said, Mr. Nicas had a bad morning." He waited a moment. "Don't challenge me, Scud. There will be no hiding from me or my associates. Understand?" Ace paused. "I have already arranged for delivery . . . *tomorrow.* Do you have any questions?"

Scud stumbled over his words. "No, Mr. Nicas."

"Good. The plan is in motion. I'll text you the time and place for the meet. Make sure you're ready."

"Yeah, got it."

Ace lifted the mug of coffee from the table and held it close enough to his mouth to hide his lips, but far enough away to avoid any unintentional contact. "Where is your partner?"

Scud's words tumbled from his mouth in an incoherent array of rambling excuses.

"I didn't ask for an explanation. I asked you, 'where is your partner'?" Ace repeated.

Scud chomped on some ice from his cup. "He's in a field.

Dead," he whispered, the rasp of his voice making the words nearly imperceptible.

"Can you handle this on your own?" Ace asked.

"Yes."

"Or should I send someone to . . . help?"

Scud's lips tightened. "I said I got it."

"You best not disappoint. This operation means a great deal to me . . . more than I can express. *I* do not deal well with disappointment. Do you understand?"

Scud chomped on another piece of ice. "Got it, Mr. Nicas."

"Excellent. I will be watching."

(12)

CLAY LABORED WITH EACH STEP. His feet felt raw and beaten like tenderized steak. He could hardly wait for football to start, just so he could finally get a new pair of shoes. His damp T-shirt clung to his chest, and except for the thin Mohawk strip, his head was lobster red. Under his breath, he cursed the thin soles on his shoes and his stupidity in leaving his cap and shades in his pack, buried somewhere at the bottom of the wagon.

Glancing up ahead, Clay noticed a few of the kids sitting on the back of the wagon, stealing a free ride. They sucked water from orange Gott jugs, laughing and joking while the remainder of the group toiled behind. Clay glowered at the young boys hitching a ride, not that they noticed or would even care. Still it made him feel better, like somehow, by persevering through his pain, he had earned a moral victory.

"Punks," he muttered under his breath. "I wouldn't ride even if they asked me."

"Me neither," Jimmy confirmed. "Real men walk, right, Clay?" Jimmy turned toward his hiking partner and flexed his upper body with exaggerated manliness.

"Right," Clay agreed quietly.

"What was that? I didn't hear you," Jimmy prodded.

Clay did his best muscle-man chest flex, pounded his chest, and grunted loudly. “Whoa, ho, ho—real men walk,” he shouted into the air.

Clay noticed kids turning in response to his overzealous gorilla grunt. He looked away in embarrassment.

Jimmy slapped Clay hard on the back. “Nice! See, embarrassing can be fun . . . real fun.”

(13)

EMILY ENDED THE CALL WITH Agent Stark and stuffed the phone into her pocket. Her jaw clenched and she stretched her fingers as if preparing to scratch them down a chalkboard or across Agent Stark's face in a painful but therapeutic release of tension. She leaned against the driver's door as erratic thoughts of fresh opportunity and Stark's angry words swirled together in a cloud. Thrasher was right. Stark was grumpy, more so than usual, but in a way he had a right to be. The thought of her good news contrasted with Stark's grumbling annoyance brought a sliver of a grin to her face, and then the idea that she could escape from Stark's supervision—*forever*—made her smile.

Emily ran a hand through her hair and then tightened her ponytail as her stomach bubbled with a combination of nerves and excitement. A new team, new responsibility, and a new town; the possibilities were endless. Stark may not have liked being the bearer of good news—he made that very clear—but despite his threats, Emily's confidence surged and her dreams of career advancement soared.

She turned to open the car door but watched for a moment as Paul fiddled with his cell phone. Her smile faded and her lungs deflated with a gasp. Leaving Stark also meant leaving Paul. *What should I do? Will he understand?* she wondered. As if hearing her thoughts through the glass, Paul turned and flashed a smile.

Emily climbed into the black SUV and slouched behind the wheel. She closed her eyes and her shoulders rose. Then they dropped as she exhaled through pursed lips. Emily felt the weight of Paul's eyes pressing against her, and then he cleared his throat.

"Emily . . . everything okay?" he asked. Emily remained focused on breathing deeply as she gripped the steering wheel. Paul waited a moment, but the silence persisted. "Okay, then. What's next, boss?"

Emily scrunched her nose and tightened her grip on the steering wheel.

Paul's eyebrows furrowed. "Maybe we could visit the address where the truck is registered or run the owner's name through our databases for an alias? Or maybe we could research the name of the individual supposedly buried in that grave?"

"Paul, just give me a moment. I'm trying to think."

Paul bit his tongue as he absorbed the brush-off. He placed one hand gently on Emily's, but she pulled away. "Thinking about what?"

Would telling Paul about the offer for her new assignment make things better or worse between them? How would their relationship change in the short time she had left in Kansas City? She shrugged off the thought. It didn't feel fair to question how Paul might react, but still, she wondered. Emily didn't respond to Paul's question, but she watched as he turned away and looked out the passenger-side window across the bank parking lot.

"You're acting kind of strange. Is there anything you'd like to share?" he asked.

"No."

"Would you like me to drive while you *think*?" Paul asked, irritation creeping into his voice.

"No, Paul. Seriously, just . . . just relax."

Paul flinched and then turned and stared at Emily for a moment, but she remained still. He fidgeted and then returned his gaze out the window.

"Come on, boss. We're a team." He paused for a moment. "Hey, I've got a crazy thought. Why don't we think about the same thing so we can come up with some answers . . . together," Paul suggested.

Emily opened her eyes with sharpness, but quickly softened as she looked at her boyfriend. Her mouth quivered as she started to speak, but she stopped herself and then took another calming breath. "Sorry, Paul. I'm frustrated."

"The usual Stark stuff?" Paul asked.

Emily smiled in recognition of Paul's observant question. "Yeah, something like that." She paused, thinking, and returned her attention to the case. "I'm just not connecting the dots between the cemetery, the truck, and the other crimes. What's the common link?"

"Let's focus on what we know, starting with the truck."

Emily was thankful for the change of subject. "Agreed. We know the same truck has been identified at various crime scenes over the past week," Emily said.

"So what are the crimes and how are they connected?" Paul asked.

"Last week, there was a home invasion in Liberty. An old couple was bound to their chairs for about an hour while two masked men rummaged through their things."

"What was taken?" Paul asked.

"Nothing. At least nothing the couple noticed. Jewelry and cash were left untouched in a drawer next to the bed. Afterward, neighbors reported seeing a red-and-beige truck parked in the driveway."

Paul half chuckled and shook his head. "Bold."

Emily nodded. "Three days ago there was a break-in and vandalism at a museum in Independence. Some glass cases were shattered, and some books were strewn around, but nothing valuable was taken."

"And now we've got a possible grave robbery from an otherwise empty casket," Paul added.

Emily's head bobbed in agreement. Her brow furrowed as she considered the seemingly random crimes.

"Okay, there is definitely something unusual going on," Paul said, "but why are *we* here? Is Agent Stark just trying to tweak you again? Giving you another lame assignment to mess with your mind?" Paul waited for a moment, but Emily didn't respond. "From what you've described, there haven't been any federal crimes committed. What's the FBI's jurisdiction?"

Emily's eyes narrowed, her lips tightened, and then her eyes brightened with recognition. Her cheeks moved, almost imperceptibly, like she was trying to speak, but her mouth wouldn't open.

"Emily, what's going on here? There's something you're not telling me. What is it?" Paul questioned.

Without answering, Emily turned the key in the ignition and pulled from the bank parking lot. "We're done here."

"We are? Where are we going?" Paul asked.

Emily quickly considered her options and then made a decision. She bit the inside of her lip and hoped that an immediate detachment at work would help ease the transition in their personal relationship. She prayed silently, hoping that she was making the right decision. Feigning confidence, she blurted out her plan. "I'm taking you back to the field office to follow up on our leads. You know, shake the bushes and see if you can find any connections."

Paul crossed his arms, glaring at Emily. "Are you benching me? Seriously?"

"Of course not, but I need you at the office." Emily remained focused on the road, her hands placed responsibly on the steering wheel.

"What's happening here?" Paul murmured. "What did Stark say to you?" Emily ignored the questions. "You trust me, right? You can tell me if something's bothering you." Paul turned to look at his girlfriend, but her stoic eyes remained focused on the road.

The couple rode in tense silence back to the Kansas City field office, both anxious for the drive to end.

(14)

LIZ WALKED A FEW STEPS ahead of Clay while Jimmy pulled up the rear. Bishop Taylor and the wagon led the way.

Many of the kids, and even some of the adults, took turns riding on the back of the covered wagon. Clay watched jealously but wasn't prepared to show weakness by hopping on the wagon. He didn't need rest or a sip of cold water badly enough to declare his wimpiness to the world.

From behind, Clay heard the clippety-clop of horses. He turned to see four men riding in single file, their stern eyes focused on the wagon ahead. Each man wore a crusty cowboy hat and chaps; one even had a leather vest with tassels. Each had a bedroll tied to the back of the saddle with a rifle rolled inside. Two of the men were tall and slender. Another was short and squatty, while the fourth, presumably their leader, was broad and weathered. The man sat with perfect posture on the mountainous animal with his cowboy hat pulled low. His black handlebar moustache and stubbled face screamed, "Get out of my way!" The shadows hid what Clay imagined were cold, hollow eyes. As the man passed, Clay noticed that the man even smelled tough, with a balanced mix of musk, horse, and campfire.

Clay glanced back in time to see Jimmy grin and then pull down the brim of his hat as he tried to look as dangerous as the man on the horse. Clay took a couple of quick steps forward and tapped Liz on the shoulder, motioning her to look at Jimmy's artificial toughness.

Liz's eyes drooped and her face remained expressionless as she looked at Jimmy. "That's the most pathetic thing I've seen all day," she said in exaggerated monotone.

"Maybe, but the day is still young." Jimmy pointed toward the wagon. "Come on, guys. This doesn't look good. Let's see what's going on up there."

Abandoning his spot at the back of the hikers, Jimmy held the top of his hat as he jogged toward the wagon, which had stopped in the middle of the gravel road. Three of the horsemen surrounded the wagon with their weapons in hand, while the fourth circled the group on his horse, rounding them up like he was rustling cattle.

The leader sat astride his horse at the front of the wagon. When the entire group was gathered close, he tipped his burnt-brown hat. Clay was right; his eyes were steely and his expression grim. "Ya'll Mormons don't belong here!" the large man bellowed in a high, tenor voice. The warm breeze carried his words, but it wasn't as intimidating as Clay had expected. The inconsistency between the man's look and his voice caused a thin smile to appear. "You best get out, while we let ya," the man spat.

Clay snickered at the man's coarse but cheesy manner. Liz snorted and tried to maintain a straight face. Clay mumbled something under his breath, and Liz elbowed him as she tried not to laugh.

The leader glowered at Liz and Clay as he dismounted his horse. His mouth twisted as creases surrounded his squinting eyes. He walked toward Clay. Liz's feet shuffled backward, but Clay stood firm.

"You think this is funny . . . *boy*?" the man asked. The tip of his boot grazed the worn toe of Clay's sneakers. The man stood so close that Clay could smell peppermint on his breath. Clay remained silent. "You think you're special, don't ya?" the man roared, gazing around the group. "All you Mormons do . . . think you're special . . . think you're better than the rest of us. You're about to learn how wrong you are," the man growled, backing Clay into the side of the wagon. The mob leader reached his rough, meaty hand toward Clay's throat but stopped as Bishop Taylor stepped forward and called out.

"You will not touch the boy or anyone else here! Leave us to our journey in peace."

The men still on horseback laughed and aimed their weapons at Bishop Taylor.

The leader turned from Clay and Liz to the bishop. Clay sighed deeply but silently, surprised by the frantic beating of his heart. He looked at Liz. Her shoulders rose and fell with her rapid breathing. Clay reached at his side and clasped her hand, offering what little support and comfort he could spare. Her sweaty palm didn't squeeze back, but it didn't pull away either.

"You think you're pretty tough, don't ya?" the man seethed. He spat. "We'll see."

"Yes, we will," Bishop Taylor responded.

The leader spoke. "I know what you did down at Crooked River. You murdered a man. Don't think we is going to let that stand. Everything you have will be ours," the man said, spitting again. "Everything," he repeated. "I'm gonna take it from ya. Your land, your pride, your gold—your life! And if your women and children get in the way, we'll take them too. Yep, we'll take it all," he said with a menacing chuckle.

The group stood in silence, the only sound coming from the huffing of a horse and then the cocking of a shotgun. Clay spun around to see Jimmy pointing a weapon directly at the mob leader's chest. Seconds later, additional weapons cocked and pointed at the other mobbers on their horses.

"We don't want trouble," Bishop Taylor said, holding his hands in a conciliatory position.

The mobbers laughed. "You are trouble." Backing away, the leader grabbed the reigns of his horse, placed his foot in the stirrup, and gracefully mounted his animal. "We'll be seeing ya again . . . soon." Gently tapping the side of the horse with his heel, the mob leader rode back in the direction from which he came, the others close behind.

"Whoa! Who was that guy?" Clay whispered in Liz's ear.

Liz exhaled and smiled. "He's actually our old stake president," she said and then laughed. "Really nice guy, but I had no idea he could act so creepy. That was crazy," she said.

Clay looked down at Liz's hand still wrapped in his and then let go, wiping his moist palm on his shorts.

"Don't worry, Clay. I won't take it the wrong way," Liz offered.

Clay attempted to smile, but it was more of a grimace. *What is the "wrong way"?* he wondered. *Did she think I was making a move, or did she think I was scared?* Neither was good, he decided.

"Hey, Jimmy," Clay called out. "Who was he supposed to be?"

"Maybe Colonel Bogart, leader of the mob militia, but probably just one of the mobbers. Doesn't really matter," Jimmy said.

Nicki joined the group. "We may have taken a little creative license with that one," she said, grinning.

"Kind of gives you a flavor for the times though, *don't it*?" Jimmy said with a heavy drawl.

The crowd was humming as kids and leaders took a moment to get drinks before continuing the hike.

"Do you really think people were like that?" Clay asked.

"Heck yeah," Liz jumped in. "They burned houses, looted stores. They . . ."

Jimmy cut Liz off in mid-sentence. "Obviously, not every Missourian was an evil redneck." A grin crossed his face, the kind he usually got before doing or saying something ridiculous, but then he flattened his lips into a line and furrowed his brow.

"Uh-oh," Nicki said. She covered her mouth with her hand as she whispered to Clay and Liz. "He's going to try to get all serious on us."

Clay shrugged. "I didn't know he had it in him."

Jimmy smiled. "You know me so well." He paused for a moment and wiped the grin from his face, literally. When his hand passed in front of his face, his grin was gone and his expression serious.

"Sometimes we think of all Missourians from the 1830s as mobbers. It's kind of natural when we read journal accounts of the horrible things that happened back then. But that's no truer than thinking that every Mormon at the time was a wonderful, peaceful, faithful person. It just can't be true. I'm sure there were plenty of

Mormon hooligans who did their share of stirring things up."

"Hooligans, huh? Well, I guess, but—" Liz began.

"And you might think of it from the Missourians' point of view," Nicki suggested.

"I don't think so," Liz said. "Nothing justifies burning houses or killing or stealing land."

Jimmy nodded. "Agreed. Although, we killed one of the mobbers at Crooked River," he reminded. "Was that justified?"

Overhearing the conversation, Bishop Taylor joined in and placed his hand on his daughter's shoulder. She looked at the offending hand but didn't shrug it off.

"Liz, think of the fear the Missourians must have felt. They were individualists living on the western frontier of the country. From their perspective, they were invaded by a massive group of northerners trying to dominate an area of a southern state. The Mormons had a new religion that sounded fanatical to some people. The Missourians were suddenly overrun by a people with different political, social, and religious traditions. And the Mormons stuck to themselves. I don't think it's surprising at all that the native Missourians felt suspicious and defensive."

Clay listened carefully, but although the bishop made sense, Liz's indignation felt right. His sunburnt forehead crinkled. "This whole thing is nuts. Battles—mobs—apostles dying." He paused for a moment and then gazed into Bishop Taylor's eyes as if preparing for a challenge. "The mobber said that he would take everything the Mormons had, their land . . . and *gold*." Clay shrugged. "What gold?"

Bishop Taylor laughed. "Ah, you were paying attention," he said. "Our mobber kind of fudged his lines on that one." He smiled as he looked into the sky as if trying to find his thoughts in the clouds. "You know, there is actually a pretty interesting legend about Mormon gold. There have even been a few treasure hunts over the years."

Jimmy's head cocked with interest. "Really?"

Clay's eyes widened and his eyebrows rose. He saw Liz flinch, and he wondered if she was surprised by her father's admission.

Excitement shone in the bishop's eyes as if he were preparing to tell a ghost story around the campfire. He opened his mouth but then closed it as he peeked at his watch. "Oh, we're behind schedule. We've got to get moving." He turned to the rest of the group and shouted. "We head out in one minute. The mobbers may be back. We must gather to Far West for safety."

Bishop Taylor turned to Clay, Liz, Nicki, and Jimmy. "Of course, it's all fantasy and rumors. The gold, I mean. It doesn't really exist, but it's kind of a fun story." He glanced at his watch again. "I'll have to tell you about it later."

"But . . ." Clay said.

Bishop Taylor grinned. "Sorry. But it's time to move out."

(15)

Scud pulled the pickup truck to the shoulder of the road and flashed his hazard lights. He waited for a minivan and a tiny SmartCar to pass and then pulled back onto the quiet rural route. The engine roared and the monster tires turned slowly as he crept along, his eyes searching for his turn. Spotting the dirt road, he turned to the right. After a half mile, he made a left onto what appeared to be little more than a farm road with field grass growing in between the tire tracks.

Vast fields flanked the road on each side. Tall grass littered with thistles and weeds pressed against the rusty truck as it crawled over deep ruts. Putting the truck in park, Scud pressed a button activating the four-wheel drive. He inched forward. One tire leaned into the first giant rut, causing the truck to tilt toward the driver side, then he emerged on the other side. The dirt road became even and the grass, though still high, appeared to be casually maintained.

To his left, a line of trees stretched forward. Near the edge, a blue plaque with the profile of a man's face indicated he was in the right place—Haun's Mill.

Scud glanced at the informational placard but didn't care enough to read. The history of the place didn't interest him; only his current assignment mattered. The truck tires followed the dirt path and then halted as the line of trees cleared into a view of the small creek below.

Pulling a manila envelope from the glove box, Scud poured out a wide scrap of yellowed parchment. He set the paper on his lap and then removed the scroll from the seat. Unrolling it carefully, Scud laid the opened scroll next to him and flattened it gently. Picking up the scrap, he held it like a piece to a jigsaw puzzle, examining the contours and shape. His eyes transferred to the scroll as he searched for the proper placement.

After a moment of searching, he set the scrap next to the scroll. The piece was loose, but it fit. He read the section of the scroll immediately before the torn edge, and combined it with the previously missing scrap. Together they made sense.

Tossing the items onto the seat, Scud climbed out of the truck and lowered the tailgate. He grabbed the shovel and a small white pail and then walked into the trees. He peered down the steep bank into the shallow water and wondered how a mill could have ever functioned on such a mild stream. He climbed down the bank and hopped across the stream on wobbly stepping-stones. On the other side, he climbed out of the stream gully, using the shovel as a walking stick. Emerging atop the ridge, he searched the forest. He walked deeper into the woods toward the largest tree he could see and then veered to the right. He walked a short distance and stopped, his thin lips curling into a smile.

In front of him was a stack of rocks in a loose pyramid formation. The bottom stones were flat and wide, forming a stable base for the round rocks stacked on top. The cairn rose three feet high, marking the spot. Stepping close, Scud kicked off the top rocks, and then again, and again, until only the bottom layers of rocks remained. He bent over and hefted each remaining rock from its place until the formation was reduced to its foundation.

Using the shovel, Scud pried up each flat rock from the foundation. Underneath, the black dirt was pressed firm. Scud took a deep breath and then plunged the shovel into the dirt.

Sweat flung from his face with each shovelful of dirt he tossed aside. He dug for twenty minutes, but missed his dead partner after the first ten. Scud's chest heaved as sweat drenched his shirt. Stabbing the shovel into the ground again, Scud's arms vibrated as the shovel struck stone. He tested the soil surrounding the point of contact and then cleared the dirt from the top, scooping it out of the hole with the white pail. Standing inside the hole, Scud found the corners of a flat stone and stabbed again with his shovel.

The flat stone appeared to be approximately two feet square. Using the shovel as a lever, he pried the stone cover, revealing a simple wood box beneath. Scud slammed the shovel downward, splintering the wooden lid. Bending over, Scud looked inside, but the deepness of the hole combined with the shady trees made the darkness impossible to pierce. Scud lowered his hand and prepared to reach into the box, but he stopped as he took a deep breath.

His eyes hardened with courage, and he plunged his hand inside, scraping his arm against the splintered wood. His fingers searched the wooden box and then grasped the cool object. He gripped tight and pulled an inch-wide roll of tin out of the box. He held it in front of his eyes, made a face, and then shoved the artifact into his pocket.

(16)

CLAY GLANCED AT LIZ, A sly expression decorating his reddened face. "So, Liz, what do you know about this Mormon gold?" he asked quietly.

Liz walked silently beside Clay, her eyes focused on her black army boots. "I'm not sure I should say anything. My dad might get mad."

"Why would he get mad? And, seriously, how mad can he get? He's the bishop."

"Yeah, right," Liz said. "He can still get ticked. Trust me."

Clay's lips scrunched as he thought. "I'm sure it's okay. Besides, he said he'd tell us the story later. We're just doing a little studying. Call it preparation. We're really doing it for him, so we don't have to bother him with so many questions." Liz's head shook softly as she considered giving in to Clay's request. "Liz, come on. What are you afraid of? I won't tell anyone," Clay promised.

Liz slowed her pace, causing her to fall even farther behind the rest of the hikers to ensure the privacy of their conversation. Her whisper sounded like a mild rustle of leaves in the wind.

"What did you say? Can you say that again?" Clay asked.

"Yeah. We can't hear you either," Jimmy said from a few paces behind.

Liz's head swiveled as she looked at Jimmy and Nicki. She covered her face and rubbed her forehead.

"Forgot we were here, didn't you?" Jimmy asked. "Don't worry. I get that a lot." Jimmy took a few quick steps to catch up, and Nicki followed. The group walked slowly with Liz in the middle.

"You guys are funny," Liz said, dismissing the sudden interest in the story as simple chatter. "There's not much to it. Like my dad said, it's just a story."

Clay rubbed his Mohawk with eager anticipation. "Of course. We know that. It's just an old legend. Nothing to it, I'm sure," he said as he glanced toward Jimmy.

Liz's expression brightened. "Well, there are actually two different stories that I know about Mormon gold. The first one involves John Whitmer. Do you remember who he was?" Liz asked.

Clay and Jimmy looked at each other and shrugged. "The name sounds familiar," Clay admitted.

"Yeah, but there are tons of Whitmers from early Church history. I can't really keep them straight," Jimmy admitted.

"Okay, John was one of the original Eight Witnesses of the Book of Mormon."

Jimmy and Clay both nodded sheepishly, like they should have known that. "Yeah, of course, Eight Witnesses. Continue please," Jimmy said, trying to sound as official and intelligent as he could manage.

"So, John Whitmer saw the gold plates from which Joseph Smith translated the Book of Mormon. He was also the first Church historian." Liz looked for a hint of recognition from either Clay or Jimmy, but their expressions were vacant. "Didn't you guys ever go to Sunday School?"

Only Nicki nodded with understanding. "He lived near Far West, but when the Mormons were kicked out of Missouri, he stayed behind."

"Ah, yes. Very interesting," Jimmy droned.

Liz laughed. "You have no idea what we're talking about, do you?"

"Umm . . ."

"Just plead the fifth, Jimmy," Nicki suggested.

Jimmy turned toward Liz and looked her square in the eye. "In accordance with legal counsel, I will not incriminate myself further," he said with a curt nod and a goofy grin.

Liz just shook her head. "You're an *adult* leader, right?"

"So you're saying John Whitmer stayed at Far West when the rest of the Mormons were forced to leave?" Clay asked. "Why . . . and how? How was he able to stay behind?"

Liz looked at Clay, a confused expression crossing her face. "Actually, I'm not sure why he was able to stay."

"Maybe he had some friends in high places," Jimmy suggested. "Friends that protected him."

Liz's eyes flashed with recognition. "No, I remember. He was adamant about staying at Far West, so he quit the Church."

"Quit the Church?" Clay asked skeptically.

"Well, yeah. According to the rumors, someone high up in the Church asked him to stay in Missouri to keep an eye on things, hoping that someday they'd be able to come back to their homes and farms," Liz said. "The only way he could stay was to act like he quit the Church."

"So he 'acted' like he quit the Church so he could stay at Far West to keep an eye on '*things*'?" Jimmy made air quotes with his fingers and raised his eyebrows.

"Yeah, '*things*.' Land. Homes. *Gold*," Liz confirmed with a glimmer in her eye.

"Now we're talking," Clay said enthusiastically, and then his nose scrunched and his eyes narrowed as he thought. "Um, question . . . where did the gold come from?"

Jimmy scratched his head. "Everyone knows the pioneers were poor as dirt."

Liz gazed into the sky for a moment, concentrating to remember the tale. "Well, remember, John Whitmer was a witness to the 'golden plates.' "

"So maybe some Missourians thought the Mormons brought gold with them," Clay said.

"You have to admit, it kind of makes sense, at least for someone who doesn't believe in angels and prophets and stuff," Liz suggested. "The gold had to come from somewhere, right?"

Clay nodded. "So people just assumed the Mormons had gold."

"Exactly. So the legend says that John Whitmer stayed behind, buried the gold somewhere, and that's all I know. Story number one."

Jimmy nodded. "Cool."

"What evidence could anyone possibly have that could back up a story like that?" Clay muttered.

"You know, none of the witnesses of the Book of Mormon ever denied their testimony of seeing the gold plates. That would include John Whitmer," Nicki said.

"For someone wanting to believe that there is Mormon gold hidden around here, maybe that's all they need to prove the story that John Whitmer only pretended to leave the Church. And why else would he pretend to leave the Church to stay in Missouri unless he was staying to guard a treasure? I mean, who leaves the Church but stands behind their testimony for the rest of their lives?" Clay asked.

Jimmy grinned. "Actually, people fall away from the Church for lots of reasons. Doesn't mean they don't believe. But there's a big difference between believing and doing," Jimmy said. "HUGE difference," he repeated, stretching his hands out wide.

"Whatever," Clay said with disappointment. "You said there were two stories," he reminded Liz.

"The second is even less believable than that one," she warned.

"Lay it on us," Jimmy prodded.

"In the spring of 1838, Joseph Smith told David W. Patten to get his affairs in order so he could serve a mission."

"So?"

"So Patten did. He sold everything he had so that his family would be taken care of while he was gone. He bought gold," Liz said, completely unconvinced of her own words. "Of course he died at the Battle of Crooked River and never made it on his mission, but he was prepared. Right before he died, he was able to talk with his wife and tell her where the family treasure was hidden so she could take care of herself. When the Mormons were forced to leave Far West, she paid her way to Illinois but left the treasure behind, expecting that she would come back some day."

"That's it?" Clay asked, with a low grumble, clearly unimpressed.

Liz shrugged. "That's it."

The foursome walked in scorching silence along the back roads of Caldwell County. Jimmy's hands clasped together and his fingertips wiggled with giddiness. "I love a good treasure hunt."

(17)

SUPERVISORY AGENT RICK STARK SAT on the back corner of Paul's credenza. He folded his arms as a grin creased his thick face. His graying red hair wove together like steel wool, and his lazy gray eyes stared at the back of Paul's head. A single button held Stark's navy-blue jacket together in the front, but it looked like it was ready to pop.

Paul watched Stark's reflection in his monitor. At first he pretended not to notice the heavy mouth breathing, but then he thought better of ignoring his direct supervisor. Paul punched one last key on his keyboard and then swiveled in his chair.

"Agent Stark, lovely surprise," Paul said. The instant the words left his mouth, Paul knew he had oversold his cheerfulness. Paul's eyebrows rose, and his mouth exposed his teeth in a pained grin.

Stark chuckled. "Did your little girlfriend get tired of you already?" Stark asked. "I didn't expect to see you back here so soon. You two aren't having troubles, are you? That would make me feel all sad inside."

Paul sat still. "No. Everything is fine, thank you."

Stark swiped his hand across his forehead with an exaggerated sigh of relief. "That's great news. I sure wouldn't want there to be any tension in the workplace."

Paul crossed his arms to mimic his supervisor. They stared at each other for a moment, and then Paul nodded as if prodding Stark to speak. "Is there something I can do for you?"

Stark smiled. "Nope. Just checking up on my newbie. I want to make sure your first day with our team is the best it can be," he said, slathering his words with condescending optimism.

Paul's eyes met Stark's. "Thank you, Agent Stark." Paul waited for a response, or better yet, for Stark to leave, but Stark's butt remained plastered on the corner of the credenza.

"You did fine last time we worked together," Stark said. "I'm sure you'll do fine now as well."

"Fine? You mean when I—" Paul bit his tongue and grimaced, knowing he had said too much.

Stark pretended to finish his statement, "When you . . . almost got fired for your disregard of FBI protocol. Yes, I remember it well."

The two men stared at each other, and then Stark rose and prepared to walk away but then turned back to Paul. "But I'm sure you'll do great. How could you possibly fail with a great trainer like Agent Mathews?" he said with a guttural snort.

Paul's eyes narrowed with disgust.

"I'm sure you're busy, so I'll let you get back to, well, whatever Agent Mathews pawned off on you." Stark laughed. "She ditched you on the first day. That's pretty good." He laughed again and then walked away.

Turning back to his computer screen, Paul noticed a coworker staring in his direction over the low partition. Paul tilted his head up with a gentle nod and returned to his investigation.

"Okay, now," Paul mumbled to himself as he began typing. "What do petty crimes in Richmond, Liberty, and Independence have to do with anything?" Paul stopped typing for a moment. His head cocked as he thought. "Let's give this a try," he mumbled to himself and then continued typing.

Paul read the search results of his query, and he smiled. His head bobbed expectantly. "That's better. Now we're talking."

Paul scribbled on a notepad and then continued his search with renewed hope.

(18)

EMILY DROVE THE BLACK SUV down a tree-lined lane in Liberty, Missouri. The homes were simple, but the yards were neat. Cars were parked tightly against the rounded curbs, blocking passage of two-way traffic. Emily pulled to the side, allowing a vehicle to squeeze down the street, and then she continued. She glanced at her phone's display to ensure she had the correct address. And then she pulled into a driveway and parked beside a metallic seafoam-colored Cadillac.

Buttoning her jacket, she knocked three times on the exterior glass screen. She waited for a moment and then knocked again. She prepared to ring the doorbell but stopped when she heard an unusual scraping sound coming from behind the door. She placed a hand on her weapon and then waited another moment. The inner door opened, revealing a frail woman with a sweet expression and thinning white hair, hunched over her walker.

Emily smiled at the woman through the glass screen. "Hello. I'm Agent Mathews with the FBI."

The woman gazed at Emily. She blinked twice. "Huh? What did you say?" she hollered through the glass.

Emily couldn't hide her amusement. Her smile broadened as she reintroduced herself . . . loudly. She held her badge for the woman to see.

The feeble woman stared some more and then unleashed a tirade of profanity. Emily tried to hide her shock, but the language spewing from the old woman's mouth was filthy. Not even Agent Stark spoke that way—at least not in public.

"What do you want now?" the old woman bellowed.

Emily tucked a tendril of blonde hair behind her ear and replaced the badge in her pocket as she evaluated the old woman. Did someone really tie this old woman up during a home invasion? Gagging the woman made more sense, but binding her arms and legs to a chair seemed like overkill.

"Are you Luetta Barlow?" Emily asked.

The woman nodded.

"May I come in?" Emily asked through the glass.

The woman grunted something obscene, then turned and walked away. Emily watched through the screen as the woman scooted slowly down the entry hallway. Emily reached for the screen door handle and entered the home, following the woman to the living room.

The home was dated—the floor had a green shag carpet from an era best forgotten, and a sparkling cottage-cheese-style texture covered the ceiling. Old metal art of a fishing village hung on the wall and a plant dangled from a ceiling hook in a macramé cover with large brown beads.

The old woman lowered herself onto a mustard couch that was covered in protective plastic. To her left a bookshelf towered to the ceiling. Emily glanced around the room and shuddered at the 1970s decor. She pulled a wooden chair from beneath the plant and sat directly in front of the old woman. Emily hunched her shoulders as she leaned in to make eye contact, but the old woman's eyes darted nervously.

"Is something wrong?" Emily asked, surprised by the woman's evasiveness.

"Just get on with it, will you?" she hissed.

Emily sat up straight, her pleasant expression becoming all business. "Okay then. You reported a home invasion about a week ago. You were tied up, but nothing was taken from the home. Is that correct?"

The woman glared at Emily. "No."

Emily thought for a moment. "No . . . to which part? That was your official report to the police," Emily reminded. "You and your husband were bound while two men searched the house. Right?"

The old woman didn't respond.

Emily sighed as her eyes surveyed the room. "Is your husband home? Perhaps it would be better if I spoke to him."

"No."

The woman's cold eyes glared at Emily. Emily felt the anger and expected that had the old woman not been confined to using a walker, she would have pounced and bloodied her fists on Emily's face. The irrational hostility confused Emily.

"You obviously aren't interested in my help, but I'll make you a deal," Emily said. "As soon as you answer my questions, I will leave and never bother you again." She paused for a moment, waiting for a signal of acknowledgement, but the woman's expression remained stern and unyielding. "Until then, I will be happy to stay and talk with you . . . as long as you like."

Emily stood, approached the bookshelf, and scanned the books. Some were new, at least new within the last decade, but most were old. The leather bindings were cracked, and a thin residue of powder that had once been glue stuck to some of the volumes. Emily reached for a leather-bound book. Her hand hovered in place for a moment and then she glanced back at the woman as if sensing increased anxiety. The woman scooted to the edge of the sofa and reached feebly toward Emily with her mouth hanging open. The plastic crackled beneath the woman's movement.

The grin returned to Emily's face. "Is there something you'd like to tell me?" She waited.

"No. You little—"

Emily cut her off before she could continue with another string of obscenity. "Or is there something about these books that makes you nervous? Look, I don't know what your problem is, but the sooner you tell me, the sooner I get out of here. I think we will both like that."

The woman glowered. Her false teeth sloshed around inside her mouth as she prepared to speak.

"Tell me about the night the men came to your home. What were they looking for? And where is your husband?"

The woman grumbled. "Frank stays at the nursing home. That night, he wanted to get out. He came to watch *Wheel of Fortune*."

"Okay. Good. This isn't so hard, is it?" Emily muttered. "But the men didn't take anything?"

"Nothing I noticed . . . at first."

Emily's ears perked up and her weary eyes brightened. "So they did take something. What was it?"

The woman's eyes darted around the room, finally resting on Emily. No, her eyes were fixed on a spot over Emily's shoulder. Emily turned back to the bookshelf. On the top shelf, a quarter of the way toward the left hand side, a book was missing.

"May I?" Emily asked, pointing to the chair. Emily thought she detected a slight nod from the woman, so she proceeded. Pulling the chair to the bookshelf, she stepped up to view the empty slot more closely. A thin line of dust covered the shelf in front of the books, but the space was clean. Pulling out the book to the right, Emily glanced at the title—*Civil War Legends*. She turned it in her hands and then placed it back on the shelf. She picked up the book to the left of the space—*Missouri Treasure Hunters*.

Emily shook her head. "What book used to be here?" she asked, pointing to the empty space.

Again the old woman was reticent. "It's Frank's. I don't know what it was."

Emily stepped off the chair and smiled at the woman. "You're lying to me. Why?"

"Ask the police," the woman hissed. "I told them. Lot of good that did."

"So you told the police about the missing book?"

"I told them, but they didn't care."

"Do you know anyone who drives a beat-up red-and-beige pickup truck?" Emily asked.

The woman's eyes darted to the side, avoiding eye contact. Emily repeated the question, more firmly.

"No. But I've seen it before."

"Where?"

The old woman sighed, and her teeth jostled in her mouth. "The nursing home. I seen it once or twice."

"That's not in the report. Why didn't you tell the police?" Emily asked.

The old woman glared at Emily. Her lips creased. "They know. Oh yeah, they know."

Emily replaced the chair below the hanging macramé. "Thank you. It's been a . . ." she trailed off, not wanting to finish the sentence. The old woman muttered a slur under her breath. "I gotta go." Emily left the woman sitting on the sofa.

An exultant whistle blew from Emily's lips as she quickly exited the house. Finally, she got what she came for—but even better, her interview with the old woman ended without bloodshed.

*****

"Agent Stephens here," Paul said, answering his phone while still typing on his computer. "Oh, hi, Emily."

Paul cleared his screen and typed in a new search and paused momentarily. "Frank Barlow lives at Shady Creek Nursing Home. I'm sending the address to your phone right now. I can meet you there in twenty minutes," Paul said. He stood, listened, and then plopped down in front of his monitor. "Okay, boss. I'll stay right here . . . yeah, sorry, I won't call you 'boss' anymore . . . okay . . . sure will . . . got it," Paul said, responding to Emily's orders. "Yep, will do."

"I'll check with Thrasher about forensics on the casket, get bios worked up for Frank and Luetta Barlow, and check out the officers of record on the Barlow home invasion. Check. Anything else?"

Paul leaned back in his chair and rubbed his hair with his free hand. He held the receiver away from his mouth as he exhaled an exasperated sigh. He stared at his watch. "Yes, I'll wait here until I hear from you . . . boss."

(19)

WHILE MOST HIKERS COLLAPSED TO their stomachs and rested their faces on the prickly grass, Clay kicked off his shoes and socks and walked a short distance to a pond at the edge of the field. He dropped to his knees to splash his face but paused as he noticed the thick algae film covering the water. He pressed aside a line of cattails and skimmed his hand across the surface, moving the green froth to the side.

He stared at the water with apprehension. His eyebrows scrunched and his upper lip curled with disgust. Leaning forward with his hands propped at the edge of the pond, Clay took a deep breath and submerged his reddened face into the cool water. Gentle bubbles rose to the surface as he exhaled. The water immediately relieved the heat that had caused his temples to pound. After a moment with his head submerged, Clay lifted his head out of the water and wiped away the remnants of pond scum that had gathered around his face and on his thin strip of hair.

Clay lay on his back with his raw feet set in the water, his toes digging into the cool, soft mud. He closed his eyes for a moment. His breathing slowed as he inhaled through his nose and exhaled out his mouth. For the first time since daybreak, his feet didn't hurt and his head didn't feel like it was ready to spontaneously combust. Clay heard approaching footsteps but ignored them, content with his soothing comfort.

"So, Clay, that's pretty brave of you," Jimmy said, breaking the silence. Clay raised his hand to block the sun from his eyes as he peeked at Jimmy. "You do realize that's a lagoon, right?" Jimmy asked.

Clay squinted at Jimmy. "Pond . . . lagoon, I don't really care what you call it. It feels gooood."

"No, Clay. You don't understand. It's an old septic lagoon . . . you know, for sewage. There must have been an old house around here at some point," Jimmy said.

Clay's eyes popped as he jumped to his feet. He danced, wiggled, and squirmed and then flung the frothy scum from his legs.

Jimmy backed away, his hands raised in front of his face to ward off flying goo. "That's cute. You look like a four-year-old waiting for a potty break."

Clay lifted his shirt and wiped forcefully over his thin strip of hair, attempting to remove any potential sewage remnants. He completed his dance and wiped a clean area of his shirt across his lips one last time and then spat.

Jimmy smiled at his young friend. "Well, you know what? Maybe that's not a lagoon after all," he said, peering into the pond thoughtfully. "Nope, I was wrong. It's okay, Clay . . . just a pond."

"You little turd," Clay began, glaring at Jimmy.

"No, the little turd is actually . . ." Jimmy started saying as he pointed behind Clay's ear. "You want to get that? It's kind of gross."

Clay wiped his shirt on the back of his ear and then cringed at the large piece of green foam that remained on his shirt. He shuddered. "Thanks. I guess."

"If you're feeling better, how about we start setting up camp?" Jimmy suggested.

"We're camping here? Is this Far West?" Clay asked.

"Yes and no. We're camping here, but it's not Far West. We'll actually finish the last five miles of the hike in the morning."

"So where are we? What is this place?"

"Camp. I thought I just said that," Jimmy responded.

"Yeah, I got that much, but . . ."

"I'm just joshing you. Charles C. Rich once owned this land.

In fact, right around that clump of trees over there is the remains of the C. C. Rich cabin. The landowner is letting us use this for camp tonight. Girls will be in this field and the boys will be all the way over there," Jimmy said, pointing past a line of trees into another field.

"C. C. Rich? The guy from Crooked River, right?"

Jimmy nodded. "That's me," he said, tipping his hat.

"Hmm. So if we're setting up camp, does that mean it's almost dinnertime?" Clay asked.

"Not really. But the sooner we get camp set up, the sooner we can start dinner, and then the real fun begins." Jimmy paused as he turned in place, scanning a small strip of clearing that broke through the trees to connect the two fields. "I think I saw the chickens we're going to be eating later. Shh . . . listen."

Clay listened and heard the clucking of chickens and then the loud crow of a rooster. "We're going to eat live chickens?"

"Gross. No way. We're going to kill them, pluck them, and then cook them first," Jimmy said with a sly grin.

"Seriously? Great. Can't wait."

(20)

On a dirt road outside the township of Mirabile, Scud sat in the driver's seat of the parked red-and-beige pickup, his white-knuckled fists gripping the wheel. Shielded by the overgrown brush and saplings pushing up between rusty barbed wire, he hunched low in the seat.

He watched as tents popped up in fields on opposite sides of a thick line of trees. Three campfires burned on a dirt path as food was transferred from a covered wagon. Chickens clucked in cages, and cast iron dutch ovens were prepared near the fire.

Scud pulled his phone to his ear and waited while it rang. When the unpleasant greeting ended, he spoke. "We've got a problem."

Scud heard Ace breathe heavily into the phone. "Already? That didn't take long."

Scud flexed his jaw. "I'm looking at a field full of campers, maybe thirty-five of them. I'll need to wait to extract. Tomorrow, maybe." Scud listened to the silence on the other end of the line. "Mr. Nicas?"

"You are not authorized to wait. We need that piece now. Make. It. Happen."

Scud sunk lower in his seat as Ace's voice intensified. Though no one was close enough to hear, he felt exposed in the daylight. "Tonight. I'll come back tonight."

Ace chuckled. "See, that isn't so hard. Text me with the new time, and I'll have a team meet you for loading. I'm warning you, Scud. Don't mess this up."

Scud listened as the line went dead. His phone vibrated and his finger hovered over the photo file. He didn't want to look. He opened the new photo Ace had sent him of Alex Nicas. He cringed, instantly wishing he hadn't looked.

Scud opened the truck door but stopped when it started to creak. He looked at the bustling activity on the other side of the fence, and when there was no reaction to the door squeak, he opened it the rest of the way and hopped to the ground. He closed it softly and then crept down the fence line further from the group.

Crouching in the tall grass, Scud gazed through the brush at walls of gray timber. Propped up by wires and vertical supports, the front walls of the cabin were mostly straight, with large gaps between each horizontal beam where the chink and daubing had once been. His eyes focused toward the back of the cabin, where the gray wall collapsed inward, but then his attention was wrenched away as three boys scurried past.

Returning to the side of his truck, Scud considered his options for gaining access to the cabin without being noticed. He reached to the small of his back and felt the handgun tucked into his pants. The cold steel provided clarity and courage. Even with the large group nearby, it wouldn't be too much of a challenge. His business would be brief, and if anyone got in his way, well . . . he'd take care of it, just like he had taken care of Jack.

A chicken fluttered and then clucked as a man pulled it from a cage. Scud watched as the man snapped its neck and then placed the chicken on a stump, burying the hatchet and chopping off its head with an easy swing. Two boys who stood nearby cheered, but the girls and another boy looked away. The executioner handed the chicken to one of the boys, and Scud grinned as he watched the boy pluck the feathers with disdain. Scud's attention refocused on the hatchet buried in the log. Behind the log, a shotgun leaned against a tree.

Scud noticed the shotgun with a scowl and then cursed quietly. He thought for a moment and then considered the best time for his return. He squinted at his watch and nodded.

Climbing back into his truck, Scud started the engine. The oversized tires inched along the road, turned around, and then sped off, kicking up dirt and dust. The missing muffler rattled the peaceful rural silence as the truck groaned back into town.

*****

Clay held the dead chicken by its feet and plucked each feather individually as if pinching the head off a pimple. He held the fowl at arm's length, trying not to throw up his meager lunch.

The sound of spitting gravel and a revving engine stole Clay's attention from the chicken carcass, and he watched as a pickup truck sped down the road and out of sight. Clay scowled at the loud disruption but then groaned as he continued plucking feathers from the limp chicken.

(21)

PAUL LEANED AGAINST A BRICK pillar outside the front door of the Shady Creek Nursing Home. He glanced at his watch and then dug into his pocket for a Jolly Rancher but only found empty wrappers. Paul straightened as he saw Emily's black FBI-issued SUV pull into the lot. He sucked in and then blew out the air through puffed cheeks, hoping Emily was in a more cheerful mood.

Emily held a phone to her ear and slammed the SUV door. "Fine, Stark, I understand. I'll get back with you later," she said and then stabbed the "end" button on her phone as she walked past Paul, ignoring his presence. She burst through the front door of the rest home like a doctor entering the ER. Paul's head tilted back and wagged.

"Great." His eyes locked on the back of Emily, and he followed her through the doors knowing he had miscalculated.

"Where's the administration office?" Emily asked a nurse in camouflage scrubs. The nurse pointed down a hallway and then continued in her original direction.

The farther down the hallway Paul walked, the more pungent the smell of institutional cleaning supplies and urine became. The rest home smelled like a freshly cleaned bathroom at the bus station.

Emily held out her badge as she entered an office suite. The director looked up from a stack of papers and smiled wearily.

"Can I help you?" she asked.

Paul stood in the doorway as Emily took a seat across from the director and set her credentials on the desk. "Frank Barlow. May we speak with him?" Emily asked.

The woman's cheeks looked chubbier when she smiled. "What could old Frank have done to get you two out here today?"

Emily looked into the woman's eyes. "Frank Barlow. Please tell me where I can find him."

The director's smile vanished, and she emulated the agent sitting across from her. She looked at her watch. "Dining area. Probably working on a puzzle. He'll be wearing a bowling shirt."

"What color?"

"I don't know, but he always wears a bowling shirt."

Paul grinned. "You take the residents bowling often?"

"No." The woman's cold glare cut through Paul. "If you don't mind, I'm kind of busy here."

Emily stood, brushed by Paul, and headed toward the dining hall.

Paul remained in the doorway. "She really is a sweetheart," Paul told the administrator, but she only focused on her pile of paper.

"Mmhmm. I'm sure she is," she said, not looking up.

"Right. I'm leaving now," Paul said, motioning with his hand. "Oh, one question first. Do you keep a list of vehicles permitted in the employee parking?" The woman looked up. "It would really be helpful if I could get a list of employees and what they drive," Paul said. "I'll be back for the list."

The woman's eyes narrowed. "Fine. Give me a few minutes."

Paul nodded and then headed toward the dining hall where he joined Emily, standing behind a half-wall and staring into the dining hall. He studied Frank Barlow through the wooden spindles as if imagining him behind bars. The man was old. Super old, just like Emily had described his wife.

"Is everything all right?" Paul asked Emily.

Emily stared through the bars for another moment and then broke her silence. "I'm trying to psych myself up for this."

Paul grinned. "I've seen you interrogate hit men for the mafia, and you didn't have to get psyched up for them."

Emily's mouth twitched into a smirk, and she turned to look at Paul. "Yeah, but I just spoke to this guy's wife. If he's anything like that old hag, heaven help me."

Paul placed a hand on Emily's shoulder, but she shrugged it off. "What's going on?" Paul asked. "You're in a weird funk today."

Emily turned back to look at her subject through the bars. He wore a red, green, and beige bowling shirt. "Paul, why are you here? I asked you to stay at the office. I wish you would do what you're told." She turned and looked at her boyfriend. "Stay here."

Paul cringed. He remained behind the wooden spindles as Emily took a seat across from Frank Barlow. "I'm really glad we're working together. This is like a dream come true," he whispered softly. He pulled out his phone and dialed.

"Thrasher. Please tell me you've got something on the contents of the casket," Paul whispered into the receiver.

"Yeah. I got it," Thrasher replied. "Don't know what it means though."

"And . . . ?"

"It's brick. Small remnants."

"Brick? Why was there a brick on a pillow inside a casket?" Paul wondered out loud. "Was there anything else?"

"Yeah, paper."

"What kind of paper?" Paul asked.

"Old paper. Brittle. Yellow. The tech team's running more tests to determine manufacturer and age. I'll let you know when I have more," Thrasher said.

Paul hung up and stared at the phone as he thought. "Paper and brick," he mumbled. Leaving his post behind the wall, Paul pulled out a chair next to Emily. He watched the old bowler fit two puzzle pieces together and then silently search for another.

"Mr. Barlow, why are you ignoring me?" Emily asked. The man didn't respond.

Paul waited a moment, but when the man didn't speak, he leaned close to Emily and whispered in her ear. "They found brick and some kind of old parchment in the casket." Paul looked back at the old man in time to see his gray eyes twinkle and his lips curl up with excitement. The man swallowed as he stared at the agents. "What?" Paul asked as he noticed the man's attention.

Frank set his puzzle piece down and looked squarely at the agents. "Tell me about the casket. Where was it?"

Emily's lips tightened. "I just spoke with your wife, Mr. Barlow. You two are a lot alike." She shifted in her seat and leaned forward with both arms on the table. "You want to know about the casket?"

He nodded.

"Good. First answer my questions about the home invasion: the books, the truck. Give me what I need, and I'll tell you a little something about the casket," Emily enticed.

Frank Barlow sat tall, his hunch disappearing instantly. He smoothed his white hair back with a comb from his chest pocket as he grinned at the agents. "Deal."

(22)

PAUL FURROWED HIS EYEBROWS AS he finished the phone call, and then he returned to his seat. He sat tall with his hands folded on the table in front of him. His eyes narrowed, studying the codger in front of him, and he struggled to keep his mouth closed as a yawn nearly overpowered him. Beneath the table, he tapped his knee against Emily's. She raised her eyes from the tabletop and removed her hands from their planted position on each cheek.

Emily brushed a strand of hair behind her ear and sat taller. "Mr. Barlow, I'm sorry we wasted each other's time. We're getting nowhere." Emily stood, looked at her watch, and shook her head.

Paul stood and leaned close, whispering in Emily's ear. "I spoke with Thrasher again. They found trace elements of gold in the casket and on the brick fragments."

Emily turned to face Paul. "Gold?"

Frank Barlow smirked. His saggy cheeks and loose teeth tightened with interest. "Whoa there. Did you say gold?"

"We'll call if we need anything else," Emily said, grabbing Paul's elbow and moving toward the exit.

"You never asked me about gold!" the old man shouted. "I know lots about gold."

Paul turned. "Mr. Barlow, you seem pleased to waste our time.

Why should I believe that you have anything of value to share?"

The phlegm in the old man's voice rattled. "I haven't been forthright with you kids."

"You don't say . . ."

"But you need to understand, gold changes everything. Do you hear me boy? *Everything.*" The man licked his lips and muttered to himself.

Emily continued for the exit, but Paul held firm as he considered the man. "How does gold change everything?" He looked at his watch. "And you'd better make it quick."

Frank Barlow swallowed. "Boy, you'd have to be an idiot not to know."

"Really?"

"One piece of the puzzle doesn't show you much of the picture. Right?" The old man rubbed his forefinger and thumb against the corner of his mouth, removing the gathering spittle. "All your questions surround the real picture, but gold is the missing piece that ties it all together. Gold is everything."

Emily stood near the doorway. "Gold, huh? Clearly you're a fan."

The man's head nodded. "Of course. Kind of a family tradition," he said. A raspy cough escaped his throat. He rubbed his hands and then flexed them as if limbering up to play a concerto. "I admit I wasn't honest with you. Didn't see the point. What are you going to do, throw me in jail?" he asked craggily.

Paul rolled his eyes. "You could be a helpful and concerned citizen. After all, we are trying to solve the case of your home invasion."

Frank Barlow brushed the comments aside like he was swatting at a gnat. "I will help you understand, but you must swear."

"Swear to what?" Emily asked.

His yellowed dentures flashed with a broad smile. "I want to see it. The gold. I want to touch it."

"The gold from the casket? There are only trace elements," Paul said.

"Don't be stupid. The gold bricks. I want to touch the gold bricks," Barlow said. "My grandfather spent his whole life searching for the bricks. I want to touch them. Swear."

"You're saying there are bricks of gold? How many?"

The old man cleared his throat as he thought.

"Ten bricks? Fifty?" Paul asked.

Barlow mouthed the words but the sound was less than a whisper. "Dozens."

Paul rubbed his chin, grinning. "Really?"

Frank Barlow raised both eyebrows.

Paul squinted at the old man. "Okay, we'll see what we can do."

"No." Frank Barlow raised his shaking hand to his mouth and spit into the palm. "Agent Stephens, swear," he said, extending the hand to Paul.

Paul looked at Emily and scowled. "I'm not shaking that." He turned to the old man. "First, tell us everything we want to know, and if the information you provide assists us in solving our case, I'll arrange for you to see one of these 'supposed' bricks of gold," Paul agreed. "Take it or leave it."

Frank Barlow nodded with satisfaction.

"Tell us about the truck from the home invasion," Emily said.

"And the book that was removed from the shelf," Paul added. "What does any of this have to do with gold?"

Frank Barlow rubbed the back of his head, causing his white hair to stand up. "Always follow the money, boy. You should have learned that by now."

"Yeah, I got that."

"The grave robbery—the book—the museum theft—all have two things in common."

"Go on."

"Each event was literally gathering a piece to a puzzle." The old man giggled. "The puzzle is a map." He clapped his feeble hands together, barely making a sound. "At the end of the map—GOLD!"

Paul eyed the man skeptically but couldn't keep from smiling. The thought of piles of golden bricks was irresistible, and the man's enthusiasm was contagious. He tried to hide the excitement from his voice. "You said there were two things in common."

The old man nodded. "The truck, of course. I know whose it is. He doesn't think I know, but I know."

"Who?"

"All in good time. I'm telling you the 'who' and the 'why.' I'm still trying to figure out the 'how.' Remember . . . you swore," he said, wagging his finger.

Paul pulled the chair out from the table and took his seat. Emily smirked as she joined him. "Okay, Mr. Barlow—talk."

(23)

CLAY GRIPPED THE FOOTBALL AND cocked it back. He waited and then fired an arching spiral that flew in front of the lowering sun. He connected with his receiver in stride. A younger boy lined up wide and waited for the ball to be returned. Clay held the ball as if under center and yelled, "Hike." The boy sprinted fifteen yards down an imaginary sideline and then cut hard to the left, crossing directly in front of Clay. The ball hit his hands and then fell to the ground.

"Don't worry about it, kid. Nice route," Clay said, wiping the perspiration from his face.

"Come on, Clay," Jimmy hollered as Liz motioned with her hand. Jimmy and Liz gathered with the rest of the group near a pile of wood stacked like a teepee.

Clay held up a finger. "One more—quick."

The kid hurried back to the offensive line as Clay took one last snap. The younger boy ran a short buttonhook route, turning just as the ball met his stomach. He clutched the ball as he fell to the ground gasping for breath. Clay hurried on his blistered and chigger-bitten feet to the young boy.

"Great catch, kid. Nice!" Clay said as he reached down. The boy accepted Clay's hand with a smile, still gripping the ball against his body. "Come on. It looks like they're ready to start."

Clay joined the group as Bishop Taylor lit the bottom of the bonfire. The red sun lowered behind the trees, and the fire caught, crackling high into the night.

"A bonfire. Just what we need on a muggy night, eh?" Jimmy said, nudging Clay.

Within moments the heat became unbearable, and the group of youth and leaders backed farther away and sat in the grass. Bishop Taylor stood in front and began the fireside with a song and prayer.

"How many of you felt like giving up today?" Bishop Taylor asked.

No one answered at first, but his eyes searched the crowd and eventually found an unwilling volunteer. One hand rose, and then a couple of others. "How many of you are exhausted and sore?" More hands rose. "How many of you wondered if I had gone crazy bringing you on this trek? And how many are wondering what the point is?" Bishop Taylor waited as the rest of the hands rose, including Jimmy's and some of the other adult leaders.

Bishop Taylor smiled as he looked around the group. His eyes stopped on Liz. "Me too. The lesson I need to learn may be different than yours. I hope by the end, we'll each figure out our own personal answer. It's been a really long day, and we all need our rest." Then, hopping back into character as a member of the Crooked River rescue party, he continued. "We have made some mistakes today. We have freed our brothers from the mob but the price has been heavy. Brothers and mobbers alike have fallen. I have received word that news of our battle at Crooked River has reached Governor Lilburn Boggs."

"Is he going to help us?" an adult asked from the audience.

Clay smiled, recognizing the question was a plant.

Bishop Taylor's face became gloomy. "The Governor blames the Mormons. He claims that the Mormons' actions at Crooked River prove a direct threat to the peace and safety of the citizens of Missouri. He has issued an order authorizing the extermination of any Mormon who refuses to leave the state."

Clay looked at Liz. His eyes widened. "Is that for real?" Liz nodded. "Seriously?" he confirmed.

Bishop Taylor continued. "We must be watchful. Those who

seek to destroy us are pursuing us, and they now have legal authority to harass us and expel us from our own lands. The Prophet has asked us and other settlements in the area to gather to Far West for safety. Tomorrow morning we will get up early and finish our trek to Far West."

The bishop nodded, and Jimmy moved to the front of the group. Jimmy lifted the brim of his cowboy hat and spoke in what was supposed to be a gruff cowboy accent. "Our bellies are full and our tents are up. Get some rest. We all need it. But be on the lookout tonight." Jimmy gave some further instructions and then called on a young woman to close with a prayer before dismissing the youth to their tents.

Clay turned toward Liz. "Um, good night," he said, extending his hand for an awkward handshake.

Liz studied his hand and then shook. As Clay turned to walk to his camp, she patted him on the shoulder. "Good night, Clay."

Clay lay on top of his sleeping bag and stared through the mesh tent top. He scratched at his chigger bites, and with each motion his sticky, sweaty body clung to the fabric of the sleeping bag. His legs throbbed and his feet burned like he had walked over the hot coals of the bonfire. He sipped from his water bottle and removed his shirt, hoping for some rescue from the stifling humidity. Lying on his back with his hands behind his head, he thought of the battle and hike and plucking chickens. He thought of Liz and about how happy he was to finally be able to rest. *What a day.*

Even though it was early compared to his usual bedtime, Clay drifted to sleep. His eyes closed for what felt like mere minutes when the crack of gunfire filled the camp.

(24)

CLAY'S CHEST WAS HEAVING WHEN he sat up. The other kid in his tent was already climbing through the nylon tent door when Clay threw his shirt on and stuck his head out. Another gunshot fired. "What the . . . ?" He looked at his watch, surprised to see it was almost 1:00 a.m. Leaving his shoes next to the foot of his sleeping bag, Clay hurried across the grass to the bonfire, where the young men and the adult leaders gathered.

"Clay. Good. You're here," Jimmy said as he motioned for the boys to gather around. Another crack of gunfire killed the silence.

"What's going on?" Clay asked.

"The mob has found us," Jimmy said, nearly out of breath. "They've surrounded the camp. We need to get out of here."

Clay's shoulders slumped with a sigh. *Crap. Another reenactment.* "Right. I'm going back to bed." Clay turned back toward his tent but stopped when he felt a firm hand on his elbow.

"Clay, I need your help," Jimmy said, his words dripping with melodramatic desperation. "Boys, I need all of you. You have two minutes to gather your sleeping bags and be right back here. We're hiking out." The moans nearly drowned out the next gunshot. "Quickly. Two minutes," Jimmy said, and then he winked at Clay. "See you soon, buddy."

Gunfire surrounded the camp as the boys returned to the fire with their sleeping bags. "What about the girls?" one boy asked.

"Yeah, seriously. If we're in danger, don't we kind of need to protect them?" Clay asked.

Nicki smiled. "I'm glad you asked, but actually, no. The mob only wants the men because of what they did at Crooked River. They won't bother the women if you're gone. The best thing you can do to protect us right now is leave."

"Okay, whatever," Clay said. "But what if you're wrong?"

Jimmy ignored the comment. "Is everyone ready?" He looked into the drooping eyes of the gathered boys. "Good. Let's go."

With his sleeping bag thrown over his shoulder, Clay walked barefoot behind Jimmy with his shoes tied around his neck. "Anyone have a flashlight?"

"We'll walk by the light of the moon," Jimmy said. "We don't want to let the mob see us."

"Of course. 'Light of the moon.' Why not?"

Jimmy led the group as they shuffled their feet through the tall grass. They hiked from the field along the clearing where dinner had been prepared. The rattle of gunshots fell farther behind as they walked through the field where the girls were camping and farther past the skeleton of the C. C. Rich cabin.

They hiked a short distance along a gravel road and then entered a gate leading to another field.

"I think this will do it, boys," Jimmy said as he threw his sleeping bag to the ground. "Let's get some rest." The boys dropped their bags and spread them out on the grass.

"Rest, huh? Are you sure this time?" Clay asked

*****

Scud huddled in the shadows against the gray cabin timber. He listened to the surrounding gunfire and watched with confusion as a group of boys walked past the cabin with sleeping bags hanging from their arms.

He tensed as the yellow shovel handle slid down the gray log wall and fell out the doorway, mere feet from where the boys walked. He watched the boys to see if anyone would notice, but no one did. He loosened the grip on his gun as the boys filed past, crossing the gravel road into another field.

Scud looked to make sure no one else was coming and then picked up the shovel and continued digging.

*****

"Jimmy . . . you still awake?" Clay asked as he lay on top of his sleeping bag, looking up at the stars. He leaned up on his elbow and looked around at the other boys curled in their bags. The distant gunfire surrounding the old camp had long since faded, and the cicadas buzzing in the trees provided the only sound. "Anybody awake?"

Clay waited for an answer, but the encampment remained silent. He slipped on his shoes, stood, stepped over a sleeping boy, and then followed the trail of trampled grass back toward the road. He could see the distant light of the fire at the base camp, and he slowed as he approached the edge of the field. Clay crouched next to the barbed wire and strained his eyes to see down the street. The truck was still there, nestled against thick shrubbery on the side of the road.

Clay held his breath while he listened and watched the shadows, but the night seemed still. He wiped his sleeve across his forehead and sucked a morsel of spit in his dry mouth. Then he felt the sudden weight of two hands pressing down on his shoulders. He gasped as he stood and spun around.

"Jimmy!" Clay's breathing raced. "You're awake!" Clay proclaimed in a harsh whisper.

"Nothing gets by you, Clay. That's one of the reasons why I like you," Jimmy said in full voice.

"Shhh!" Clay held a finger to his lips and motioned for Jimmy to squat down.

"What are you doing? Come on. I'm tired. Let's get some sleep," Jimmy urged, mimicking Clay's earnest whisper.

"I noticed something tonight when we were hiking to our new camp in the middle of nowhere. I didn't want to say anything because . . . well, I thought I was just being a paranoid wimp."

"That *is* highly possible," Jimmy agreed.

"I just wanted to check it out to see if I really am a wuss. Look," Clay said, pointing down the road to the truck. "I saw that truck today."

"So? It probably belongs to someone on the trek or maybe one of our fake mobbers we had come shoot up the place earlier."

"Maybe, but that thing spun out of here earlier. Not very responsible for an adult leader."

"Clay, be fair. Not everyone is as mature as I am," Jimmy said with a smirk.

"And when we were hiking past the cabin, I thought I heard something."

"It was probably a raccoon, or maybe a dingo," Jimmy suggested as his eyes widened.

"A dingo? No. It was heavy breathing. I thought some jerk was trying to scare us. I kept waiting for someone to jump out, but then nothing happened. I saw the truck a few minutes later and . . . I just wanted to check it out," Clay said.

"Look, Clay, I'm nothing if not a protector of young men and young women," Jimmy said in a thick British accent as he struck an awkward pose. "You go back and get some sleep, and I'll check it out. I'll see who's on watch at the fire and if they know who the truck belongs to. Okay? There's nothing to worry about."

Clay opened his mouth to complain but stopped as Jimmy held a finger to his lips. He watched Jimmy slink toward the truck and look in the driver's side window.

Jimmy turned back to the fence line. He motioned with his hands and mouthed something Clay couldn't understand.

Clay looked around to ensure the continued absence of any lurking serial killers and then crept onto the road and walked toward the truck. He felt guilty, but not enough to actually obey Jimmy. He placed a hand on Jimmy's shoulder, nearly causing Jimmy to fall into the bed of the truck. Clay smiled at the reaction. "You deserved that."

"No graduation tassels or fuzzy dice hanging from the mirror. No planner lying on the seat. Just lots of garbage—and it's not any better back here," Jimmy said as he lowered the tailgate to get a better look. "Piles of dirt and rock, tools . . . nothing to see here, Clay. Now go back with the boys. I'll be there in a few minutes."

Clay didn't budge.

"Clay . . . seriously . . . go."

"I'm not sure I like 'Dictator Jimmy,' " Clay said.

"Yes. I know. I'm drunk with power. Please, go back and . . ." Jimmy stopped and his head swiveled. "Did you see that?"

"What?"

Jimmy focused his eyes on the gate near the main field. "There's someone out there," Jimmy said, peering into the darkness.

"Who is it?"

"I can't tell. Wait, there," Jimmy said, pointing. "Two of them."

Clay nodded as his vision acquired the subjects.

"Great. Looks like we've got a couple sneaking off. Let's see if we can put a little fear into these kids," Jimmy said with a grin. "Hide behind the truck."

Clay and Jimmy hid in the shadows between the truck and the bushes, waiting for the ideal moment to leap out. Clay listened and peeked around the truck as the couple moved closer. The man held the woman's right elbow with his right hand as he walked behind. "I don't know, Jimmy. They don't look like a happy couple."

Jimmy shook his head, scowling. "No, they don't."

(25)

CLAY KNELT BEHIND THE TAILGATE and lowered onto all fours for a better view of the approaching couple. Crouching down he had a clear view of their feet. His chin dropped and his lips parted with disappointment as he recognized Liz's thick combat boots and funky socks. He'd only known her for the day, but he expected more from her than sneaking off in the middle of the night to make out with some greaseball. Judging by the pair of ratty sneakers marching alongside her black boots, "greaseball" felt accurate, but then he examined his own worn shoes.

Turning to Jimmy, Clay whispered, "See if you can sneak around the other side. After I pop out to scare them, you'll be there when they turn to run." Clay smiled, but he was pretty sure he shouldn't be enjoying it this much. Jimmy nodded as he turned and started crawling through the thick shrubbery to gain the desired position near the front of the pickup.

As the couple moved closer to the truck, Clay watched with anticipation, eager to teach Liz a lesson. Clay rubbed his Mohawk and waited. He watched as the feet marched closer, and then as the heels of the combat boots dug into the gravel and dragged forward. Clay looked to his right and saw Jimmy trying to navigate his way through the shrubs, and then he looked back at Liz's shuffling feet. Clay was preparing to pounce as the approaching mumbles drew near. Then the shuffling feet stopped at the front of the truck.

Clay peeked around the side of the pickup for a better view. He winced as he saw the filthiness of the man with Liz and then shuddered as the man pulled a handgun from the back of his pants. *Oh crap, oh crap.*

Liz clutched a metal container, about the size of a bread box. The man held her elbow in one hand and his weapon in the other. Their mumbles became audible.

"I did what you said. I brought the box. Now let me go," Liz spat.

The man scratched his head with his trigger finger. "Shut up. You're coming with me."

Clay heard Liz gasp. He turned to find Jimmy, who appeared to be stuck in the middle of the shrubbery, or maybe he had seen and heard the same things and was keeping a low profile. Clay turned back to Liz. His heart raced, and he swallowed hard as he heard Liz whimper.

"Please. Just let me go. I won't say a word. I didn't see anything. I promise. I was just out walking, that's all," Liz pleaded.

The man released Liz's arm and stabbed the gun against her chest. "Just walking?'" Scud laughed. "You're a stupid girl. You know that? Shut your mouth and get in the truck." The man opened the driver's-side door and motioned for her to climb in.

Clay remained crouched behind the tailgate, paralyzed. *What do I do? I can't let her go. Gun.* As the thoughts scurried through Clay's brain he heard someone yell.

"Who goes there?" Jimmy shouted. The goon spun in surprise. "Liz, RUN!" Jimmy yelled again. Clay turned toward the sound of Jimmy's voice. He appeared to be stuck behind thick foliage.

The man pushed Liz toward the door and jabbed her back with the gun. "Get in. NOW!"

Liz climbed in as the man shoved from behind. He moved back to the front of the truck, and his eyes searched for the man who had yelled. He raised his gun and fired two blind shots into the bushes, which mimicked the militaristic ambiance of the camp. The man hopped in the cab, slammed the door, and started the engine.

Clay recognized the roar of the truck as it came to life. He looked at the position where Jimmy had been hiding but couldn't see him. "Jimmy?"

The truck lurched forward, and Clay stood. He placed his hand on the tailgate as the wheels began spitting out gravel. He pumped his legs and held on to the gate as the truck gained speed. His hand reached farther into the bed of the truck and found a handhold where the tailgate folded down. His feet dragged across the gravel and dirt, and then he swung one leg up onto the truck, and then he lifted the other. He held on. As the truck slowed at the end of the road, Clay rolled into the bed and crawled beneath a canvas tarp.

As the truck made a sharp turn to the right, Clay peeked from beneath the tarp and saw Jimmy running down the middle of the road, waving his arms.

(26)

JIMMY GASPED FOR AIR, HUNCHED over in the middle of the road. He listened to the truck careen around the corner and roar away. He sucked in air, then changed course and raced back toward camp. Reaching the fire, Jimmy panted as he tried to speak.

"Liz . . . Clay . . . truck." Jimmy stared at the two sentinels sitting around the fire, hoping they would express a glimpse of understanding. They didn't even blink. Jimmy struggled to calm his breathing but couldn't. "Gun!" His breathing became heavier. The camp guards looked at him. Moving beside them, Jimmy stood one man up and quickly patted him down. The man squirmed but was too surprised to react or stop him. Jimmy felt the keys and reached into the guard's pocket. He held up the keys. "Car . . . where's your car?"

The man pointed to the distant edge of the field.

"I need . . . to borrow . . . car. And this." Jimmy reached into the man's other pocket and removed a cell phone. He started running toward the cars parked on a side road at the far edge of the field. "Tell the bishop. They have Liz . . . and Clay!" Jimmy yelled back.

Jimmy forced his breathing into a controlled pattern, like a running back racing for the end zone. Behind him, he heard the men move into action as they raised an alarm.

Approaching the cars, Jimmy held the key and pressed the auto-unlock. The car's horn chirped and the lights flashed. Jimmy hopped into the dark Dodge Charger and peeled out heading north.

At the main blacktop intersection just outside Mirabile, Jimmy sat wide-eyed as the Charger faced north. He looked to his left and then to the right down HH highway, wondering which direction the truck had gone. He turned in his seat and looked to the south and then straight ahead to the north as D highway followed the rolling hills. There were no signs of traffic in any direction.

Jimmy's head listed to the side. "I don't know what to do." He rolled down the window and screamed. "I DON'T KNOW WHAT TO DO!" He lowered his head into his hands. "Heavenly Father, what do I do?"

Jimmy sat still and then raised his head. He looked again in every direction, but there was nothing. Then, straight ahead, far in the distance, he saw the hint of taillights emerging from the darkness of a low valley.

Without thinking, Jimmy stomped the pedal to the floor. The car blasted forward and the instant momentum pushed his back against the seat. He held the wheel tight with both hands, urging the vehicle to speed toward the distant lights. The car quickly accelerated to a safe speed, but Jimmy pressed down again, following a curve in the road. The tires squealed as they hugged the corner, and then Jimmy pressed down harder when the road straightened. Grabbing the borrowed cell phone from the seat next to him, Jimmy dialed and waited.

"Yeah," a shaky voice on the other line responded.

"Paul, it's me."

"Jimmy, do you have any idea what time it is?" Paul croaked.

"Shut up and listen. I need your help." Jimmy listened as he imagined Paul shaking the cobwebs from his sleeping mind. "Something happened!"

"Hold on, Jimmy. You're still on the trek, right? Where are you?"

Jimmy thought for a moment as the car continued to accelerate along the straight rural highway and bounced over a slight rise. "Heading north, I think. Two kids from church were taken from camp."

"What?"

"Clay was worried about a truck, so I was checking it out, and then Liz showed up and the guy had a gun. He forced her into the truck, and he shot at me a couple of times. Clay jumped into the truck bed, and I think I'm following them now."

"Jimmy, don't take this wrong, but you're not making any sense. Are you being serious?" Paul asked.

Jimmy recognized the skepticism. "Yes, I'm serious. Get some cops, FBI, National Guard—I don't care. But HELP!"

"Okay, Jimmy. Just relax. You said you *think* you're following them now. What do you mean?"

"They were way ahead of me. I saw some lights, so I followed. I have no idea where I am."

"Can you describe the truck? And do you still see the lights you're following?"

Jimmy paused, scanning the road ahead. "It's a red-and-beige truck, but I can't see them now." Jimmy listened to the silence on the other end of the phone. "Paul?"

"Did you say a red-and-beige truck? Is it old? Jacked up?"

"Uh, yeah, how did you . . . Wait, Paul, I think maybe they turned off, or . . . HOLY CRAP!" Jimmy clutched the steering wheel as he hit the apex of a hill and started downward, *Dukes of Hazzard* style. When the wheels reconnected with the pavement, the car swerved but he held it steady. Placing the phone between his shoulder and ear, Jimmy positioned the car on the center line and stepped on the gas. "I haven't seen the lights for a while but . . ."

"Jimmy?"

The tires squealed again. Jimmy slammed the breaks and cranked the wheel as the road curved sharply to the east. Jimmy's shoulder slammed against the side of the car and the phone dislodged from his ear, and it skittered out the window. He struggled to regain control of the car. Jimmy's heart pumped like the pistons in the Charger's engine. He gripped the wheel, pressing again on the gas, and sped past a sign that read "Far West Temple Site." He glanced to his right as he passed a black iron gate surrounded by trees. He refocused on the road ahead.

Jimmy leaned forward and flipped off his headlights for a moment, hoping to reacquire the taillights of the truck. Nothing. He flipped the lights back on as the road curved to the west. He muscled the steering wheel, willing the car to stay on the road, and then made another sharp turn back to the north. After finding a long straight away, Jimmy flipped off the lights again as the Charger descended into a farm valley.

A short distance ahead, he saw the hopeful glow of red taillights. Jimmy's chest heaved, his body tense with excitement. "Thank you."

(27)

PAUL NEARLY FELL ON HIS face. He pulled on his shoe while hopping out the door and then leaned against the wall for balance. With the top of his pants unbuttoned and the back of his shirt untucked, Paul patted down his cowlick. He held his keys and cell phone in one hand and a small spiral notebook between his teeth as he moved hastily toward the elevator of his apartment building. Once inside, he filled his pockets with the sundry items and voice-dialed Emily.

"Paul?"

Paul winced as he heard the exhaustion in Emily's voice. "Emily. Good. You're still awake," he said, hoping his cheerfulness would quickly rub off.

"Paul, what's going on?" Her voice was barely a whisper. "Is everything all right?"

"I just had a call from Jimmy. Two of the kids from the trek have been taken."

Paul heard the rustle of Emily's waking motions and then the sound of the phone dropping. A moment later she spoke. "Trek? Taken? Taken where? What are you talking about?"

It took every ounce of patience Paul possessed to allow Emily time to awaken her mind. "The youth trek for the kids in the ward. They're somewhere up around Far West. I was talking to Jimmy, but the phone went dead." Paul paused, listening to the silence on Emily's end. "Emily, Jimmy described the vehicle that took the kids. It's an old red-and-beige pickup truck." Paul waited for Emily's response, but he only heard breathing. "Emily?"

Emily's voice came alive and echoed through the phone. "Paul, we've got to get out there."

"Uh . . . yeah," he said in a more condescending tone than he intended. The elevator dinged, and Paul raced to his black SUV in the underground parking. He pointed his key and pressed the button to unlock the door and start the ignition. "I'm on my way. I'll be at your place in four minutes."

"My place . . . mmhmm . . . okay . . . I'll be waiting."

"Oh, and Emily. Grab your notes from talking with Old Man Barlow. They may come in handy. I'll wake up Thrasher and get him over to the office."

"Got it. I'll call Stark to let him know we may have a new crime connected to the others." Emily paused. "Paul, what's going on here?"

Paul shook his head. "I have no idea."

"We can't let anything happen to those kids. Got it? We can't."

"We won't, Emily. Just get ready. I'll be there soon."

(28)

CLAY HUDDLED BENEATH THE TARP in the back of the pickup truck. He carefully set aside a shovel and inched his way in between a mound of dirt and a pile of rocks at the back of the bed near the cab. Craning his neck and raising his head, he attempted to peek through the rear window into the cab but quickly lowered his head again, determined to stay out of sight.

Clay laid his head on his arm, straining to listen to the activity in the cab. He recognized Liz's voice but couldn't understand what she was saying. The roar of the unmuffled tailpipe made it impossible to decipher the words, yet Clay could feel the tension inside the cab. The driver yelled, and Liz became silent. Clay remained still.

With his eyes adjusted to the darkness, Clay studied the rest of the filthy truck bed. Rocks, dirt, buckets, shovels, rope, and . . . Clay sighed as he recognized what looked like a pile of clothes crammed between a bucket and the wheel well. He glanced at the rear window of the cab and then extended his hand toward the pile of clothing, but couldn't reach it. He shifted his position and put out his hand a little farther, but it still wasn't far enough. His middle fingernail scraped at the bucket, but he still couldn't reach. Lying on his stomach, Clay slithered toward the wheel well and stretched again. His eyes darted again to the cab, hoping he was out of the line of sight of the rearview mirror.

Clay grabbed for a handful of cloth, but the truck crested the road, causing him to loft into the air and crash down. His hand knocked over the bucket and his chin slammed on the hard steel of the truck bed. Clay grabbed the clothes and scurried to the back of the truck. His breathing raced, and he cursed himself for making such a loud noise. He hoped the sound of the crashing bucket and the thud of his body hadn't alerted the driver to his presence. He looked up, expecting the rear window to slide open. Clay picked up the largest rock from the pile and gripped it, ready to hammer any hand that should reach in his direction, but the window remained closed, and the truck continued speeding along the rural road. Clay rubbed his chin and exhaled.

After a few more minutes of roller coaster–style riding, the truck slowed. Grabbing a shabby scrap of clothing, Clay wrapped a piece of shirt around a rock and then repeated the process on a second rock and then a third. The truck stopped, and Clay tossed the rock onto the road. The truck turned to the right, Clay tossed another wrapped rock into the road. He looked up to the rear window, expecting to be discovered, but the trucked continued on.

Convinced that the driver was still unaware of his presence, Clay ripped the remaining clothing into small shreds and tied each scrap around his bread crumbs, occasionally tossing another out the back of the truck to mark the direction of travel.

(29)

EMILY CLIMBED INTO THE PASSENGER seat of Paul's SUV as she spoke frantically into her phone. Ending her call, she set the phone on the center console and pulled a rubber band from around her wrist. She removed the black FBI ball cap from her head and pulled her hair into a ponytail and then threaded it through the opening in the back of the cap.

Paul continued talking on his phone, but his eyebrows rose as he looked at Emily. *Dang.* She even looked good in a plain white T-shirt and ball cap, in the middle of the night with no makeup. Paul ended his call. Though the situation didn't really warrant the compliment, Paul couldn't resist. "Nice!"

Emily lowered her head and raised her eyebrows, smirking at Paul and waiting for him to return her gaze. "Seriously, Paul?"

Paul shrugged with a goofy grin. "Can't I appreciate my girlfriend a little?"

Emily's expression flattened. Her shoulders rose as she took a deep breath and wagged her head. "Let's try to focus on what's important."

Paul knew she was right. Of course they should focus on the missing youth, but can't he say something friendly without being reprimanded? His spirits instantly deflated. "What's with you lately? You're kind of being a . . ."

Emily's eyes hardened. "Being a *what*, Paul? What am I being?"

"I think you know," he said as his eyes focused on the road. They traveled a moment in silence, and then Paul changed the subject. "Let's review the situation. What do we know so far? Do you want to go first, or me?"

"Go."

Paul glanced at Emily, hoping to find some hint of gentility in her demeanor, but her gaze was steely and her lips curt. "I called Bishop Taylor at the campsite. They'd already started a head count after they realized something was wrong. Apparently Jimmy ran through camp and borrowed someone's car keys and cell phone. He said Jimmy and Brother King had taken a small group of boys farther from camp. He's going to finish the camp inventory and get back with me in the next ten minutes. What do you have?"

"I spoke to Thrasher. He'll be at the office within fifteen minutes. He'll coordinate communications from there. He'll also review maps and satellite images of the area," Emily said.

"Good. How recent are the images he's looking at?"

Emily lowered her chin and looked at her boyfriend. "I don't know, Paul. I said he will review them when he gets to the office."

"Sorry, boss," Paul said. "What about Stark?"

"He's being Stark. He's working on getting air support—kind of. I want a helicopter to help with the search, but he's dragging his feet. He says it's an unwarranted expense unless we can provide evidence of an abduction."

"You're kidding. What's that supposed to mean? He doesn't believe me? I was talking to Jimmy and . . ."

"Let's just say Jimmy made an impression the last time they met. Stark doesn't trust Jimmy. He wants verification first." Emily watched the road as they sped toward the I-35 ramp. "Do you know where we're going?"

"North."

"Sounds very specific."

Paul's grip on the steering wheel tightened. "Bishop said they're at the C. C. Rich cabin near Far West. Far West is about an hour north of Kansas City, so I'm driving north."

"Would you like me to program the GPS for you?" Emily asked, slipping into her sweet southern drawl.

"Yes, boss. Make yourself useful."

(30)

BISHOP, I'VE GOT YOU ON SPEAKER. Emily Mathews is here with me. We just passed Liberty, so I think we're still about forty-five minutes away. What did you find out?"

Bishop Taylor started to speak, but he caught on his emotions. He tried again. "We're missing two kids. A new kid named Clay and . . ." The bishop coughed and cleared his throat as he struggled to speak. His pained words chopped at the silence "And . . . my daughter . . . Liz."

Paul listened as the bishop muffled a sob. He looked at Emily and nodded, then scratched his head. Emily picked up her phone and dialed. She spoke quietly but earnestly into the phone as Paul continued speaking with Bishop Taylor. "I'm sorry. Bishop, we're on our way. Nothing's going to happen to your daughter or Clay. What about Jimmy? Is he there?"

Bishop Taylor cleared his throat, and his voice became firm. "You'll find them, Paul. I know you will."

"Bishop, what about Jimmy?"

"He took Brother Conrad's car key and cell phone, but we haven't heard from him."

"What kind of car is he driving?" Paul asked.

Paul heard the bishop cover the receiver and yell, "Brother Conrad, what kind of car are you driving?"

Brother Conrad gave a muffled response as he described his car.

The bishop started to speak, but Paul cut him off. "Got it, Bishop—2012 Dodge Charger. Navy. I've got to go. Make sure everyone stays put. We'll be there soon."

"Hurry!"

"Yeah." Paul hung up the phone and instantly dialed again.

"Thrasher. Check out a 2012 Dodge Charger, navy, registered to Jason Conrad. Check for GPS. Send me coordinates as soon as you have them."

"Got it." Thrasher hung up.

Paul set his phone down and exhaled as Emily also ended her call. "Well?"

Emily smiled. "Helicopter's lifting off in ten. It will meet us at the camp. How much farther?"

Paul looked at the clock and then at the GPS. "It says thirty-five minutes, but we'll be there in twenty," he said, pressing the gas pedal to the floor.

(31)

THE NAVY CHARGER STOPPED AT the intersection of D Highway and Old 36. Jimmy shifted into park and stared to the west and then to the east. He stared again in each direction and then climbed out of the car. The taillights had disappeared over two minutes ago without a single red glimmer of hope since. He placed his hands behind his head, his forehead creasing and his lips tightening. Jimmy's deep breathing intensified into a low growl as his mouth curled into a frown, and then he screamed.

To the west he could see a gentle glow from the next town over, but otherwise the night grew perfectly dark. The rural roads were free of streetlights and traffic, and the clouds had covered the moon and stars sometime during the night. Jimmy listened to the distant barking of dogs and then turned toward what looked like an abandoned gas station on the corner. A canopy light had turned on.

"Everything okay out there?" a shirtless man yelled as he walked into the graveled yard.

Jimmy looked at the man who was standing next to a rusty bus on blocks, but he didn't respond. He looked at his watch and then again down Old 36 Highway to the west and east. Then he saw it.

"Can you hear me out there?" the shirtless man yelled. "I'm calling the cops."

Jimmy ignored the threat. He took a few steps to the east, closer to the canopy light and a small mound in the road. Jimmy bent over and picked up a rock that filled his palm. He untied a scrap of blue fabric tied around it. He stared at the rock for a moment and then ran back to the Charger. He tossed the rock to the floor on the passenger side, climbed in, shifted into drive, and hit the gas as he headed east.

*****

Clay tossed another rock out of the truck and then secured himself against the back of the truck bed as the pickup turned onto the four-lane highway. With a burst of acceleration, the truck roared to highway speed as Clay held on. Looking out the back of the truck, Clay could now see occasional vehicles driving the opposite direction. It looked like he was returning to civilization.

He felt the prying lights of a semitruck approaching from behind. Hoping the truck driver would see him, Clay waved a cloth low in the pickup bed, but the semi changed into the fast lane and passed. Clay watched, determined to get another vehicle's attention no matter what. He waited, but no other vehicles approached, and then the pickup's blinker turned on. Clay tossed out two rocks as the pickup took the off-ramp and then again at the stop sign as the truck turned north.

Clay studied the passing scene as the pickup headed down what appeared to be the main street of a small town. Few lights were on. The gas station lights were lit, but there wasn't a car in sight. The pickup rolled through a stop sign and passed the Missouri Star Quilt Shop, Hy-Klass grocery store, and then a brick building with a lighted sign in front: J. C. Penney Library. Clay had no idea where he was, but he memorized the familiar name, hoping it would be easily identified. After another minute he passed Penney High School, and then the dark town fell farther behind as the pickup once again headed into the even darker countryside.

Clay tagged another rock with a scrap of fabric and tossed it onto the road, then the sky lit up as lightning flashed and thunder cracked. The air thickened and then the first drops of rain cooled Clay's skin. The truck continued traveling north.

(32)

THE TIRES SQUEALED IN DISTRESS, hugging the road as Paul navigated another tight turn. Emily held tight to the handle as Paul raced along the black road. Paul looked at his watch and then at the GPS. He smiled.

"Twenty minutes exactly," Paul said with satisfaction as they entered the small township of Mirabile. He followed the GPS directions and turned down a small road and around a bend. The camp was unmistakable. Two dozen kids and leaders stood next to a bonfire as flashing lights of local law enforcement lit the darkness with red and blue.

Paul slowed and then pulled through a gate and into the field near the fire. "You take the law, and I'll take the bishop," Paul suggested.

Emily nodded. "Let's do it."

Exiting the SUV, Emily approached the local sheriff's deputy while the adult leaders and youth thronged around Paul and bombarded him with questions.

Paul held up his hands and motioned for everyone to calm down. "Bishop Taylor, where are you?"

The bishop moved to the front of the group. "Brother Stephens, thank you for getting here so quickly," he said, placing an arm on Paul's shoulder.

"Of course, Bishop." Paul leaned close to the bishop's ear. "Please call me Agent Stephens and call Emily Agent Mathews while we're on duty. It's just that . . . the local law needs to know who's in charge."

Bishop Taylor patted Paul's back. "Of course. You're in charge here. What can we do to help?"

"Did anyone notice anything unusual, anything out of place?"

Bishop Taylor made a face and looked like he might throw up. "To these kids, the whole day's been kind of weird. I mean, it was unusual by design. We've had mob attacks and a gun battle, and . . ."

Paul scratched his nose as he thought. "Okay." He raised his hands to quiet the crowd again. "Does anyone have any information about Liz or Clay, or Brother Younger?"

The crowd went dead silent.

"Anybody?" Paul asked again. The crowd remained silent for another moment and then burst into a cacophony of questions. "This isn't working. Bishop, please," Paul said, motioning toward the SUV. He opened the door, the bishop climbed in, and then Paul followed.

Bishop Taylor's head wagged back and forth. "I can't believe this is happening."

"Bishop, I need you to focus. Why would anyone want to take Liz? Have you seen anyone or anything unusual since you've been here at camp?"

"Paul, I don't have a clue. It doesn't make sense. Why would this happen? Why Liz? And why Clay? They barely know each other. As far as I know, they just met today."

"Is there anything unusual about Clay? Does he have any kind of past? Drugs? Gangs? Any problems like that we should know about?"

"Clay and his mother just moved here . . . nasty divorce—domestic abuse. They showed up one day with nothing except a couple of suitcases. Sad situation, but nothing I know of would relate to this. I don't think Clay's dad even knows where they are. Clay seems a little depressed and out of place, but I think he's a pretty good kid."

Paul looked out the window. The kids and other leaders hovered around the fire, and Emily was speaking to the deputy. Paul shook his head. "This is so odd."

Bishop Taylor nodded. "You're telling me."

"No. I mean . . . look, Bishop, I'm going to share a couple of things with you. Can you keep it confidential?" Bishop Taylor lowered his head and raised one eyebrow. Paul smiled. "Of course you can. Sorry."

"What is it, Paul?"

"Emily and I have been investigating a case today that I think is tied in with this abduction, but I'm not sure how."

"What do you mean?"

"We've been investigating a grave robbery from Richmond. Analysis of the casket indicated there were traces of gold, brick, and some kind of parchment in the casket. A witness identified a red-and-beige truck at the scene. That same truck is connected to a break-in at the Community of Christ Temple in Independence. At first we thought it was just vandalism, but it turns out some historical materials were stolen from the museum."

"What was taken?"

"Just some pages from a journal."

"A journal?" Bishop Taylor asked.

Paul nodded. "The same red-and-beige truck is also connected to a home invasion of an old lady named Luetta Barlow. The only thing taken from the home was a book. The lady wouldn't tell what the book was, but it was placed between books about the Civil War and treasure hunting. When we tracked down Mr. Barlow at a local rest home, he wouldn't tell us anything either. That is until we mentioned gold."

"Gold?"

"Yeah. Gold. We have gold at the cemetery, and then there's Mr. Barlow's extreme interest in gold and treasure hunting. He finally admitted his missing book is about LDS Church history in northern Missouri, but he isn't a member of the Church."

Bishop Taylor linked his fingers together and used his thumbs to rub his hands as he thought. "You don't have to be a Mormon to be interested in LDS Church history," he began, as if talking to himself. "Especially around Caldwell County."

"Of course not," Paul agreed. "But—"

"What was the book? The book from the house? What's the name?"

"Emily has the notes. We'll get her over here in a second," Paul said.

"What about the journal from the temple? Who's journal was it?"

Paul searched his memory. "It wasn't really a full journal. Just some random pages really. Who was it?" Paul quizzed himself. "John Whitmer," he said, finally remembering. "Yes, John Whitmer."

"Hmm. That's interesting."

"What's interesting?" Paul asked.

"John Whitmer was one of the Eight Witnesses who saw the plates. The plates were said to have the appearance of gold."

Paul scowled and a moan seeped from his lips. "Of course. I'm so stupid."

"And where did most of the Whitmer family live after the Saints left Missouri?"

"Richmond?" Paul asked.

"Exactly."

Paul stifled a yawn, covering his mouth. "Sorry. This is obviously more than coincidence, but the grave in Richmond didn't belong to John Whitmer."

"Well, that's true."

"How do you know?" Paul asked.

Bishop Taylor smiled. "Easy, John Whitmer is buried in the Kingston Cemetery, not Richmond."

"But nothing happened in Kingston," Paul said. He thought for another moment. He typed in Kingston Cemetery into his GPS. "Huh . . . Did you know Kingston is only eight miles from here?" Paul looked at the Bishop. "Wait here, please." Paul exited the SUV and quickly joined Emily at the patrol car.

"Agent Stephens, this is Deputy Blair," Emily introduced. "We've got local law enforcement watching for the pickup and the Charger."

"Good. Has anything unusual happened up around these parts today?" Paul asked.

Emily grinned. "Funny you should ask. There was a disturbance at one of the local cemeteries today."

"Kingston?" Paul asked.

"Yeah, how . . . ?" Emily asked.

Paul glanced back at his SUV and at Bishop Taylor behind the window. He leaned close to Emily. "This guy's been to Richmond,

Kingston, and now here. All in one day. He's escalating his timeline and becoming more brazen. We need to get to that cemetery. Maybe we'll find something to explain what's really going on here."

"Agreed. Why don't you—" Emily began but was cut off by the heavy chopping sound of rotating blades. A spotlight beamed from above, and a black FBI helicopter lowered slowly into the field. "Perfect," she yelled over the sound of the rotors.

"I'll take . . . Bishop Taylor . . . to the cemetery!" Paul yelled. Emily looked at Paul quizzically. Her eyes focused on his mouth as she tried to read his lips. "Bishop might be helpful. You take the chopper. Find Jimmy." Emily nodded in agreement.

Running to the SUV, Paul climbed in the driver's side. "Bishop, you feel like going for a ride?"

"Will it help find Liz and Clay?" Bishop Taylor asked.

"I'm hoping."

"Well, let's go, Paul. What are you waiting for?"

Paul checked his mirrors and backed out of the gate but stopped. He watched as Emily climbed into the helicopter and lifted off. Paul studied the faces and body language of the young men and young women surrounding the fire. Their faces expressed a mixture of fear, worry, uncertainty, excitement, and awe. Just like him.

(33)

THE TRUCK PASSED THROUGH ANOTHER town, came to a stop, and turned east near a grouping of large grain silos. Scud looked back at the town in the rearview mirror, but it was just like the first town. Dark.

Lifting his shirt to his nose, Scud blew with loud success and then looked at the gooey snot. "Whew, that was a good one." He picked up the brick from the middle of the seat and smirked. Liz shivered from the nose-blowing sound and crammed herself even farther into the corner against the door. Scud held the brick in his hand and stared, imagining the gold shining from underneath the caked layer. He glanced to the road and then again at his brick.

"Hey! Watch out!" Liz screamed, pointing at an abandoned car on the shoulder of the two-lane road.

Scud looked up. He dropped the heavy brick onto the seat and swerved, barely missing the car he had drifted toward. The truck lurched across the center lane and the rear fishtailed as he overcompensated. With both hands back on the wheel and his eyes on the road, he resumed his course in the correct lane.

"Whoo-whee!" Scud proclaimed. "You awake over there little girl?" he asked. He wiped his mouth on the shoulder of his shirt and gave a redneck laugh. "I nearly messed myself on that one."

Liz's fists clenched to the shoulder strap of her seat belt. "Why don't you just let me out?" Liz asked, a sob escaping from her throat.

"I'm just a kid. I don't know where you're going or what you're doing. I'm no threat to you."

"No, you're not," Scud said, licking his lips. "But you sure are cute. Business will be done soon, and then we can celebrate." Scud reached to the center, and his fingertips raced along the seat like a crawling spider. He stopped just before touching her leg.

Liz stifled a shriek.

"What? Don't you like wealthy men?"

Liz looked around the cabin of the truck as a tear ran down her cheek. She noticed the brick, hamburger wrappers and empty soda cans, sundry tools, a stone, a wooden box at her feet, and pink gum stuck to the dash where it had once held a picture. "Wealthy? I guess your house must be *super* nice." She wiped her cheek.

Scud smiled at the insult. "Not yet it's not, but it will be. I'll get myself a house with ten rooms and a swimming pool and the baddest truck you've ever seen. I'm thinking black and silver. Sounds nice, huh?"

"Don't care. Wealthy or not, you're still trash," Liz responded with cool indifference.

Scud's grin turned to a snarl, and he refocused on the road. "Stupid girl. I can't be trash when I'm rich. And you might want to be nicer to me."

Liz's sob turned to a laugh. "Be nice to you? Did I hurt your feelings? Forgive me for wondering how a scumbag like you plans to be rich. You probably rob gas stations and pizza shops. It looks like it's been very lucrative. Rich? Yeah, right."

"Shut up!"

Liz smiled nervously. "I did hurt your feelings. Awww."

"I will be rich. I'll get my gold. I don't care what a bratty girl thinks." Scud leaned forward in his seat and pulled the gun from the back of his pants. "I just think it would be smart for you to show a little respect," he said, holding the weapon up as a reminder.

Liz swallowed and then nodded.

"We'll be there soon. You'll do whatever I ask, and then we'll see what happens next," Scud said. "But you really should be nicer."

Liz nodded again. "Where are we going, anyway?" Liz asked.

Scud cleared his throat as if collecting a year's-worth of phlegm. "It's got a name I can never remember, but the map calls it the Mormon Shrine." He lowered his window and spit.

Liz's eyes widened and her head flinched. Her bottom lip dropped, and her voice sounded like a croak. "Mormon Shrine?"

Scud's eyes narrowed, and his lips curled up, exposing a blackened side tooth and dark chew grit littering his teeth. His head bobbed. "Yep. Mormon Shrine."

(34)

THE WHEELS OF THE CHARGER skidded to a stop, and Jimmy hopped out. He stepped in front of the headlights and picked up another rock. He examined the familiar cloth wrapped around it and then gazed into the sky as the clouds passed in front of the moon. A drop of light rain landed on his nose. He shook his head, climbed into the driver's seat, and slammed his door. He tossed the rock onto the passenger-side floor with the others. The tires squealed again as he stepped on the gas and continued north out of Hamilton.

"What am I doing?" Jimmy muttered, flipping on his brights. The light sprinkling of rain dappled the windshield, then it intensified, forcing him to turn on the wipers. His head listed from side to side, and he rubbed the crease in his forehead as he thought about Clay and Liz on their way to some unknown destination. *Maybe they've already arrived. The guy has a gun. What's he going to do to them? Maybe I missed the turn. Maybe I'm heading in the wrong direction. Maybe I'm too late.* Jimmy rubbed his aching eyes. "I'm so lost." Jimmy maintained his course, his heart racing to match the speed of the Charger.

He hadn't seen a cloth-tied rock for a few minutes, and the pounding rain turned to instant steam on the road and hood. "Please, tell me what I should do," he said before inhaling a cleansing breath. "I . . . need . . . help." He waited for a moment as if expecting to hear a voice speak back, but he only heard the gentle hum of the engine. "Please . . . I have to save them."

The Charger's hemi purred, but the gentle sound intensified into a low growl and then a heavy *thwat . . . thwat . . . thwat . . . thwat.* "Great!" Jimmy cursed as he checked the gauges. RPM's are okay. Engine temp okay. Gas okay. Tire pressure okay. The rapid rhythm continued sounding in his ears.

"Jimmy."

He locked his jaw open and rubbed his ear but he could feel the *thwat . . . thwat . . . thwat . . . thwat . . . thwat . . .* through the back of his seat, and then he heard his name again.

"Jimmy."

"I'm losing it." His breathing sped up as he considered the possibility that his heart was about to explode, but then the sound disappeared and the rhythmic feeling in his chest normalized.

The blood rushed to Jimmy's ears, and he became intensely aware of the heavy sound of each breath. His eyes darted from the road back to his gauges, then out the side windows as he searched for lights or any semblance of civilization along the darkened highway. The pounding rain stopped and the night became still.

Jimmy tightened his grip on the wheel and swallowed with a gulp. Then the percussion of the *thwat . . . thwat . . . thwat . . .* entered his body and attacked his ears as a beam of light brightened a round spot on the road in front of the speeding car. Jimmy stomped on the gas and entered the light. He shielded his eyes with his hand as the light entered through the windshield, and then he slammed his foot on the brake as a black helicopter dropped into view directly in front of his car.

The Charger fishtailed on the wet pavement. Jimmy held the wheel and closed his eyes as he felt the car start spinning. He opened his eyes again to see the black helicopter rising out of the car's path. The lights strobed and the world became silent. Jimmy felt time slow as the car spun toward a thin cluster of trees on the side of the road. Then time caught up and the car slid between the trees and into the mud of a farmer's field. Stalks of corn slammed against the windows as the car came to rest. Jimmy blinked slowly.

He smelled pollen in the muggy air and then recognized the rhythmical *thwat* of the helicopter. He breathed deeply and assessed the narrow gap between the trees and a power pole the car slid through. He watched the helicopter land on the road behind him. Jimmy took another breath and threw open the door. Bolting from the car, he ran deeper into the cornfield.

"STOP!" yelled an amplified voice. Jimmy turned to look but kept running, blocking the sting of cornstalks with his outstretched arms. The voice from the helicopter repeated. "STOP. JIMMY. STOP."

Jimmy slowed down. Hiding in the corn, he bent over with his hand on his knees as he gasped for air. He looked at the helicopter in the middle of the road. He wiped a hand through his rain-dampened hair and smiled when he saw Emily step from the helicopter. The rotors on the helicopter slowed, and the high pitch squeal of the engine died.

"Jimmy! It's okay. It's me," Emily said into the handheld helicopter microphone. She waited for a moment. "Where are you?"

Emily tossed the CB mic onto the helicopter seat and walked toward the corn. "Jimmy?" Cornstalks rustled. She moved closer. "Jimmy. Come on out," she yelled.

Jimmy hid for a moment longer as he regained his composure. Then he stepped from the corn. "Hi there, sweet cakes," Jimmy cracked. His brows knit together and his lips tightened as he attempted to hold in tears of exhaustion and worry.

"Nice try, Jimmy. You don't need to try to be cheery," Emily said, wrapping her arms around his neck and placing her cheek next to his. "Really, it's okay, Jimmy. We'll find the kids," she promised.

Jimmy smelled the comforting bouquet of Emily's perfume and laundry detergent. "I can't even tell you how glad I am to see you." Jimmy pulled Emily closer and squeezed. A tear ran down his cheek onto the top of her FBI cap. He wiped his face and then released her as he started waving his arms. "It's crazy. I was praying for help when this beam of light suddenly shined from heaven."

"You don't say."

"No, really. Shined from heaven, I tell you. It's a miracle."

"Actually, it's GPS on the car you stole," Emily countered.

"Stole? I borrowed . . . forcefully . . . maybe. So I guess you're here to arrest me then," Jimmy said with a forced smirk.

Emily's eyes narrowed as she lifted the brim of her cap. "It's a good idea, but no. Where are we, Jimmy? What are you doing here?" Emily turned in place, looking into the vast darkness surrounding them.

"Well, I can't say exactly where *here* is. I've been following the truck I told Paul about. I haven't seen it for ages, but every once in a while, and at every turn, I've found a rock."

"A rock?"

"Yeah. A rock wrapped in a piece of cloth. Clay climbed into the back of the truck when it took off with Liz. I think he's leaving bread crumbs for me to follow."

Emily grinned, and her head bobbed with admiration. "Smart boy."

"The breadcrumbs brought me here, but I have no idea where they're going," Jimmy's voice cracked and he cleared his throat. "I'm not even sure I'm still on the right track, but I don't know what else to do."

"Well then, I guess we'd better keep looking, don't you think?"

Jimmy's eyes scrunched as he struggled to hold in his emotions. "This is all my fault. I'm responsible for those kids."

"Come on. Let's hop in the heli and see if we can spot them."

Jimmy began to nod, but then it turned into a shake. "No. If Clay's still dropping crumbs, I need to find them. I'll drive, and you can scan from above."

"You don't think you're going to keep driving after that incredible exhibition of skill, do you?" Emily asked. "The panicked spinning was a nice touch."

"Yeah. About that, thanks for running me off the road." Jimmy grinned. "But I do have to say, it wasn't your most 'Christian' act of kindness."

"My pleasure. Look, we'll ride together, but I'll drive, and you look. Dan will be our eye in the sky. Deal?" Emily asked.

"Deal." Jimmy grabbed Emily again and planted a kiss on her cheek. "It really is a miracle, you know."

Emily looked at Jimmy and offered a modest nod. "Sure thing, Jimmy. Let's go find the kids."

(35)

AFTER A FEW MINUTES OF searching the gravel, dirt, and the sometimes-paved streets of Kingston, Paul and Bishop Taylor pulled onto an alley road behind an old brick school.

"You think this is our spot?" Paul asked. Bishop Taylor shrugged his shoulders. After another moment, the alley became a narrow dirt path leading to the Kingston Cemetery. "Okay, this is it," Paul said, stopping the car at the crest of a slight rise. The headlights shone across the hill of headstones. "Any ideas how we can find the Whitmer grave?"

"Yeah. Easy. We'll look for a sign. Pull ahead a little."

Paul's eyebrow rose. "I didn't really have you pegged as a sign seeker, Bishop. What are you expecting exactly?"

Bishop Taylor's stern gaze allowed only a hint of a smile. He pointed through the windshield. "A sign." A white metal sign was atop a short green post with an arrow pointing to the John Whitmer grave.

"A sign. Right," Paul said with a chuckle.

Stopping at the sign, Paul pointed the car in the direction of the arrow and turned the brights on. They climbed out of the car and walked a short distance until they found another sign. They stopped at the grave.

"We don't seek for signs, but we follow the ones we're given," Bishop Taylor said with an uncomfortable smile that quickly faded into his usual scowl of concern.

The tall limestone marker was shaped like a chalice, and a more current granite slab lay across the grass, commemorating the John Whitmer gravesite. To the right of the slab, the grass was matted, and remnants of piled dirt had turned to mud.

"Everything looks intact . . . kind of," Paul said.

"Yeah, but—"

A harsh but uneven voice startled him from behind. "What's your business here?" A flashlight clicked on.

Paul shielded his eyes with his left hand. "Hey, easy there, old timer. You mind lowering that light a bit."

The light lowered gradually until it rested upon the weapon Paul extended toward the man. "Oh, uh, sorry to bother you. I'll be going," the man volunteered, backing away. Paul identified himself, and the man sighed in relief. "Sorry to startle you boys," the man said. "But after the trouble we had here today, we're just keeping a closer eye on things. You understand."

"Are you with the sheriff's department?" Paul asked.

The old man moved closer and laughed, hacking up a series of coughs. "No. I'm not law. I'm with the historical society."

Bishop Taylor stepped toward the man and extended his hand in peaceful greeting. "Can you tell us what happened today?"

"Well, I trust you boys and all, but can I see some ID first?" he asked.

Bishop Taylor nodded and motioned. "Paul . . ." Paul pulled his badge from a pocket and held it into the light as he gave Bishop Taylor a friendly *I'm in charge* look as a reminder. Bishop Taylor mouthed the word, "Sorry."

"You've got to understand. This kind of stuff doesn't happen around here. This is a quiet town."

"I bet everyone was talking about this. Am I right?" Paul asked.

The old man coughed and laughed. "You got that right, but what is so important that brings the FBI out in the middle of the night?" the man quizzed.

Paul bent down to touch the mud at the side of the granite marker and then wiped it off in the moist grass. "Look, this is part of an ongoing investigation. Can you tell me what happened?" Paul's voice took on a less friendly edge.

"A little grumpy, aren't you?" the man accused. "You can call me Brother Dave."

Paul stood and met the man with a steely stare. "What happened?"

The old man scowled. He scratched his bald head and then adjusted his suspenders. "Fine, since you're going to be that way about it. Most people don't know that this county is unique from every other county in the entire United States."

"Are you talking about the Mormon history?" Bishop Taylor asked.

"That's right," Brother Dave said with a smile. "This county was created by the state legislature in 1836 for the sole purpose of Mormon settlement."

"I bet the locals love to hear that," Paul said.

"There's a plaque about it at the courthouse, but it's not all that well known, and just because it was created for Mormon settlement 175 years ago doesn't mean others don't have the same right to be here."

"Agreed. Let's try to stay on track here. You were going to tell me what happened at the gravesite today," Paul reminded.

"That's what I was doing. You need to understand a little bit of history to understand what happened. Do you know anything about the Mormons?" the man asked.

Paul grinned at Bishop Taylor. "Yeah, we know a little something."

"Then you may know that the Whitmers were important in the early Church history."

"Yeah, I got that much."

"Do you also know that the Whitmer family claimed to have a stone that allowed the holder to see the future?" the man asked.

Paul rolled his eyes. "Sir—*please* tell me about what happened *today*."

Bishop Taylor fidgeted with his watch. "I'm familiar with stories of the seer stone. The family's claims of possessing and using this stone actually led to friction with the Church and their eventual decision to leave the Church."

The old man's closed fist covered another hacking cough. "Their 'decision to leave the Church'?" The old man coughed as he laughed. "That's one way to put it. And where is that stone today?"

Bishop Taylor looked at Paul, who was staring into the man's eyes. "I don't know. Where?"

"Well, I don't know either. Not anymore. Yesterday I would have told you that the seer stone was placed in a stone box beneath this granite slab. But today . . . I have no idea."

Paul squinted and he motioned for the man to lower the light a little more. "Finally. So someone stole a Whitmer family artifact from below this memorial?"

"That's what I've been saying," the old man said with a snort.

"Okay, then answer me this question. Why would someone care enough about a 'seer stone' to dig up a graveyard in Kingston?" Paul asked. He waited for a response but was interrupted when his phone started to ring. He pulled it out of his pocket and looked at the display. The harsh ring continued to pollute the quiet night. "And why would this same person be interested in stealing a book about Church history, journal pages, and some kind of old scroll from a casket at the Richmond Cemetery."

The old man looked at the ringing phone in Paul's hand. "Are you going to get that?"

"There's nothing of intrinsic value there," Bishop Taylor noted. "All that stuff is interesting, but basically worthless."

"Except for the gold," Paul corrected.

"Whoa there! You didn't mention anything about gold," Brother Dave said. "What kind of gold?"

Paul's eyes scrunched together in confusion. "The shiny type." He looked at his ringing phone and pressed a button to disconnect the call.

Bishop Taylor stepped in. "Agent Stephens, I think he's asking if the gold is in coins or jewelry, or bars? What was the form of the gold?"

Paul thought for a moment. "We found remnants of brick, so we're speculating that we have gold hidden beneath a layer of mud brick."

Bishop Taylor and the old man looked at each other with slack jaws. "That changes everything," the old man said.

Paul's phone started to ring again.

"What is it with old men and gold?" Paul asked. "What does that change? What does it mean?"

The old man smiled, but a heavy frown covered Bishop Taylor's face. "I know exactly what it means," Bishop Taylor said. "And it's not good."

"Not good? It's fantastic!" the old man said. "The 'seer stone' is a key to finding the Mormon gold. Maybe it doesn't really see the future, but I'll bet it helps find the cache of gold." He whistled with glee.

Paul shook his head and then looked as his phone began screeching again. "How much gold?" he asked, shouting over the obnoxious chime of the phone.

The old man's bushy eyebrows rose. "More than I've got."

Bishop Taylor swallowed hard. "Forget about how much gold there is. What this really means is those kids are in serious trouble."

Paul nodded and then hit a button and placed the phone to his ear. "Yes . . . Good." Paul pulled the phone away and mouthed to Bishop Taylor. "Agent Mathews has Jimmy."

"What about the kids?" Bishop Taylor asked.

Paul continued listening to his phone and relayed information to Bishop Taylor. "Jimmy was following the truck . . . North on Highway 13 toward Gallatin?"

"Gallatin?" the old man asked.

Paul nodded and waved off the old man. "Yeah. It seems like they're going even farther into the middle of nowhere."

"You know Gallatin is the county seat of Daviess County, which was created at the same time as Caldwell County. You see, the Legislature split Ray County up and created the two new counties. Caldwell was for the Mormons and Daviess was to be shared by the Mormons and the locals." Paul shrugged off the old man and turned away, covering his free ear with a finger, but Bishop Taylor continued to listen. "Daviess County is rich in Mormon history too," the old man said. "Long time ago there was a crusty old local who used to give tours and spin yarns about Mormon history in the area."

"Clayton Barlow?" Bishop Taylor asked. The old man nodded. Bishop Taylor grabbed Paul by the shoulder and turned him around. "I think I know where they're going." Paul held up a finger and continued talking on his phone. Bishop Taylor grabbed Paul by the shoulders and stared into his eyes. "Paul, I know where they're going," he repeated.

"Hold on, Emily." Paul held his phone out so Emily could also hear Bishop Taylor. "Bishop, what are you saying?"

"Daviess County. They're going into Daviess County."

Paul grimaced. "Daviess County? Why? What's in Daviess County?"

"Adam-ondi-Ahman."

The old man nodded. "Yep. The old Mormon Shrine."

(36)

Agent Stark threw the door of his cruiser open and stepped out slowly. He stood beside his car in front of the bungalow-style home in Kansas City, Kansas. He rubbed his eyes and patted down his fuzzy red-and-gray brillow-pad hair as he watched the second cruiser pull up behind him. The rain fell gently on his navy FBI windbreaker, and he zipped up the front.

"Who are you?" Stark asked with his usual charm.

"I'm Specialist Sever," the young man responded, climbing out of his cruiser.

Stark squinted into the darkness. "I asked for Jacobson or Croton. What are you, some kind of intern?" Stark asked, not because he wondered, but because he wanted to show Sever who was boss.

"Intern? No." The young man chuckled. Stark stood stone-faced. "Um, yeah, I don't really know why I was assigned, sir. My supervisor called me with the address, so I'm here. What can I do?" Sever asked.

"I don't know what you can do. That's the problem." Stark cracked his neck and slammed his door. He leaned against the car and glared at the young specialist. "Why would they send me a know-nothing? And why does this crap always happen in the middle of the night?" Agent Sever shuffled his feet but didn't answer. "What's your specialty?"

"I'm a psychologist," Sever answered.

"A psychologist? Fantastic." Stark eyed the young man, halting his eyes on the weapon holstered at Sever's hip. Stark pointed at the weapon. "You know how to use that thing, champ? Or is it just for show to make you feel like a grown-up?"

"Sir, I'm fully certified with my weapon and—"

"Shut up." The falling rain tapped rapidly on Stark's jacket. He wiped the rain from his thick hair and continued staring at the young specialist.

Sever's eyes shifted nervously as the rain matted his straight hair against his forehead, making him look like an abandoned puppy. "Are we going to stand here all night, sir?" Sever asked.

"I'm thinking about it," Stark said.

"Well, as long as you're thinking, do you mind telling me our objective—sir?" Sever asked.

Stark smirked. "You see this house?" Sever nodded. "It belongs to a bad guy who does bad things."

"He sounds really terrible," Sever said. "Does this bad guy have a name?"

"John Ferguson—goes by Jack. Runs with a tough crowd. He steals old ladies' purses, gets cozy with a few petty drug traffickers, that kind of thing. He's an average low-life punk."

"Okay so why are *we* here?" Sever asked.

"We traced the auto registration of one of Ferguson's buddies. The guy's name is Melvin Scudder. Another punk who happens to drive a red-and-white pickup truck we're following. ID of the truck led us to the owner's cousin, and then a roommate, and ultimately here."

"Well, all right. Let's go get them."

"Oh, they're not inside. The truck's been spotted up north. It appears they've been on a crime spree, but tonight things were taken to another level when a couple of kids were abducted from a church camp. We've got a warrant."

Sever slicked his hair back and smiled. "So we're here to connect the dots?"

"What are you grinning at?" Stark asked, annoyed that anyone standing in the rain in the middle of the night could appear so genuinely excited and happy.

"This is what I do, sir. I connect the dots of a person's behavior, personality, and environment. You know—psychology."

"So you're telling me that you might actually be useful?" Stark asked. He waited for a response but received only another extended grin from his junior partner. "That's what I needed to know. Let's go."

Stark led the way up the concrete steps. He walked between piles of boxes, beer cans, and mechanical junk that created a corridor to the front entrance; an old air conditioning window unit and lawn-mower parts, fishing poles, and a plastic dog shelter lined the walk. Stark approached the door to look in through the window, but the glass was covered from the inside with a Confederate flag. He kicked aside a box and attempted looking through a slit in the blankets that hung like curtains on the side window.

"What do you see?" Sever asked.

"A redneck."

Sever fumbled for his weapon but halted as Stark flashed an angry glare and motioned with his hands to calm down.

"You okay there, champ?" Stark asked, his head shaking as he returned his attention to the door. He nodded to Sever, and they both unholstered their weapons. Sever held his weapon down, pointing at the porch while Stark held his raised beside his head. Standing at the side of the door, Stark balled his left hand into a fist and pounded three times. He waited. No lights. No barking dog. No movement of any kind. He pounded again. "FBI! Open up!" He waited again, but the silence in the house persisted.

"Back up, Sever. This is my favorite part." Stark took a step back and kicked. The door crashed open. "I never get tired of that."

Stark stepped into the dark house and flipped on his flashlight, holding it parallel with his gun. His nose twitched as the smell of musty filth assaulted his nose. He shined the light to the left and motioned for Sever to check upstairs. Stark turned to his right, careful not to kick a can lying in his path. He entered the living room, shined his light around, and then moved deeper into the house as he cleared each room. "Clear downstairs!" he yelled.

Stark flipped on the lights in the kitchen and turned on the rest of the lights downstairs. "Come on down, Sever. I'm eager to hear your enlightening psychological conclusions about our suspect." Stark snapped on his dark latex gloves and began thumbing through books and knickknacks that covered a large plastic container that was being used as a coffee table. He looked toward the stairs. "Sever, get your butt down here." Stark moved to the entryway and looked up the stairs. "Sever!"

Sever appeared at the top of the stairs, his usual jolly grin absent. "Sorry, sir, but you are definitely going to want to see this. Now."

(37)

SCUD TURNED OFF THE ENGINE and pulled the keys from the ignition but left the lights beaming forward. He dangled the keys in front of Liz. "Be right back."

Hopping down from the driver's seat, Scud walked to the bed of the truck. Liz heard a heavy thump and the sound of small items scattering across the metal bed. She turned in her seat and looked through the sliding rear window. She saw Scud hold up a pair of bolt cutters, but then she turned around in her seat, staring straight ahead at a sign that read, *Adam-ondi-Ahman.*

With bolt cutters in hand, Scud walked to the white metal crossbeam that blocked the entrance. He opened the bolt cutters and snapped the chain that locked the barrier closed. He walked the beam back, swinging it flush against the fence. Scud hopped back in the truck and turned the key. The engine roared.

"We're here. No one is around. Can't you just let me go?" Liz asked.

Scud's usual tobacco-riddled grin forced Liz to scowl and turn away. "But we just got here," Scud drawled. "We haven't even had any fun yet. You'll stay a little longer, won't you?" Liz's head wagged. "Now listen, I'm trying to be polite because I like you. I need your help." Scud's face grew long, and the smile disappeared from his face. His voice lowered. "Trust me. You want to be useful." He paused for a moment. "See, it's so much nicer to be polite, don't you think?"

Liz nodded.

Scud turned off the headlights and shifted the truck into drive. The gravel crunched quietly beneath the tires as he headed to the left.

*****

The truck pulled forward, exposing a lump on the road.

Clay tucked his knees into his chest, closed his eyes, and remained still, hoping he wouldn't be noticed. He listened to the truck pull away. As the rumble of the engine softened, Clay rolled onto his knees and looked at the trees that lined the left fork of the road. Climbing to his feet, he felt the pained familiarity of gravel beneath his worn soles. He winced at the sharpness of the rocks and followed the truck into the darkness.

(38)

AGENT STARK GRIPPED HIS PHONE, waiting for Thrasher to pick up on the other end.

"Yeah."

Stark held a hand near his nose to block the odor wafting up to his nostrils. He stifled a gag. "Thrasher, we need a coroner and a forensics team. ASAP."

"What'd you find?" Thrasher asked.

Stark stared at the carnage in front of him. "Soup. I've never seen anything like it. This is . . . uh . . . we need that forensics team, a meat wagon, and the M. E. down here, now."

"Agent Stark, I've got something else!" Specialist Sever yelled from the adjoining room.

"Fantastic," Stark mumbled. "I'll get back with you, Thrasher." Stark hung up.

Taking another look at the carnage on the floor and walls of the bedroom, Stark walked out the door into a less vomit-inducing filth. He peeked through the door into the next room at Sever, expecting another grisly discovery, but instead of grime, beer bottles, and decomposing human tissue, he saw a sterile office with plastic sheets lining the walls and an empty mahogany desk set at the center. A high-back leather chair was pushed in to the desk, and in each corner an air filtration tower stood four feet high.

"Somebody wasn't impressed with the cleanliness of this house,"

Sever said as he opened a closet door. "This is a refuge. Empty. Clean."

"Anything in the desk?" Stark asked, walking deeper into the room. The desk drawers hung open. Stark rubbed his finger along the inner corner of the top drawer and then looked at his finger. "Nothing."

"Like I said, clean," Sever said. "Whoever worked in this room was an outsider. He didn't belong here. He was fastidious and even more disgusted by this place than we are."

"Impossible."

Sever grinned. "He has a healthy ego and a taste for the finer things. He's determined, but most important, he's our killer."

"How do you know that? And maybe 'he' was a 'she,'" Stark proffered.

"No, definitely a 'he.' The mahogany desk is thick and blocky, definitely masculine. The leather chair demands attention. He wants to feel powerful."

"Who would know it? I doubt he was holding board meetings in here. The room may be clean, but the rest of the place is a pit."

"You're right about that. The scene outside this room is definitely an embarrassment, but the chair provides him a level of comfort he's accustomed to. It helps him to cope with the rest of this . . . environment."

"So what's with the desk?" Stark asked.

Sever pulled the chair out and set one knee on the hardwood floor. He leaned under the desk and wiped his gloved hand. "The floor's as clean as the desk. I don't see anything that would tell us what he was doing in here."

Stark plopped into the raised, black chair. "The guy was short." He scooted the chair in to the desk and sat with his hands folded in front of him. The door to the hallway was in front and to the right. Against the left wall, Stark could tell the plastic covered a window. Plastic covered nearly everything. "Well, look at that." Stark stood and the chair rolled to the back wall.

"What is it?" Sever asked.

Stark walked to the window and bent down. "Plastic is

everywhere, right?" Sever nodded. "Except right here," Stark said, pointing at an electrical outlet.

"Is it for the air purifiers?"

Stark looked at the purifiers in each corner and listened to the gentle hum. "They're running, but they must use some kind of battery. I don't see any power cords. Something else was plugged in here and I'm betting that something was sitting on that desk."

"A computer."

Stark scoffed. "Of course, a computer. Your dot connecting is *really* impressive. Laptop or desktop?" Stark asked.

Sever squinted for a moment as he thought. "Desktop. He's been working in here for a while, and he likes the feel of substance, power. Whoever worked in here is precise, clinical. But judging by the room next door, he's also brutal," Sever said.

"Right. What would this guy be doing in a place like this at all? Why would he lower himself to be here? And what drove him to butcher the person in the next room?"

"I think it's possible there might actually be two bodies in there," Sever said, shuddering. "But there are so many pieces it's hard to tell."

"So we find the short anal-retentive computer guy who separates himself from pure filth with walls of plastic and air purifiers while sitting at an oversized desk in an oversized chair, and we'll find our killer," Stark said.

Sever snapped off his glove and ran a hand through his wet stringy hair. "Not only will we find our killer, but we'll find his computer. That computer could hold the key to understanding the 'why' of all of this."

"And when we understand the 'why' to this scene, we'll understand the connection to the abductions up north . . . maybe. Let's get to it." Stark pulled out his phone and hit a speed dial. "Yeah, Thrasher. We're going to need you here too. You might want to wear your galoshes."

"Still raining?" Thrasher asked.

Stark peeked into the room covered in gore. "Don't know, but trust me, you're going to want them."

(39)

PAUL STARED AT THE EMPTY road and then looked in the rearview mirror at the silhouette of the cemetery on the hill behind him. He listened to Bishop Taylor's heavy breathing. "Are you doing okay, Bishop?" he asked, breaking the silence.

"No."

Paul wanted to offer words of encouragement and support. He wanted to promise things would work out, that Liz and Clay would be safe, but he didn't want to lie, especially to his bishop.

"Okay, Bishop, I know it couldn't be the gold plates, but is it possible there is a stockpile of Mormon gold somewhere around here?" Paul asked.

Bishop Taylor shook his head. "I'll admit I've had some fun in the past speculating about the legends. I may have even let my imagination run away with things on occasion, but no. It's absurd. The whole idea that there is a pile of Mormon gold is absolutely ludicrous."

"Well, someone believes it," Paul countered. "Is our suspect just a crazy coot, or is there some reason for him to believe the stories? He's taking some big chances. In his mind, the risk must be acceptable." Paul looked at Bishop Taylor, who stared blankly ahead.

"For years, there was an old guy from the Gallatin area who perpetuated these myths. He used to give tours of Adam-ondi-Ahman to Church members who visited the area. I read somewhere that he talked about 'Mormon caches' around Spring Hill." Bishop Taylor chuckled, but there was no joy in his voice. "He even used to show visitors piles of rocks he claimed were remains of ancient altars. It was later discovered that local farmers would dump the rocks they cleared from their fields because they knew Mormon pilgrims would carry them off as souvenirs."

"So what are the 'Mormon caches'?" Paul asked.

The bishop shrugged, and his voice wavered with weary coldness. "Who knows? Maybe the old man made it all up. Maybe it was old stockpiles of rifles from the militia at Gallatin. But I can tell you what it wasn't. Gold. Impossible. It wasn't gold."

Paul cleared his throat. He looked at Bishop Taylor and raised a questioning eyebrow.

Bishop Taylor sighed. "I'm fine." He looked at Paul and wrung his hands together. "But Liz is out there somewhere. And Clay."

"So tell me. How can you be so sure there wasn't any gold?" Paul asked. Bishop Taylor scoffed as if he had just been asked how he knew Bigfoot didn't exist. Paul lifted his hand. "Hey, I'm just trying to keep you thinking about something other than Liz."

Bishop Taylor grinned sheepishly. "Paul, the Mormons were so poor, they settled Caldwell and Daviess Counties as part of a government land program. They laid claim to tracts of land. All they had to do was show that they had made improvements to the land and they would have first bid when it came up for government auction. It was cheap. Super cheap, like a dollar an acre. They had to claim land this way because they were too poor to purchase it any other way. Unfortunately, they were forced to leave the state before they could ever receive their claims." He looked at Paul. "Are you following me?"

Paul wasn't convinced.

Bishop Taylor continued. "Then, when the Mormons fled to Illinois, they purchased swampland because they couldn't afford anything else. Does that sound like a people who had stockpiles of gold?" he asked. His voice sounded weary yet anxious, interested yet annoyed. "Really, who in their right mind would live in utter destitution when they had stashes of gold?" He breathed heavily as he closed his eyes.

Paul patted the bishop on the shoulder. "It just doesn't make sense, Bishop. It's like this guy has been collecting puzzle pieces to a treasure map that leads to gold. There must be some compelling reason."

Bishop Taylor shook his head. "If I was inclined to search for gold in northern Missouri, I wouldn't be looking to find it from the Mormons."

Paul's eyebrows furrowed as he thought. "What do you mean by that? Is there another possible source?"

Bishop Taylor turned to Paul. His chin lowered and his eyes pierced the darkness. "Paul, did you ever pay attention in your Missouri history classes?"

Paul flipped on his brights and smiled as they exited Hamilton and continued north along Highway 13.

"Sometimes. Why?"

"Well, after the Mormons were forced to leave their settlement at Diahman—that's what the locals called it—the area was resettled. People moved into the homes vacated by the Mormons, and they renamed the township Cravensville. Now, during the Civil War, Missouri was a hotbed of activity. Is any of this starting to sound familiar?"

Paul nodded. "Sure, I've heard of the Civil War," he said with an embarrassed grin.

"Good for you, Paul. Anything else?"

Paul thought for a moment. "Cravensville? Interesting, but nope."

"You're really going to owe me some consulting fees on this one."

Paul smiled. "Please, go on," he said with a flourish of his hand.

"Okay. Listen up. In 1862, the Union tried to stop some Confederate reinforcements from joining in a battle at Independence, and there was a skirmish at Cravensville. One of the captured Confederate soldiers tried to bargain for his life by telling the Union officers about a stash of gold that was hidden during the battle. When the Union officers couldn't find the gold, the prisoner was executed by firing squad. Even after the execution, stories of the gold stash leaked out and the legend grew."

"Yeah, I can see that," Paul admitted.

"Old Clayton Barlow could have mixed the stories of the Mormons and the Confederate gold together to make his tours more interesting. After a while, he probably couldn't even remember what parts of the story were true."

"Clayton Barlow? That's the name of the guy who gave tours to the Mormons?" Paul asked.

Bishop Taylor tilted his head. "I'm pretty sure. I studied up a bit before our trek, but I can't swear to the name."

Paul scratched his head and let out an exultant laugh. It felt strange and sounded even stranger. There hadn't been cause to laugh all night. Paul shook his head from side to side as a grin covered his face.

"I'm sorry, Bishop. I don't mean to make light of the situation or anything, but this is all starting to make a little bit of sense." Paul laughed again. "Unbelievable. Clayton *Barlow*. That's great!"

(40)

THE HEADLIGHTS BEAMED ON A wide cluster of three rocks in the middle of the road. Emily pulled over, and Jimmy hopped out of the Charger. He stooped over, picked up the cloth-wrapped rocks, and then climbed into the passenger side.

"I guess that means we turn left," Jimmy said, tossing the rocks onto the floor, but Emily held up a finger as she spoke on her phone.

"Yeah, Paul. GPS puts us about seven minutes out. Where are you?" Emily asked. She listened and then sighed. "Paul, which is it, fifteen or twenty minutes?"

Jimmy's eyebrows rose with surprise when Emily spoke brusquely to her partner. "Is everything okay?" Jimmy whispered.

Emily didn't respond. "Fifteen? Good. Hurry."

Emily listened some more as her perma-scowl faded and a smile broadened across her face. "Really? Clayton Barlow. Are you sure? Have you verified ancestry with Frank and Luetta Barlow?" She waited for a response. "Okay. Let me know as soon as you hear back from Thrasher." Emily thought for a moment as she listened to Paul. "Yeah, that puts a whole new spin on the book stolen during the home invasion. Maybe Clayton Barlow left notes that lead to the gold . . . Interesting. Hold on a second. Let me get Stark and Thrasher on conference call." Emily pushed a couple of buttons and then dialed. "Thrasher. Hold on a minute." She dialed another number and waited, "Stark, are you there? Good. Can you all hear me?"

Paul, Stark, and Thrasher all responded in the affirmative.

"Thrasher, what do you know?" Emily asked, shifting the Charger out of park and turning north.

"On my way to Stark's crime scene. Still waiting on research about the Barlow connection." Thrasher went silent.

"Is that it? What else do you have?" Paul asked impatiently.

"John Ferguson owns the home, and Melvin Scudder is registered on the pickup."

"Yeah, we got that."

"No other names on the title, but I'm searching census and utility records to see if anyone else is registered as an occupant. It may give us a lead on our John Doe at the house," Thrasher said, exhaling into the phone.

"We'll have forensics over here in a few minutes. We'll see what they can find, but I'm not hopeful," Stark said.

"Why not? What's wrong?" Paul asked.

"The crime scene's a mess. It's going to take a while to sift through the identifiable body parts and blood. We're estimating this soup is fresh today, and the house in general is a disaster. It's going to take them days to separate any useful clues from the filth," Stark said.

"We don't have days," Paul snapped. "What are the chances our John Doe is this Ferguson guy?"

"Gee, I hadn't considered that. Thanks, Paul." Stark spat. "We're checking it out. But are you guys ready for this?"

"What is it, Stark?" Emily asked.

"Thrasher thinks he can find an electronic fingerprint from our clean room. When I say clean, I mean this place is clean. There's nothing here, but Thrasher can . . . Hey, Thrasher, explain it."

Thrasher grunted into the phone, and Emily held it away from her ear. "Computers are all about data. In and out. That's all they do. They process."

"So . . ."

"We know there must have been a computer hooked up in this

room. We know where it's been. We know the road it traveled. All I have to do is back trace the data streaming to and from this house. Kind of like tracking a cell phone user by the towers his phone pings off, only in reverse."

"You can do that?" Emily asked.

"Well, kind of. I can trace the streams of information. If I'm lucky, I can see who he communicated with, IP addresses, that kind of thing," Thrasher said. "If I can locate the user's Internet signature ,I can track him. See where he's been and when. From there I can piece together what he was doing."

Emily smiled. "Amazing, Thrasher. Our chopper is over Adam-ondi-Ahman now. Reports are normal. Nothing unusual. Everything's dark. I'll be there in two minutes, and Paul is a few minutes behind me."

"Look, these two kids are with this Scudder guy. We know he's a bit of a thug, but do we think he's working alone or should we expect a mob of bad guys?" Paul asked.

"This guy's not alone," Stark said. "He could be with at least one jerk friend, if he didn't already kill him, and judging from the extreme filth, dishes, and multiple sleeping areas in the house, contrasted with the spotlessness of the clean room, there are *at least* a few other guys living here with him. Or he has more personalities than is possible for a sane man. Subtract one or two dead guys upstairs, and he's likely still got some help."

"One or two dead guys? You can't tell?" Emily asked.

"No. And Specialist Sever claims the guy working in the clean room is separate from the others. He wouldn't live in this muck. But he's connected somehow. He may or may not have his own agenda and crew," Stark said.

"Great."

Emily tapped on the breaks as the GPS began beeping. The display directed her to turn left in one hundred feet. "Guys, I'm here. Notify me the instant you know anything," Emily said.

The other lines dropped off the call except Paul. "Emily, I'm right behind you. Wait for me. I'll be there in—"

Emily hung up and muted her phone as she turned left onto the gravel drive. "Jimmy, let's see what we can find." Jimmy nodded. "We don't know how many others there may be, so we're going to take it slow."

Jimmy cleared his throat and swallowed as he looked at one road veering off to the right and the other to the left. "Which way?"

Emily studied the drive as the forks headed in opposite directions. She turned off her lights and stopped the car. Her shoulders rose as she sighed. "Great question."

(41)

After an excruciating day of hiking along the back roads of Caldwell County, the last thing Clay wanted to do was hike another gravel road, but he trudged forward. The gravel stabbed through his shoes, and his legs were already reminding him of their exhaustion. Clay looked ahead at the road, which curved into a roundabout parking area at the center of a well-designed grove of trees.

Stepping into the grass, Clay spotted his target and leaned behind a tree. The red-and-beige pickup truck was backed up next to a small restroom facility on the west side of the parking area. The dim light above a drinking fountain illuminated the tailgate of the truck and the man standing next to it. For the first time, Clay looked into the face of Liz's abductor. The grimy man hovered near the tailgate and occasionally leaned over. It looked like he was moving pieces on a chessboard. After each move, the man looked at his work. Clay decided to move closer.

Keeping to the shadows was easy—the grove provided ample darkness, and the moon remained mostly covered by passing clouds. The ground was dry, but a cool breeze tickled the back of Clay's neck ,and the fresh smell of a summer shower approached.

Making a wide berth, Clay crouched and circled the drive, moving from tree to tree. When the man turned away, Clay darted across a trail that led down the hill through another grove of trees. He resumed his cover behind a large rock and held still. Clay waited another moment and continued through the trees to gain a better vantage point.

Liz remained in the truck with her head propped against the glass. Clay waved when he thought she might be looking his direction, but she didn't seem to notice. Clay moved closer. His shoes inched through the freshly cut grass and then raced from behind the last tree to the small bathroom facility. Clay leaned his back against the wall and peeked around the side.

"Would you get out here already, you lazy little—" Scud said.

Liz rolled down her window and spoke in his general direction. "That's not very *polite* of you." Scud removed the weapon from the back of his pants and tapped it on the metal of the truck bed. "Fine." The door squeaked as she threw it open and then slammed it shut.

"Keep it down," Scud growled.

"So why do people call you Scud? Did your parents lose a bet?" Liz asked as she approached the tailgate.

Scud thought for a moment and then spit. "Because I'm as deadly as a Scud missile."

A chortle escaped from Liz's lips. "Okay then. Sorry I asked."

Clay smiled at her sass. He waved his arm again trying to get Liz's attention, but she didn't notice. She turned and stood with her back to Clay, blocking his view of the tailgate. Stepping carefully around the building, Clay peeked around the other side. The light was brighter there, and he felt exposed, so he pulled his head back and listened.

"So what is all this junk?" Liz asked.

Scud laughed. "This is wealth. This is my future," he said.

"Has anyone ever told you that you're kind of . . . um . . . dramatic?"

"That's sweet. Thanks," Scud said.

Clay's head cocked with confusion. Liz's comment didn't sound like a compliment, but Scud didn't seem to notice. *He's not playing with a full deck and he's got a gun. Wonderful.*

"It just looks like old paper and some rocks," Liz said.

"Yes. But where will the old paper and rocks lead us?" Scud asked.

"Into the middle of nowhere?" Liz asked. "Wait, we're already here."

Scud placed his weapon in the back of his pants and pulled out a pocketknife. He flipped it open and locked the blade in place. Picking up the heavy brick from behind the other items he whittled away a large piece of the exterior mud brick. He held it in front of Liz's eyes. "You see that?" Scud asked. "Gold. And there's lots more of it."

Clay leaned around the corner to look at the brick but Scud's body blocked the gold from his view. Clay saw Liz's eyes widen. With Scud's back to him, Clay leaned further out from behind the building and waved his arms. Liz yelped, and Clay quickly retreated back behind the corner of the building.

"Where'd you get that?" Liz asked.

"Doesn't matter," Scud said. "What you should be asking is 'where is the rest of it?'"

Clay leaned his back against the wall, out of view of the others. He turned his head and tried to listen.

"Seriously. You want me to help you find gold?" Liz asked.

Her voice sounded strange, and Clay couldn't decide if she sounded worried, annoyed, or excited. He felt his chest bubble with excitement, so he figured she was likely feeling the same thing.

"That's right," Scud said. "See, I'm not such a bad guy. I'll be so rich I won't miss a bar. I'll let you keep it. You don't have anything to worry about. I'd never hurt anyone."

Clay's eyebrows scrunched together as he scowled. *You shot at Jimmy, you big dope. No way would Liz buy that line.* Clay peeked back around the corner.

"Why me? Why do you need my help?"

Scud thought for a moment. "Finding the gold is a two-person job, and my last partner dropped out. I need someone and you're it."

Liz wiped her hand across her forehead. "So we're partners?"

Scud narrowed his eyes. "That's right . . . partners."

Liz looked up, catching Clay's eye for a split second. Her left eye twitched in a way that looked like an attempted wink. "Great. Partners."

(42)

DROPS OF HEAVY RAIN PINGED on the hood of the truck. The air swirled, and the canopy of leaves rustled. Scud swept up the journal papers and parchment into his arm and rushed them into the cab of the pickup.

Clay sensed this was his moment. Picking up a rock half the size of a baseball, Clay reached back and hurled it at a boulder on the other side of the drive. The rock crashed and then skittered off into the gravel.

Scud's head lurched up as he looked around the driver's side door. He placed the papers on the seat and then looked into the darkness. He closed the door and took a step toward the noise. "Did you hear that?"

Liz looked to the side of the building and saw Clay nodding his head. "Yeah," she said. Her voice faltered with uncertainty, but it sounded like fear. "Is someone there?" Liz called out louder. Clay lobbed another rock toward the trail leading down through the grove. The rock hit the ground and rolled. "It's coming from over there," Liz said, pointing to the far corner of the parking area.

Scud stepped toward the sound as his eyes searched.

Poking his head out from behind the corner of the restroom building, Clay motioned for Liz to follow. She took two steps and then stopped. Turning back to the bed of the truck, Liz lifted the stone artifact and a rolled strip of metal and stuffed them into her pockets.

"Come on," Clay urged quietly. He tossed one more rock into the trees past the trail in hopes of luring Scud away. He motioned again for Liz to follow. She stepped cautiously and then slipped around the corner, joining Clay with her back to the cool concrete.

"You okay?" Clay asked.

Liz's smile brightened the darkness as she hugged Clay. "How did you . . . ?"

"Later." Clay stuck his head back around the corner, and he saw Scud returning to the truck.

Scud took a slow step and then waited. "Liz? Partner?"

"We've got to go," Clay whispered.

"Where?"

"I don't care. Anywhere." Grabbing Liz's hand, Clay stepped to the back of the building and raced along a line of trees before entering the grove to the south. The bitterness of Scud's calling fell farther behind and was finally swept away by the sound of rustling leaves and wind.

Holding Liz's hand, Clay ran through the trees. He looked to the sky for a hint of light, but the moon had disappeared. The blackness was complete. Then the smell of summer rain filled the air, and the patter of drops fell through the leaves.

Clay stopped and turned around, looking toward the faint light up the hill near the drinking fountain. The truck remained, but Scud was gone. "Do you see him?" Clay whispered.

Liz looked. She shook her head. "He's got a gun."

Clay nodded. "We've got to keep moving. Stay close." Clay loosened his grip on Liz's hand, but she squeezed tighter.

The rain intensified. Drops beat upon them as they navigated the darkness of the grove. Then the trees and their cover ended as the grove opened onto a plateau overlooking a lower valley. Flat boulders lined the gravel outlook, and another trail continued farther down the hill toward the valley floor.

Clay looked into the sky, and the rain beat across his face. He rubbed his hands across the side of his head like a squeegee. His clothing clung to his body. "What do we do?"

Liz looked back in the direction of the truck, but it was out of sight. Except for her black pigtails sticking out over her ears, her wet hair gripped her head. "I don't know." A string of light webbed across the sky to the south, lighting the valley below, but the sudden percussion of thunder forced Liz to take a step back. "Can he find us here?" Liz asked as another bolt of light crashed through the sky.

The rain flowed over Clay's face. "We're probably safe for a while."

Clay looked back in the direction of the truck as another clap of lightning mingled with the falling rain. His eyes widened and he pointed. He tried to speak but only a gurgle escaped his lips. He stepped backward toward the lower trail, pulling Liz with him. He pointed again.

Another bolt of lightning brightened the sky. The silhouette of a man approached. Scud walked down the hill in their direction. Clay's hand tightened around Liz's, and he watched as Scud weaved through the trees with his gun held at his side.

"Run!"

(43)

"YOU ACTUALLY WAITED FOR ME," Paul said as he stepped from his SUV and approached the driver's window of the Charger. "I'm impressed. I didn't actually think—"

"Of course I waited. We're a team," she said, trying to sound professional.

Paul leaned over and looked through the window. "Good to see you, Jimmy. How are you doing?"

Jimmy fidgeted in his seat. "Honestly, I'm about to explode here. Let's do *something*," he muttered while giving Emily an evil eye.

Paul examined the forked road. "Which way, boss?"

Emily smiled sweetly, but her eyes were full of fire. She couldn't tell if it was the added stress of the kids being abducted or the news of her pending reassignment, but the irrationality of her annoyance was obvious even to her. It wasn't Paul's fault, at least not totally, but everything he said irritated her like a needle prick to the skin or a jab to the eyes. She tightened her jaw and tried to hold her tongue, but the response flew out. "If we knew which direction to go, we wouldn't be sitting here. We're waiting for a map so we can make an educated guess." Emily felt guilty the instant she heard the tone of her response. She wanted to apologize but didn't dare show weakness.

Bishop Taylor stepped toward the Charger. "If I remember right, the left path goes to a valley overlook, and the right path goes to Spring Hill."

"Let's make this simple. Emily, you go to the right with Jimmy, and I'll go to the left. Any word from the chopper?" Paul asked, looking heavenward. "He *is* up there, right?"

"Yeah, he's up there. I just checked in, but he hasn't seen anything. He'll let me know of any change and await *my* order," Emily said.

"Okay, so what is *your* order, Agent Mathews?" Paul asked.

She sighed. "Jimmy and I will go left. You and Bishop go right."

Paul nodded. "Of course. Anything else?"

Emily looked sadly at Paul and started rolling up the window on the Charger. She didn't want to be harsh with him, but transitioning their relationship to a more "official" partnership was for the best. At least she hoped so. If she accepted the new assignment, the professional relationship was the only one likely to endure. Emily hollered through the crack. "Just get to it already!"

Paul and Bishop Taylor stood next to the SUV watching the Charger head down the south fork. "Problems?" Bishop Taylor asked.

"Apparently."

*****

Paul and Bishop Taylor headed along the north fork of the gravel road just inside the gates of Adam-ondi-Ahman. Paul turned on his intermittent wipers to clear the raindrops from the windshield. A white fence lined the road, and occasional mailboxes extended from the end of driveways.

"Missionaries live there," Bishop Taylor said. They sat quietly as the SUV moved slowly along the road. "Hey, Paul, do you mind dropping me off?"

"Excuse me?"

"Next mailbox. Let me out. No one knows this place better than the missionaries. Let me see if I can get a good map or directions."

"Not a bad idea, but I'm not waiting for you. Try not to get shot when you ring the doorbell at . . ." Paul looked at his watch. "Whoa. At 3:30 a.m."

A mailbox and driveway came into view. "Here, pull over."

"You've got my number, right, Bishop?" Bishop Taylor nodded. "Call me when you have some information."

"Will do." Bishop Taylor climbed out, but then he leaned back into the SUV. "And Paul, be a hero, but stay safe."

Paul nodded. The door closed, and he watched as Bishop Taylor took his first few steps jogging toward the white farmhouse at the end of the long driveway. Paul pulled along the dark road and removed his phone from a pocket and dialed.

"Thrasher, anything new?" Paul asked as he recognized the usual heavy breathing on the other end of the line.

"Since you asked ten minutes ago?"

"Yeah, since then," Paul said. He shook his head. *Everyone's a serious grump today*, but then he realized that this was normal for Thrasher.

"Actually yes," Thrasher said in his low guttural growl. "Barlows are all related. Clayton Barlow is Frank Barlow's great-uncle."

Paul smiled. "Perfect. Anything else?"

Thrasher was silent on the other end of the line. "You want some scary coincidence?" Thrasher asked.

"What do you mean?"

"We have another family connection," Thrasher said.

Paul bit the side of his lip. "What is it?"

"Did you know the area surrounding Adam-ondi-Ahman was later named—"

"Cravensville," Paul answered, proud that he could show off a little.

"Yep. Do you know who it was named after?"

Paul racked his brain for a split second or two, but after realizing Bishop Taylor hadn't told him that part, he conceded that he wasn't as smart as he was pretending to be. "Gotta be honest. That one's kind of slipping my mind."

"Cravensville is named after the founder, John Cravens."

Paul's mouth hung open. "John Cravens?" He laughed nervously. "You're not going to tell me he's related to Judge John Craven, are you?" Paul waited for a response, but while Thrasher didn't speak, Paul could feel the frown oozing through the phone. "Thrasher, you're not telling me Judge John Craven is related to the guy who settled Cravensville. Are you?"

"Somewhere along the line, Craven dropped the 'S' at the end, but . . . yep." Paul pressed on the brakes and placed the SUV in park. He leaned his head back and stared at the ceiling of the vehicle. "Crazy coincidence, no?" Thrasher asked.

"No. A coincidence like that is impossible. Is Craven still at Crossroads Correctional in Cameron?"

"Yep."

"Find out who's been visiting, who's been writing to him, and who he's calling. I want all records for the past year," Paul barked.

"Already got them. Long list too," Thrasher said. "But there's only one name you'll care about."

"Who?"

"Nicas."

Paul rubbed his hands through his hair as his mouth opened in disbelief. "You can't be serious. Alex Nicas has been visiting Judge Craven? Please tell me our corrections department is capable of keeping a wanted fugitive from speaking with Judge Craven. Seriously. Tell me. Please."

"I never said it was *Alex* Nicas."

Paul sighed and took a deep breath. He shook his head as he glanced at his watch. "I don't get it. I'm a little tired here. What are you saying?"

"Alex Nicas is still out there, but there's no way he gets in to visit the judge at a level 5 maximum-security prison. But his half-nephew . . ."

"Whoa, hold on. Half-nephew? Is that even a real thing?" Paul asked. "Why didn't I know he has a 'half-nephew'?"

"Stephens, you're focusing on the wrong thing here. Forget Alex Nicas and forget Judge Craven. They're old news."

"Maybe not as old as we thought," Paul corrected.

"We need to worry about Acacio Nicas. Goes by Ace."

Paul flexed his grip around the steering wheel. "Ace, huh? Sounds delightful."

"Right."

"What do we know about him? Where does he live? What kind of work does he do? How close is he to his half-uncle? Does he have other family?" Paul asked.

"Yeah, I'll get back to you on that."

Paul listened for a moment and could hear Thrasher's fingers pounding the keyboard in the background. "Fine, but put a rush on it," Paul said.

Thrasher growled into the phone, and it wasn't his usual subtle growl. It was intentional. "Do you know how much I do around here?"

Paul winced and paused before answering. "Yes," he said, hoping to placate the growling agent.

"Do you realize I'm standing in a room with bloody body parts scattered everywhere while I'm tracing phantom computer activity from hours ago, while connecting the Barlow, Craven, and Nicas families?"

Paul's eyebrows rose. "Of course. I know that. You're the amazing Thrasher," Paul said, hoping his shameless compliment would earn him some brownie points.

"You're asking the impossible," Thrasher said. "I'm busy."

"Yeah. I know."

Thrasher breathed heavily into the other end of the line. "As long as you *know* it, Stephens."

"I know it. You're the man!"

"Good. We agree," Thrasher said.

"Thrasher, I need to know everything about Acacio Nicas—immediately. Oh, and see if there's any new chatter on where we might find Alex Nicas. So hurry up." Paul hung up before Thrasher could growl at him again.

"What is going on around here?" Paul asked himself. Then, the thunder crashed and lightning webbed across the sky. The downpour began.

(44)

PROTRUDING FROM THE HILL, A flat boulder created a miniature cave that sheltered Liz and Clay from the onslaught of rain. Liz's breathing raced as she clenched her hand around Clay's. Kneeling in a puddle, Liz listened for approaching footsteps, but all she could hear was the pounding storm and the stream that flowed over the boulder like a waterfall in front of her.

"We can't stay here," Clay said. "This is way too obvious. Scud will look in here for sure," he whispered.

Liz swallowed and brushed the soaking hair out of her eyes and then yanked up her long socks to cover her knees. She released Clay's hand and leaned closer to the water flowing over the edge of the boulder.

"Careful."

Liz looked back at Clay and raised one eyebrow, then refocused her attention on the setting outside the thin fall.

"Can you see anything?" Clay asked.

A flash of brilliant white brightened the sky. Liz's eyes darted from side to side, trying to take in every detail during the brief moment of light. "No." Liz backed up, her back scraping against the rock. She sat in the puddle with her knees held to her chest.

"We're going to get out of this," Clay said.

Liz's shoulders lurched as she laughed silently. "Yeah? How do you know that?" she challenged.

"Jimmy will have people out looking for us," he offered feebly. "And it will be light in a few hours. Scumbags like Scud work best in the dark when no one can see what they're doing. He won't have that cover much longer." Liz wanted to believe Clay, but his optimism felt naïve.

Their heads hunched forward to avoid hitting the low rock ceiling. Liz shivered despite the muggy heat of the night. Her soaked clothes and hair sent a chill deep into her bones. Clay lifted his arm and Liz scooted closer. He placed his large hand on her arm, sending an instant shot of warmth into her body.

"I hope you're right," Liz said. Clay remained silent. "I hope we get through this, but whatever happens, thanks for coming after me." Liz stifled a quiet cry as Clay squeezed her arm. They sat in silence.

"Clay."

"Yeah."

"Things don't always work out, you know. Bad things happen to good people all the time." She paused for a moment. "Even when they don't deserve it. Even when they pray," Liz said, remembering the reenactment of David W. Patten's death. Liz's forehead rested against her knees. "Bad things happen, Clay. There's nothing we can do about it."

"Shhhh. Let's keep quiet and listen."

"Okay."

"Go ahead and close your eyes for a couple of minutes, and then we'll need to get moving," Clay said.

Overcome by a massive yawn, Liz rubbed around the sockets of her eyes and then opened her eyes wide as if propping them up with toothpicks. She wiggled her ears, placing them on high alert. Then she looked at Clay, cradling her in the nook of his arm. Her shoulders bobbed, and then she let out a muffled sob. She leaned in closer and wrapped her other arm around Clay.

Liz appreciated the warmth of Clay's embrace, and it helped her to relax. She closed her eyes, but her mind couldn't rest. Her thoughts couldn't be diverted from Scud's ugly face. His tobacco-covered teeth and his filthy shirt covered in mud, oil, and snot. Her mind replayed the sound of his gun tapping on the tailgate of the pickup. She could see the light glimmer off the weapon and could almost smell the steel. *I could have run. I could have jumped out of the truck when it slowed. I could have screamed for help. I could have . . .*

Liz's mind clipped the thought. Her eyes popped open and her head jerked up, bumping on the low ceiling. She held the crown of her head and listened. Then she heard it again and this time the sound was unmistakable. She heard the heavy steps of Scud's shoes splashing in the water overhead. Her jaw dropped, and she looked at Clay.

"I hear it," Clay whispered.

Then a flash of lightning brightened the sky, and the low rumble of the thunder pulsed on Liz's chest. She swallowed and then breathed, faster and faster. Then the sound of splashing steps disappeared.

Clay released Liz and rose to his knees and then onto the balls of his feet. His fingers stiffened against the rocky ground in front of him like a lineman waiting for the ball to be snapped. Liz watched him stare through the falling water. Pulses of bright light and clapping thunder echoed through the sky. Clay looked back at Liz and nodded his head as if saying "get ready."

Liz crouched at the back of the mini-cave. Clay waited like a wound-up spring in a four-point stance. Then it appeared. The strobe of lightning lit up the entire valley, and they saw the silhouette of a man clomp in front of the fall. He stopped and turned in place.

"I won't hurt you," Scud said. "I just want my artifacts. That's all. Just give them back to me, and I'll let you go back to your little camp. Scout's honor," he said, raising four fingers.

Clay shook his head. He leaned forward placing greater weight on his fingertips. His toes flexed and his calves bulged. He watched as Scud turned in place and walked off to the right. Liz sighed in relief, but Clay remained on point.

"Clay, he's gone."

Clay didn't speak. He tilted his head from side to side, causing audible cracks to mingle with the sound of falling rain. The heavy drops pounded louder, and the thunder boomed as a monster web lit the sky.

Scud stepped back in front of the waterfall. He raised the gun in his hand and hunched over to look inside. Scud moved closer, pulling his hand through the falling water like he was pushing back a curtain. He inched closer, prepared to peek inside, but before he could, Clay attacked.

(45)

Clay launched through the opening and crashed into Scud like a linebacker sacking a quarterback. He dug his shoulder into Scud's sternum and drove him into the muddy ground. The gun slipped away. Clay looked up, hoping to find it, but the weapon was obscured by water, mud, and darkness.

"Run!" Clay screamed.

Liz scampered out from underneath the primitive shelter and raced to the trail leading down to the valley floor. She looked back at Clay as he beat down on Scud with repeated blows.

Just before reaching the lower trail, Liz ducked behind a tall stump that was stripped of its bark. She peered through the rain and darkness, looking for Clay. The sky lit up, and she could see a man standing over another. She swallowed and began hyperventilating. "Clay?" she whispered.

*****

Clay stood over Scud. He kicked into the man's belly, but Scud only groaned. Wiping his sleeve across his face, Clay blew out, expelling a light spray from the water running over his lips. His eyes scanned the surroundings, and the lightning flashed again, illuminating the hill. To his left, a shimmer caught his attention, and he moved toward it, hoping he had found Scud's gun. Clay stepped over the crumpled man. His eyes tried adjusting to the darkness. He took another step and then stopped and searched.

Glancing back at Scud, Clay dropped to his knees and felt the ground with his hands. "Come on," he muttered to himself. He felt nothing but slimy mud, grass, and rock. He bent closer to the ground as if searching for a lost contact lens, then his knuckles snagged against a sharp rock. He pulled his hand close to his face, but he couldn't see until the lightning flashed again. He saw lines of blood drip from two small puncture wounds. He sucked the blood from his finger and spat. Two feet in front of him, the gun lay propped against a root. He reached toward the gun but stopped when he heard a rattle mix in with the patter of falling rain.

The air above Clay cracked with blinding light and then again and again. Chills shot through his body at the constant shelling of lightning and thunder. Looking back at the gun, Clay recoiled as the root moved. He fell back and saw another root slither closer to him. Clay recognized the sound of the rattle. He looked at the puncture holes near his knuckle, and his breath exploded from his mouth like he had been sucker punched. He tried to inhale, but his shocked lungs wouldn't perform. His throat felt as if it had been crushed. He tried swallowing, but he couldn't produce enough spit.

Clay stood cautiously and backed away from the rattling snakes, leaving the gun where it lay. His foot bumped into Scud's head, so Clay lifted his foot and stepped over. He turned in place and looked down the hill toward the trail. "Liz, I think I have a problem," he said calmly.

Even in the dark Clay could see the motion of Liz's arms waving for him to come. He looked at his knuckle again and then sucked hard and spat. Clay's feet shuffled toward the grassy hill that led to the lower trail. The rain pounded his body and cascaded down his face. His hand throbbed.

The sound of mild thrashing in the puddles caused Clay to turn around, and he saw Scud reaching for him. Scud yanked Clay's foot, forcing him to the ground. He held Clay's leg, reaching for the other, but Clay planted the heel of his shoe across the bridge of Scud's nose. Scud released him and went limp on the ground.

Clay stood as if in a fog and began his descent toward the trail.

"I'm coming," he said in monotone, expecting Liz to hear and understand his muffled call. "Liz, I think I need help." Clay stepped carelessly on the wet grass and fell to his back, sliding the rest of the way down the hill, nearly colliding with the stripped stump. He stood but his knees wobbled, and he fell back into the grass.

"Clay, what happened? Are you all right?" Liz asked. She sat beside him and pulled him closer. Clay leaned into Liz. He held out his hand as if Liz would know what he meant. Liz shook her head.

"Snake. I think I just got bitten by a snake. Maybe I'm crazy," Clay mumbled as he pointed to his knuckle. "But I heard the rattle."

Grabbing his hand, Liz examined his knuckle. Her hand caressed his until she felt and then saw the puncture wounds. Then the sky exploded with a rhythmical display of lightning and thunder.

"Pretty," Clay said, leaning his head back to enjoy the display as if watching Fourth of July fireworks.

"Clay, I think you're in shock, but you're not crazy."

"Not crazy? That's good," he said. A smile covered his face, and then his eyes widened.

"Rattlesnakes are actually pretty common around here," Liz explained in her most soothing tone. Clay leaned tight against Liz as she held his head. "But you're going to be fine. Sick. But fine . . . probably," she said, trailing off when she recognized Clay wasn't listening. "Clay, you wait here," she said and lowered him gently to the ground. She propped his head on his arm to keep it out of the rain puddles.

Looking up the hill, Liz could see Scud lying still on the ground. She looked at Clay and then stood. "I'll be right back."

Stepping up the grassy incline, Liz circled far around Scud before racing back through the grove toward the truck.

(46)

Liz slowed as she neared the edge of the gravel roundabout and saw a dark sedan parked perpendicular in front of Scud's truck. She stepped backward and huddled next to a tree. She didn't recognize the car or the woman standing with her back to the grove. Liz sidestepped closer to a larger tree and watched. Her tired legs jittered with nervous anticipation.

The woman stepped away from the back of the truck and turned, her blonde ponytail slapping the side of her face. Liz squeezed her eyes shut, trying to hold back thankful tears after recognizing the FBI cap and the woman wearing it. She took an eager step forward but stopped as a hand grabbed her wrist. Liz yelped and then screamed as the hand spun her around.

Jimmy grabbed Liz by the shoulders and placed his face directly in front of hers. "Liz, it's okay. It's me." Jimmy looked into her eyes, but Liz covered her face with her arms as her sobs pierced the night. "Liz, it's Jimmy. I'm here. You're okay," he repeated, but Liz continued to cry, blocking out his words. "Emily, I've got Liz!" Jimmy yelled.

Emily was already running in their direction with a flashlight bobbing in her hand. She slowed as she approached and gently touched the back of Liz's head. She nudged Jimmy away and wrapped her arms around Liz. She cradled Liz's head, and her hand lingered on Liz's cheek. "We've got you, Liz. We've got you. We're here,"

Emily soothed, her eyes darting around the scene. "Jimmy, call Paul. Get him and Bishop Taylor over here right away."

Jimmy stepped away from the huddled women and dialed Paul's number. His bright white smile beamed. The instant Paul picked up, Jimmy started. "We found Liz! She's okay. Scared to death, but okay!" he screamed into the phone. Jimmy held the phone away from his ear as Paul screamed back with enthusiasm. "She needs her dad. Get Bishop Taylor over here right away." Jimmy hung up the phone and rejoined Liz and Emily.

Liz uncovered her face and looked at Emily and Jimmy with admiration. Then clarity and purpose returned to her mind. "Clay! He's hurt. We need to help him."

"We'll help him, Liz. Where is he? What's wrong?"

Liz sighed, equal parts laugh and cry. She pointed through the grove. "Down the hill. Near the stump."

"Can you show us?" Emily asked, and Liz nodded. "Jimmy, quick, get the car." Emily tossed the keys, and they bounced off Jimmy's chest and fell to the ground.

"Uh . . . sorry," he said sheepishly. "Light please." Emily flashed the light on the ground. Jimmy picked up the keys and ran to the Charger. Moments later, Jimmy pulled up with his window down. "Climb in."

Liz climbed in the backseat and Emily in the passenger side. Liz pointed through the grove, but Jimmy opted for the gravel trail to his left. He drove fast but in control as the trail rounded into an open gravel overlook.

"Where?"

Liz pointed again. "We went down there."

Jimmy cranked the wheel and headed down another narrow maintenance road, slowing as the path became steeper.

"There!" Liz said as the lights brightened a figure crouching in the dirt. "It's Scud."

Jimmy pressed on the gas. Scud stood in the path of the headlights and then turned in place. Then, running twenty yards, Scud jumped down from a steep embankment and disappeared. "You got him, Emily?"

"Got it."

Jimmy skidded to a near stop as Emily tossed the door open and jumped out to give chase. Jimmy pressed the gas, and the car powered forward, forcing the door closed.

"He's down there," Liz said, pointing. "Clay's down there."

Jimmy paused at the edge of the gravel plateau. Then his foot pounded on the gas, causing the Charger to lurch forward and angle sharply down the hill.

Liz turned and looked through the rear window just in time to see the beam from Emily's flashlight disappear from the same ledge Scud had gone over. Liz gulped and turned forward and saw the Charger sliding down the hill.

Jimmy turned the wheel to the right, aiming far to the side of the stump. "There he is."

As the car reached the bottom of the hill, Jimmy cranked the wheel all the way right and gunned the gas, sending the Charger bouncing up and over a berm and onto another access road. Jimmy clenched the wheel and pressed on the brake. The car stopped, its front aimed directly up the path. Liz's arms extended to her side with her fists clenching the seat. She gulped and then breathed . . . eventually.

"Let's go!" Jimmy yelled. He climbed out of the car and down the embankment, sliding on his knees next to Clay. Liz watched for a moment and then followed. "Clay, can you hear me?" Jimmy asked. Clay didn't respond. "Clay. Can. You. Hear. Me?"

Clay's eyelashes fluttered, and his mouth motioned like he was sucking his thumb.

"Good enough." Propping Clay into a sitting position against the stump, Jimmy leaned his shoulder into Clay's stomach and then lifted. "You weigh a ton," Jimmy muttered as he struggled to his feet. He shuffled toward the rise up to the access road, turned, and then walked sideways up the berm until he was on the road. He panted from the exertion. "Liz, get that door," Jimmy said.

Liz opened the rear passenger-side door.

Leaning over, Jimmy dumped Clay into the backseat. He tucked Clay's legs in and closed the door. Jimmy stood and stretched as he grabbed his back. "What happened to Clay?"

"I think he's in shock," Liz said.

"Shock from what?" Jimmy asked, stretching his fingertips toward his toes. "Oh, I'm really going to be feeling this one for a while," he muttered.

"The rattlesnakes."

Jimmy straightened at once. "Rattlesnakes? In the middle of the night?"

Liz nodded. "I think he was bit on the hand."

Jimmy looked at Liz with the excitement of a ten-year-old. "Seriously! Clay was bit by a rattlesnake?"

"Yeah."

Jimmy climbed in the driver's seat and put the car in drive. The tires spat mud and rock as the car headed up the maintenance road. "Rattlesnakes. That is the coolest thing EVER!"

Liz shook her head. "What part of 'bit by a rattlesnake' don't you understand?"

Jimmy nodded his head. "Of course. It's terrible." Then a goofy grin crossed his face. "But the girls are gonna love it."

(47)

PAUL HUNG UP THE PHONE and sat in his black SUV with a sense of relief he hadn't felt all day. He smiled with satisfaction, propped both hands behind his head, and closed his eyes. He offered a silent prayer of gratitude for the safety of the kids and the possibility that he might actually get some sleep.

This day had not gone as planned—graveyards, artifacts, abductions, and an argumentative girlfriend/supervisor. This was not what Paul envisioned when he agreed to transfer into Emily's team. He'd never seen the kind of aloofness from Emily that he saw today. Paul shook his head, unable to understand the sudden change but unwilling to accept any dire implications.

The road split directly in front of him. A sign on the left pointed to Spring Hill, and a road on the right headed north. He made a wide turn through the intersection to head toward the valley overlook to rejoin the others, but a light caught his eye. Far to the north, the temporary glow of red break lights surprised him. He stared out the window through the dripping rain as multiple sets of red lights drove straight and then turned to the left, one by one.

Paul pulled out his phone and paused for an answer. "I'm on the north side. What's your location?" He listened. "Good. You mind taking a swing around here? I've got four, yes, four vehicles exiting the area. No make or model. Too far. But a little strange for this time of night in the middle of nowhere, don't you think?"

Paul nodded as he listened to the response. "Okay. Let me know what you find. I'm heading that direction now."

Paul turned off his lights and drove straight along the gravel road. His SUV crested over a rise as he watched the red taillights disappear. He turned off his windshield wipers as the rain petered out, and then he stopped at the end of the long, fence-lined road as it exited Adam-ondi-Ahman into the small town of Jameson.

(48)

THE LARGE PICKUP HAD NOT yet come to a complete stop when Bishop Taylor swung the passenger side door open and jumped out. His feet slid from under him, and he fell to the ground, twisting his ankle. He stood up and looked for his daughter, but other than the old red-and-beige truck parked next to the bathrooms, the small gravel lot was deserted.

"Liz!" he hollered but received no response. He turned in place, favoring his right side as he searched. Then he heard a honk from behind. Jimmy laid on the horn again as he pulled up from a narrow utility road to the west of the roundabout. Jimmy stopped next to the bright yellow pickup.

Liz leapt from the car and wrapped her arms around her father. He kissed her forehead and cheeks and then hugged her again before starting another round of kisses. He held her back and looked at her dripping hair and soaked clothes.

"Clay needs help," Liz said, releasing from her father's embrace.

"Rattlesnake bite," Jimmy said, almost straight-faced.

"Are you sure?" Bishop Taylor asked. Liz and Jimmy both nodded.

"We've got lots of rattlers around here. Good news is, bites are seldom life threatening. He'll be uncomfortable for a little while, but he'll survive," the missionary said from the truck.

Bishop Taylor looked through the window and then opened

the rear door. He pulled some keys from his pocket and unscrewed a small metal vial. He looked back to the pickup. "Elder, can you help me?"

The gray-haired missionary climbed down from his truck, still wearing his pajamas and a robe. Bishop Taylor handed him the vile of oil, and the missionary anointed Clay's head. "Jimmy, will you join us?" Bishop Taylor asked. They placed their hands on Clay and offered a blessing of healing. Liz watched. "Let's get him checked out. Where's Sister Mathews—I mean Emily—I mean Agent Mathews?" Bishop Taylor said, stumbling over his words.

"Chasing the bad guy," Jimmy responded.

Bishop Taylor looked at Clay in the car and then at the yellow pickup. "Can we?" he asked the missionary.

"Absolutely."

Jimmy pulled Clay by the arms so only his feet remained propped on the car seat. The missionary picked up his feet and they transported him to the truck and lifted him onto the backseat. "I'll wait for Emily," Jimmy said.

"Liz, let's go."

Liz climbed into the backseat and laid Clay's head on her lap as Jimmy closed the door for her. Liz's window lowered. "Jimmy, there's a gold brick in the back of Scud's truck." Jimmy flinched. "And there are some old papers in the cab," Liz said.

"You ready?" the missionary asked.

"Yeah, I'm ready," Liz said. The missionary pickup backed up and turned. "Jimmy!" Liz yelled from her open window. "Thank you."

Jimmy saluted with an exaggerated motion of his arm. The truck turned and drove out of sight.

*****

Emily placed both hands on her knees and wheezed for breath. She propped one hand against a tree helping her to stand straight and then resumed her run back to the gravel parking lot. Her chest heaved. Leaning against the Charger, Emily placed both hands flat on the hood as if she was about to be frisked by a police officer. She reached up with one hand and yanked off her FBI cap and wiped her forehead with the bottom of her white T-shirt. "I think . . . I might . . . actually die," she said, watching Jimmy lean casually near the back of the car.

"Um, I'm not trying to nitpick or anything, but aren't you supposed to have a bad guy with you?" Jimmy asked.

Emily's lips tightened and her eyes narrowed. "I almost . . . had him," she said, still panting.

"Then that was *almost* very impressive. Way to go," Jimmy said with a grin, but his face turned serious when he could tell Emily wasn't enjoying the teasing. Jimmy waved his hands. "Doesn't matter." Jimmy's toothy grin returned, signaling something was up.

"Jimmy . . . what are . . . you doing?" Emily asked, noticing his arms folded behind his back.

He continued to smile. "Do you want to see something AWESOME?" Jimmy whispered.

Emily's shoulders slumped, and she sighed. Her face contorted into a weary and forced smile. "I suppose."

"Excellent. Check this out," Jimmy said and then removed his hands out from behind his back. The gold brick lay clutched in his hands, but Emily failed to notice.

She fumbled through her pockets and pulled out her vibrating phone. "Just a second, Jimmy," she said, holding the phone away. "Yeah, Paul. Where are you? We found the kids," she said, looking around. She held the phone down and covered the receiver. "Jimmy," she whispered, "where *are* the kids?"

"Bishop Taylor and a missionary took them to the hospital. A rattlesnake bit Clay," Jimmy said.

Emily's brow furrowed with confusion and her eyes bulged. "Really?" Jimmy's head nodded up and down dramatically while his lips puckered and his eyes widened. Emily looked at her friend again and then turned away, trying to stifle a grin of her own. She pulled the phone to her ear. "Apparently Clay was bitten by a rattlesnake. Bishop Taylor is taking him to the hospital. I'm sure he'll be fine. Jimmy seems to think the whole rattlesnake thing is kind of cool."

She listened. "Yes, he is an exemplar of maturity," she said with a chuckle. "Paul, where are you?"

*****

Paul slumped in his seat as he watched four large Yukons pull to the side of what looked like the "old" main street of Jameson. He took his foot off the brake and quickly placed the vehicle in park to keep his brake lights from shining.

"Jameson," Paul said, watching three men pile out of the first Yukon. "Main Street. I've got four large SUVs pulled over next to what looks like an old storefront. The place is falling in, and one of the buildings next to it has already crumbled."

"Well, get back here. We're done. Let's head home," Emily said in a way that sounded more like a command than a request.

"No. Emily, something's going on here," Paul said.

"No, Paul, come back . . . *now*."

Paul shook his head but remained calm. "Emily. Four SUVs exited the north access to Adam-ondi-Ahman just a few minutes ago and are now lined up on a city street. This is connected to our case. I don't know how, but I'm going to find out." Paul listened to the silence on the other end of the line. "I'm doing this."

*****

"Dang, Emily," Jimmy said, still holding the gold brick in his hands. Emily turned to look at Jimmy, but he averted his eyes toward the cloudy, night sky.

Emily held the phone in front of her and stared as if it were a rabid dog that just bit her. "Sorry, Paul. Send me your GPS location, and we'll be there in a few minutes." Emily hung up and waited for a moment until the GPS coordinates scrolled across her phone. "Got it. Let's go, Jimmy."

Jimmy held out the gold brick closer to Emily. "Seriously? Not even going to look. Just ignore Jimmy," Jimmy said. "Everyone ignores Jimmy."

Emily climbed in the Charger and waited. "Jimmy, you coming or what?"

"Yeah, I'm coming. Just a second." Jimmy opened the passenger door of the red-and-beige pickup. He looked on the floor and then rummaged through the glove box. He removed a hunting knife and then stabbed the front tire of Scud's truck. The tire hissed until flat. Jimmy flattened the other front tire as well and then removed the papers and scroll from the front seat. He climbed into the Charger and dumped the papers into the backseat and set the brick with the rest of the rocks on the floor near his feet. He held up the knife. "That's in case scumbag comes back and is looking for his ride."

"Ready?" Emily asked.

"Yeah. I'm ready, but we've got to have a little talk."

Emily searched the GPS coordinates and waited for the directions to pop up on her phone. "Looks like we have four minutes. What do you want to talk about, Jimmy?" she asked with weary indifference in her voice.

Jimmy folded his arms and looked out the window. Lightning flashed again and the thunder clapped as the sky threatened another downpour. "You're being mean."

Emily smiled at Jimmy's simple description. "Mean? I'm being mean?"

"Yeah. You're kind of being a brat. It's not like you, and I don't like it," Jimmy said. "And I don't think Paul likes it either."

Emily nodded her head. She forced a smile across her face, but the truth of Jimmy's words hurt. "Well, maybe that's for the best."

"'For the best'? What's that supposed to mean," Jimmy asked, turning in his seat to face her.

Emily rubbed her eyes and then sighed. Too tired to get into a long explanation of her new job assignment, she tried to brush off her friend. "This is who I am, Jimmy. If you don't like it, you can always get out," she said calmly.

Jimmy shook his head. "Bull. I don't know what this is, but it isn't you. You are way better than this. What's going on, Emily? Really? Why are you acting this way?"

Emily glanced at her watch and at the coordinates on her phone. She stared straight ahead but didn't answer.

"Emily?"

"Jimmy, drop it. Please. Just be quiet and mind your own business."

Jimmy turned toward Emily and spread his arms wide as if preparing to embrace her, but then he pulled back. "Remember that hug I gave you earlier? Well, I just took it back."

"You're a smart guy, Jimmy. You'll figure it out. Just give it some time, and it will all make sense," Emily said, shaking her head.

Jimmy glared. "I don't want to figure it out. I want you to tell me. That's what friends do. What's going on with you?" Emily turned to Jimmy and opened her mouth as if preparing to speak, but then she stopped. She closed her mouth, locked her jaw, and turned away. Jimmy looked out his side window and mumbled, "And I thought I was the one who needed to grow up."

Emily glanced over at Jimmy. A tear gathered in the corner of her eye and then streamed down her cheek. She wiped it away before he could notice and remained silent as the Charger raced toward Jameson.

(49)

EIGHT MEN STOOD IN A semicircle with their backs to the road. Paul watched from the crouched anonymity of his vehicle at the far corner of the block. He shifted in his seat and leaned toward the passenger side with his head barely peeking above the dash. He hoped to catch a better view, but the distance was too far, and with no streetlights the early morning darkness was too limiting.

"Crap." Paul leaned farther, but one of the men moved, obstructing Paul's view. Pulling the key from the ignition, he pulled on the door handle and pushed it open inch by inch. Paul slowed his breathing, listening to every creak. Slumping below the door window, he slid out of the car and placed one foot then the other onto the wet pavement. He climbed the rest of the way out and closed his door, pushing gently while holding the handle up. He released the handle, knelt on one knee at the front of the SUV, and peered around the bumper.

Paul heard a rumble of low laughter coming from the group and then watched as one man opened the back door of the last Yukon. The men spread into an assembly line and began passing small items from hand to hand before loading the items into the back of the vehicle.

With the men occupied on their task, Paul crept from behind the bumper to a dilapidated building across the street. The soft sound of new rain pattered on the ground, and his shoes squeaked quietly across the grass. With nothing to light his path, Paul walked slowly through a back alley, guiding each step with one hand on the building.

The chatter grew louder as Paul approached the end of the building, and he peeked through a narrow break separating the structures. Crouching, he watched as one man squatted in front of a pile of bricks. The man picked up each brick and either tossed it aside or handed it to the man in front of him. Paul's lower lip stuck out and his jaw pressed forward as he watched with interest. He removed the phone from his pocket, stepped behind the building, and dialed. "Where are you?" he whispered.

"We'll be there in thirty seconds," Emily answered.

Paul peeked back around the corner at the working men. "No. Hold back until I tell you. I don't know what these guys are up to, but I don't want to spook them."

"What's going on, Paul?"

Paul whispered. "I've got eight guys hovering around a crumbled building. They're loading some bricks into the back of a Yukon."

Emily grinned. "You know what that is, don't you, Paul?"

He covered the receiver and his mouth with his hand. "No," he whispered. "Please enlighten me."

"It's gold baby! Mormon gold!" Jimmy hollered, adding a "whoop!" at the end.

Paul hunched down and held his hand tighter against the phone, trying to muffle the sound. He peeked around the building, worried someone may have heard, but the men continued to work. "Mormon gold? You mean Confederate gold, don't you?"

"Huh?"

Paul shook his head. "Doesn't matter. It looks like regular bricks. How do you know its gold?"

"Because I'm holding a brick right now," Jimmy said. "It's wrapped in layers of old mud so it looks like a regular brick, but when you scrape that away . . . oh yeah." Jimmy was quiet for a moment, but then Paul could hear him smack his lips. "Hey, how much is there?"

"They've been loading for a couple of minutes. There's a pretty big pile, but they're tossing most of it to the side," Paul said. "It doesn't make sense," Paul said but stopped quickly as he heard the slam of the Yukon rear door. "Hold on. I think they're done," Paul said. "I'm moving into a better position. Where are you guys?"

"We're here, just waiting for you," Emily said.

"Good. I'm silencing your end," Paul whispered and pressed a button muting Emily's end of the call. He placed the phone in his pocket and then wiped the dripping rain from his forehead. Paul watched as some of the men climbed back into their vehicles and as others lit cigarettes. "Hmm. They're not leaving. Why aren't they leaving? They've got the gold—a lot of it," Paul said, speaking mostly to himself. He noted the rear of the Yukon had slumped from the weight.

Paul crept closer to the edge of the building and leaned his back against the brick wall. A man with bushy black hair pulled out a phone. The display lit up the man's face and Paul noticed the bulge of a holster underneath the man's arm. Paul listened. The man's tone was all business and precision, but Paul struggled to understand the muffled fragments of the conversation.

". . . yeah . . . thirty bricks . . . didn't need . . . stupid artif . . . Scud . . . done . . . got it . . ." The man chuckled but then became stern as his voice rose. "No. I'm telling you that's all of it," he said. "Thirty bricks. These things are heavy." The man listened and then spoke. "What do you mean it's not enough?" His head lowered as he continued to listen.

Paul inched closer as he concentrated on the one-sided phone conversation.

The man fidgeted. "Yes, sir. I'm sorry, sir. Please don't be disappointed. Yeah. I'll send the gold with an escort. Yeah, yeah, I'll wait for the idiot. We'll get it all, whatever it takes." The call ended.

The man whistled, piercing the rainy night silence. He waved his hand above his head and then pointed at the two vehicles at the end of the line. "You know where to take it?" the man asked.

"Got it, Alek," another man responded before climbing into the driver's seat. A second man joined him, sliding into the back.

"He's expecting you," Alek said. "Don't make him wait. Got it?"

The driver nodded, and the two vehicles came to life and then pulled away from the curb. Paul examined the dark scene; Alek remained in the middle of the street tucking his phone back into the pocket of his jacket, one man sat on the pile of bricks, and a third man smoked his cigarette as the rain bounced off his shaved head. Paul's mind raced. *Two men climbed in each of the vehicles. I have visual on three others. Where's the eighth man*?

"Two Yukons are leaving. Four men left. I don't have visual on—" Paul stopped as he felt the barrel of a gun press against the back of his skull. He swallowed and lifted his hands in front of him. "Emily, if you can hear me, now would be a good time," Paul said calmly as he stood and slowly turned.

"What did you say?" the man asked in a slow drawl while cocking his head and turning the gun sideways like a gangster.

Paul smirked. "I wasn't talking to *you*."

(50)

PAUL TURNED AND TOOK A slow step forward, causing the barrel of the gun to press firmly into his sternum. His eyes squinted in the darkness as he memorized the boyish features of the man in front of him.

"A little past your curfew, isn't it?" Paul asked. "Does your mom know you're still out?" Paul wagged his head like a big brother who was about to tattle. The pitch of his voice rose. "She's not going to like it."

The young man jabbed the gun deeper into Paul's chest and then motioned with his head for Paul to start walking. "Shut up," he said with a thick drawl.

Paul shook his head. "Now you see, that's just rude." Paul listened as the sound of an engine drew closer. "I don't really like *rude*." The young man scoffed. "You know, my mom always used to tell me nothing good happens after midnight," Paul said, looking at the watch on his upraised wrist. "And it's *way* past midnight."

The young man turned his eyes to the watch and then to the road as the navy Charger squealed to a stop, blocking the road fifty feet from the Yukons. A thin smirk crossed Paul's lips, and then he struck. Lunging forward, Paul twisted his body and slammed his elbow down on his assailant's wrist, causing the weapon to fall to the ground. Paul spun behind him and punched him twice near the kidneys.

The man fell to the ground and reached for his weapon, but Paul landed on the man's back with his elbow. The gunman collapsed flat, his face splashing in a puddle. Paul rubbed his hands over his soaked jeans and then picked up the weapon. "I don't like rude." Dragging the man toward an electric meter at the side of the building, Paul bound the man's hands with a plastic zip tie and moved back to his spot at the front of the building.

From his position, Paul could see both Emily and Jimmy kneeling behind the Charger and the men scrambling through the back seats of the Yukons. They emerged with automatic weapons.

"Emily, fall back!" Paul yelled. He grabbed the phone from his pocket and repeated, "Fall back!" One man stepped from behind the Yukon and opened fire. Bullets sprayed the Charger, connecting with rapid metallic clanks.

"Emily, are you okay?" Paul didn't wait for a response. "Stay put and hunker down." Paul hung up and made a quick call. He then leaned against the brick wall and removed his car key from his pocket. He clicked the auto ignition, and his SUV roared and the headlights beamed from the opposite side of the street. Paul took aim and fired two shots at the front tire of the first Yukon.

A second man with an automatic weapon swung out from behind the Yukon and sprayed the buildings with a shower of bullets, but the shots were wild with no identifiable target. Pieces of crushed brick exploded around Paul, covering his wet hair with brick dust. Paul lowered onto his belly and took aim at the second Yukon, punching out one of the back tires as he heard Emily unload a clip from behind the Charger. Paul ducked farther behind the wall and waited for the spray to end. He prepared to fire but stopped as he recognized the familiar sound of the chopper.

The spotlight lit up the two Yukons. "FBI. Lower your weapons," a voice called out over the loud speaker. Instead of lowering their weapons, the three remaining thugs turned their fire on the helicopter, but the chopper simply turned off the light and lifted higher into the sky, out of view.

Paul stepped out from behind the wall and took aim, exploding the Yukon's windows with his shots. "We've got you surrounded.

You've got nowhere to go and no way to get there!" Paul yelled, positioning himself behind the corner of the wall.

"Throw your weapons out. NOW!" Emily yelled.

Paul hit a button, causing his car to chirp. The engine revved and the lights flashed, giving the illusion of additional support. He then joined in the chorus of yelling as the chopper returned the blinding spotlight onto the Yukons.

"Let's see those weapons!" Paul yelled again.

"Do it now, scumbags," Jimmy growled.

Paul wiped the grin from his face. "And step out from behind your vehicles." He waited, holding his breath and praying the assailants would comply because he knew he couldn't stop them if they refused. Paul's heart skipped a beat as the first assault rifle scraped against the pavement, skidding into the middle of the street. Then another weapon scooted alongside as two men stepped from behind the first Yukon with their hands raised.

"One more. We're waiting!" Paul yelled. Another gun skidded to a stop against the others and the third man stepped from behind the Yukon. All three men stood in the street with their hands placed behind their heads as the spotlight trained directly on them.

Paul stepped from behind his corner with his gun raised. He moved cautiously toward the men in the road, and he saw Emily moving in from the other side, her weapon also drawn. Paul reached the automatic weapons lying in the street and kicked them farther away. "Got them?" Paul asked.

"Yeah. I got 'em," Emily said, aiming her Glock 9 mm at the men.

Paul removed a stash of zip ties from his pocket and bound each man's hands behind his back. When the last man was bound, Paul looked at Emily and grinned. "Nice timing."

"Where are the rest of you?" one of the men asked.

Paul winked at Emily and then forced the men to lay face down on the ground. "You surrendered your M4's to two agents with handguns," Paul said with a chuckle. "But in your defense, it was hardly a fair fight."

"Who do you work for?" Emily asked. "Where are the others?"

"And why are you still here? You got your gold. What are you sticking around for?" Paul questioned, but the men remained silent.

Jimmy stepped from behind the Charger. He patted his body down as if searching for bullet holes and moved to the men lying on the ground. Jimmy scowled, and his squint mimicked Clint Eastwood. He stood directly over the men as he said in his lowest, toughest, raspiest voice. "I just want to know one thing from you." Jimmy paused for dramatic effect. "Where's the gold?"

Paul's eyes glimmered and his cheeks lifted subtly. His eyes darted to Jimmy and then back to the captives. Jimmy's question wasn't as menacing as he intended, but Paul admired the effort. He placed one hand on Jimmy's shoulder, but Jimmy swiped it away.

Jimmy lowered to the ground and stared into one man's eyes. "I said, where is the gold?"

Paul found this second effort much more believable. He looked at Emily. His mouth twitched, and his eyebrows rose with approval. The gunman raised his head from the ground as if preparing to speak but then spat at Jimmy's shoes.

"You little—"

Grabbing Jimmy by the arm, Paul pulled him away from the scene. Jimmy's eyes scrunched. "You doing all right there, Jimmy?" Paul asked.

The tension released from Jimmy's body, and he sighed and stood loose. "It's just that I've been practicing that look. I was believable, wasn't I?" Jimmy asked. "I can't believe they didn't go for it."

Paul nodded. "Yeah. You had me shaking." He paused. "Keep working on it."

Pulling his cell from his pocket, Paul made a call. "Thanks for the help. See if you can track the Yukons, but do not engage. I want to see where these guys are going." Paul listened and nodded. "Good, go get them."

Flashing blue and red lights colored the street as two sheriff's department vehicles pulled behind the Charger. "Their timing is excellent," Emily said. "But they missed all the fun."

"Yes, they did," Paul agreed. "Let's load these guys up. I think it's time we get back to Kansas City."

"What about my car?" Jimmy asked.

"Your car?" Emily asked. She turned toward the Charger and winced at the destruction. The side was riddled with bullet holes, and the windows and tires were blown out. "I don't think *your* car made it, Jimmy."

Jimmy's shoulders slumped. "Ah man, Brother Conrad is going to be seriously ticked."

Paul nodded. "Yes, he is."

(51)

Agent Thrasher sat at the wide desk in the clean room of the filthy house. With fingers poised on the keyboard of his laptop, he inhaled the sterility of the room mixed with the coppery smell of blood from next door. His eyes wandered from wall to wall, then to the ceiling, the floor, and finally to the doorframe where Agent Stark leaned. The jowl lines on Thrasher's face deepened more than usual and his forehead crinkled as he thought. His eyes narrowed, and he licked his lips and started tapping the keys gracefully.

"Hallelujah!" Stark said from the door. "Are you getting somewhere? Finally."

Only a whisper of a grunt escaped Thrasher's lips as his fingertips crashed harder on the keys. His fingers halted momentarily, and he stared at his screen. His chubby cheeks turned from a scowl into a thin grin of accomplishment as his fingers resumed their frantic pace.

"By the way, we confirmed only one body in the other room." Stark waited, but Thrasher only raised his chin in response. "Of course not everything is there. We're not sure why he chopped the body into such small pieces. Sever called the psycho a . . ."

"An 'organized offender,'" Sever said, stepping to the door beside Stark. "And he's not a psycho—at least not clinically."

"I can't wait to hear this," Stark said.

"This perpetrator is highly intelligent and uses his verbal skills to manipulate his victims. His crimes occur away from his natural environment: home, office, and so on." Sever chuckled nervously. "In this case, he set up an entire clean room away from his typical environment to be close to his victim so he could strike at the appropriate time while still allowing a minimal level of acceptable comfort and cleanliness."

"You're just making this up," Stark accused. Sever shook his head. "It sounds psycho to me," Stark said.

"Well, I'm glad you think so, but this guy planned out his killing. He is fully aware of the criminality of what he's doing, but he doesn't kill for kicks. There's a rational purpose guiding his actions. We won't find a murder weapon because he most likely took it with him. He probably even brought the murder weapon to the killing." Sever popped a stick of gum into his mouth and smacked down. "The weapon is probably a butcher knife or a machete."

Stark winced. "Is there any good news?"

"Actually, yes. An organized offender is likely to track police progress on an investigation. You know, listen to police scanners, watch television news reports, and the like. Some even insert themselves into the investigation as witnesses. Oh, and our guy probably kept a trophy of his kill." Sever shook his head as he spoke. "This was an organized killing. I believe the excessive brutality was needful in accomplishing his task."

"You're kidding, right?" Stark asked. "How could that . . . mess possibly be 'needful'?"

"Well, he didn't do it for pleasure. There's obvious evidence of hesitation in the cutting. In some cases he even had to take multiple swipes at the flesh, but he's goal driven and determined." Sever held up a finger as though lecturing a class. "But . . . he likely succumbed to his compulsion to keep a piece of the victim, or as I like to call it, evidence."

"Then why? Why all the gore? There are easier ways to kill a person," Stark said.

"Yes, but you're focusing on the wrong thing. The brutality is simply a byproduct of his need. Maybe he did it to make identification more difficult. Maybe he's sending a message to a rival. I don't know. He's aggressive and antisocial, but most important, he feels a compulsion to be in control. We need to understand the goal that drives him."

"Agreed." Nodding, Stark scratched his rough red hair. "Okay, so I missed the good news in all of that."

Sever smiled. "He has an urge to track his killing. We can use that to manipulate him. Also, he kept a trophy."

"Trophy? What kind of trophy?" Stark asked.

"Well, we haven't found a head yet." Thrasher stopped typing and looked up from his keyboard.

"Right. No head," Stark said. He turned into the room and saw Thrasher staring at him. "What is it, Thrasher?"

"Come here." Sever and Stark walked behind the desk and stared at Thrasher's computer screen. "You gave me an idea. See this?" Thrasher asked, pointing to a box on his screen containing a dozen lines of code.

"Yeah. What is it?"

"One of these codes may belong to our guy. It's like a digital fingerprint."

"Which one is it?" Stark asked.

"Can't tell. Nothing to compare it to. I'm trolling the Internet searching for the same code in use so I can track the user, but the Internet's huge. I need to narrow the search."

Sever patted Thrasher on the shoulder but immediately removed it when Thrasher's eyes revealed their own homicidal tendencies. "Sorry," Sever said, raising both hands in defense. "You want to set a trap. You're going to tease him with info and lure him in."

Thrasher grunted. "That's what I said."

Stark clapped his hands together and then placed a hand on both Sever and Thrasher's shoulders. Thrasher uttered his usual growl, but Stark ignored him. "Let's cast our net and see what we catch."

(52)

PAUL RUBBED HIS EYES AND closed them for the split second the SUV sat at the stoplight before pulling onto the highway. He shook his head fast enough to make his cheeks jiggle, then he widened his eyes. His jaw popped as he yawned.

"Doing okay, buddy?" Jimmy asked from the backseat. Paul yawned again in response.

Emily's mouth flew open as the contagious yawn overcame her. "Just try not to fall asleep and kill us all on the way back," Emily said, turning in her seat to face Paul. "Death by car accident isn't on my 'to-do list' today," she said with a smirk.

Paul couldn't be sure if Emily's snarky comment was a joke or a serious warning. He focused on the road and didn't respond. He didn't even grin at what he hoped was a lame attempt at playful teasing. Looking in the rearview mirror, Paul saw the two Daviess County Sheriff vehicles following close behind with his prisoners. He glanced down at the clock on his dash. "We've got about twenty minutes."

The three friends sat quietly as the blackness on the horizon began to brighten. "You guys are killing me here," Jimmy said, breaking the silence. "An accident may actually be less painful than this drive." Jimmy waited, looking at his friends. "You guys have issues."

"Jimmy, this isn't the time," Paul said.

"Yeah, it's late," Emily agreed.

Jimmy leaned forward between the two front seats. "Technically it's *early*, and I honestly don't care if you guys feel like talking. I'm just going to start and you guys can jump in at any time." Paul and Emily both looked straight ahead and said nothing. "Good. Paul, the way I see it Emily is intentionally pushing you away. Either that or she has suddenly become an angry shrew. How do you feel about that, Paul?"

Paul didn't answer.

Answering as Paul, Jimmy said, "Wow, Jimmy. That's a great question. It really makes me feel bad, and I worry about her. Can't you tell by the way I'm sulking?

"Yeah, Paul, you're right, I can tell. It's pretty obvious. And I know how you feel because Emily is being harsh to me too," Jimmy said, his voice lowering into a dramatic, sad tone.

Jimmy's voice raised an octave to mimic Emily. "You guys are just being mean to me. Things change. Our friendship is different now," Jimmy said. He opened his mouth to continue, but Emily cut him off.

"Jimmy, I'm begging you. Drop it. You're being obnoxious."

"But—"

"She's right, Jimmy. You're giving me a headache."

Jimmy smiled. "See that wasn't so hard. You're talking and agreeing already. I'm amazing." Paul and Emily shared a weary look. "Can I ask another question?" Jimmy asked.

"No," Emily and Paul said in unison.

"But it's about the case."

Paul nodded.

"Good. What's going to happen to that Scud guy Emily lost?"

Emily shook her head and folded her arms as she looked out her window. Paul grinned at Jimmy's not-so-subtle dig. "Local authorities are searching for him. They have roadblocks set. He's in the middle of nowhere with no place to run. The sun will be up soon. It's just a matter of time before they find him."

"Yeah, everything's going to be fine," Emily reassured. "Clay should be released later this morning, and I think all the kids from the trek are back home already."

"Total bummer," Jimmy said. "I was really having fun."

"We'll get some rest and then start connecting the pieces of the puzzle tomorrow," Emily said. "But overall, considering everything that's happened tonight, things couldn't have turned out much better."

"Except for Brother Conrad's car."

"Yeah, that could have gone better," Paul agreed with a smirk. "But Clay and Liz are safe, we caught some bad guys, and we're finally going to get some rest. It's a satisfying end to a long night."

Jimmy sat back and leaned his head against the rest. He looked out the window as a dark sedan pulled alongside and kept pace with the SUV. "Check out this jerk," Jimmy said.

Paul stared into his side mirror and then lifted his foot off the gas, slowing the SUV. "We'll let them pass," he said, but the sedan slowed to match the speed.

"This isn't right, Paul," Emily said. "Let's get out of here." Emily picked up the hand radio. She turned in her seat to look out the rear window as she called to the Sheriff cruisers directly behind them.

Paul checked his side mirror again as a second sedan pulled directly behind the first. Then the sedan windows lowered in unison. "Get down!" Paul yelled as he stomped on the accelerator.

The SUV lurched forward. The muzzle of an assault rifle stuck out from each of the chasing cars. The muzzles flashed, and the familiar sound of spraying bullets from the M4 assault rifles clanked against the SUV. Paul hunched in his seat as shattered glass covered his hair and shoulders. Lifting his head, Paul swerved in front of the sedan, forcing it onto the shoulder of the road, but it pulled back alongside as the gunman extended his weapon farther out the window. Paul swerved again, scraping the sedan, trying to force it off the road.

In his rearview mirror, Paul saw the first police car veer off the road and slam into a concrete barrier. The dark sedan then opened fire on the second police cruiser, forcing it from the road as well. The tires blew and the engine caught fire. The sedan then pulled beside the stalled police car and unleashed a fiery hail of bullets. The shooter waited a moment as the cruiser was consumed by flames.

Paul drove down the center of the road, swerving defensively from side to side, blocking the chasing sedan from pulling alongside. "Stay down, Jimmy!" Paul screamed. He looked back to see Jimmy already lying across the seat with his hands covering his head.

Emily lowered the passenger side window and held her Glock ready. "Make them come to my side," she said.

Swerving to the left Paul blocked one of the chasing sedans, creating an opening on the right side of the road for the other. Emily hunched low in her seat and waited. The sound of bullets pounded against the rear of the SUV as it sped toward the front of the vehicle. Paul swerved to the right and then back again. He nodded at Emily.

Kneeling on the seat, Emily leaned out the window and took aim. She unloaded five tight shots into the driver's side of the windshield and then climbed back inside. The sedan pressed forward with an additional spray of bullets. "I think I just made them mad!" Emily shouted.

"Hold on!" Paul yelled. He lifted his foot off the accelerator and stepped on the brake. The SUV tires screeched across the pavement as the vehicle fish tailed through the middle of the deserted highway. Paul held the wheel tight as he adjusted. The first sedan swerved onto the shoulder and past the SUV. The second sedan braked and waited in the middle of the road directly behind the agents. The first car swung back and turned so that the bumper was faced directly at Paul.

"What now?" Jimmy yelled. "What do we do?"

With one vehicle in front and the other behind, Paul gripped the steering wheel. "First, we split the defense. Then we ram them."

Jimmy's head popped up from the backseat. He saw the car positioned in front of them, and then he turned to see the other twenty yards behind. "We what?" he shouted.

Emily nodded. "Yeah."

Throwing the lever on the steering column into reverse and pressing the accelerator to the floor, Paul gritted his teeth, peering out the back window. The SUV hurtled toward the stationary sedan behind him. The gunmen quickly climbed out of the car and aimed their weapons as the SUV smashed into the sedan's grill and plastered the hood into the windshield.

Emily fired through the windows, and Paul shifted into drive and started racing toward the sedan in front of them. Paul kept his head low as Emily sat on the window ledge with her foot wrapped around the seat belt for balance. She shot at the sedan as they drew close, but the men didn't blink. They sat in their seats, content to play chicken. Paul aimed directly at them, watching their expressions as the SUV approached collision, and then he swerved. Emily fell further out the window but flexed her leg in the seat belt to hold her steady as she climbed back inside. Paul saw the rush of fear in Emily's eyes. Her fingers trembled as she buckled up.

"Are you okay?"

Emily's head bobbed. Her cheeks filled with air and then she blew out.

Paul looked in the rearview mirror, expecting to see the sedan resume chase, but instead he saw the thugs from the wrecked sedan climb into the second vehicle and drive off the opposite direction down the interstate. Paul stopped and slowly turned the car around. He trolled past the smashed sedan and then past the burning cruiser. He pulled in front of the other cruiser that had crashed into the cement barrier and turned on his brights. He climbed out while Emily called for help and gave instructions over the radio.

Everyone in the cruiser was still. Paul surveyed the scene, wary that the sedan might return. The men inside the car were bloody, but Paul reached in the shattered driver's-side window and pressed his fingers against the deputy's neck. He shook his head with disappointment. He opened the rear door, and one of the captives slumped out. Paul pushed him back into the seat and then saw the bullet holes in his neck, shoulders, and arm and the massive amount of blood that had accumulated on the seat and floor. He checked the other prisoner, who was also dead.

Paul sighed and threw his head back. He climbed into the SUV. He tilted his head from side to side, stretched, and then wiped off his bloody fingers on his jeans. He looked at Emily and then Jimmy as the interior lights began fading. His eyes bulged when he saw

Jimmy holding his shoulder with blood oozing from between his fingers.

"Jimmy, are you hit? Emily, help me!" Paul yelled and pulled Jimmy's hand away from the wound. "Why didn't you say anything?"

Jimmy's shoulders raised and then fell with defeat. "They got me, Paul."

Paul squinted and pulled Jimmy closer so he could see the wound more clearly. Emily's head shook, and then a large toothy grin covered Jimmy's face. "It's a flesh wound," Jimmy declared happily.

Paul shoved Jimmy back against the seat. "I wish the deputies were so lucky." Paul faced forward. He stared calmly out the window and then beat the steering wheel with the palms of his hands. He grabbed the wheel, shook it, and then sat back, letting his shoulders slump as he inhaled a deep breath.

Emily glanced sideways at Paul. She tucked her hair behind her ear and then placed her hand lightly on Paul's shoulder. "You did everything you could," she said, but the words rang hollow.

Paul lowered his voice as he enunciated each word through gritted teeth. "These guys are really ticking me off."

(53)

WITH THE TRICKLE OF EARLY morning traffic stuck behind the wake of accidents and burning cars, Paul's SUV crept southward down the interstate. Despite Emily's stare, Paul didn't respond to her question. His eyes scanned the east side shoulder as the rising sun splintered through the cracked window. "There," Paul said, nodding his head toward a gap in the protective wire barriers.

"What's there, Paul? I don't see anythi—" Jimmy started, but Paul interrupted.

"Hold on." Paul gripped the wheel and pressed against the chest strap, testing its sturdiness.

Emily's eyes darted from side to side and then locked on Paul, and she sunk her fingernails into his knee. "Paul, what are you doing?" she asked, the pitch of her voice rising.

Paul cranked the wheel to the left, causing the SUV to skip down the median embankment. The vehicle bounced, and Paul slammed on the accelerator as the SUV approached the incline toward the northbound lanes. The sun shone through the windshield, blinding Paul temporarily. The SUV launched upward like a plane at takeoff. The tires bounced up the incline, squealing when they reconnected with pavement. The vehicle swayed, but Paul cranked the wheel again to the left and stabilized his steering. Maintaining his position in the fast lane, Paul loosened his grip on the wheel as a broad smile covered his face.

"*Ehh-hemm.*" Emily cleared her throat, studying Paul's expression. "I know that look. You've got a plan. Mind sharing?" Paul glanced out his window at the burning patrol car in the other lane and then slammed his foot on the accelerator.

Jimmy fell back against his seat. "Hey, buddy, injured guy back here. Do you mind?"

Paul's mouth formed into an odd combination of smile and snarl. "We're going back. Something's not right. We missed something."

Emily pulled off her FBI cap and set it on the dash as she tightened her ponytail. Pulling her weapon from the holster, she ejected the magazine and began reloading.

"Yeah, right. Guys, what am I missing here?" Jimmy asked. No one answered. "Okay then, would you at least pull over so I can hitchhike to the hospital. Gunshot wound here. I'm bleeding." He waited again for a response. "Come on. Seriously?"

"You're fine," Paul said. "It's only a flesh wound, remember."

"We're going back, Jimmy," Emily said. "Paul's right. Something's been bugging me the whole drive. Why did a group of men stay behind after the gold was loaded and gone?"

"They were still on smoke break?" Jimmy suggested.

Paul grinned. "No. They weren't finished. There's something else they were supposed to do."

"And they didn't seem to be in any kind of hurry. What do you think they were waiting for?" Emily asked.

Jimmy leaned forward. "More gold?" Paul's head cocked to one side. He didn't confirm but didn't refute the idea either. Jimmy clapped his hands and rubbed them together like a maniacal villain plotting his next heist.

Even Emily's weary eyes exuded new life. "Calm down, big boy," Emily said. "It's probably *not* gold. Right, Paul?"

"Right." Paul said. He sat quietly for a moment and then his right eyebrow rose. "*Maybe* it's more gold," he admitted quietly. Jimmy leaned forward in his seat. Paul continued. "But most important, if they're not finished . . ."

"We know exactly where they're going next," Emily said, completing his sentence.

"So we're going to wait for the guys with guns to come back and shoot at us again?" Jimmy asked. Paul confirmed the question with an eyebrow shrug through the rearview mirror. Jimmy threw one hand up. "Of course we are."

Paul eyed Jimmy and then opened the glove box. He removed a small first-aid kit and handed it to Jimmy. "For the blood."

"Thanks, Paul," Jimmy said with mock emotion. "That's so sweet."

Paul's eyes narrowed. "It's for the seat, Jimmy. You're bleeding all over the leather."

For the first time all day, Emily and Paul shared a smile.

(54)

WHOA, WHOA, WHOA! HOLD ON there," Agent Stark said. "I've got Thrasher and Sever here. Okay, so tell us again. How many suspects are we talking about?"

Rolling his eyes, Paul elicited a knowing smile from Emily. "We're not sure. That's the point, Stark. That's why this idea will work. We need to divide and conquer."

"So just to confirm, we don't know how many bad guys we're dealing with, and we don't know what they're up to. Sounds like we've got all the intel we could ever hope for," Stark said.

Paul could feel Stark's condescension through the phone's speaker. He shook his head.

"Dude, you're not paying attention," Jimmy said but then quieted as Emily motioned him to be silent.

"Who's that?" Stark asked.

"Uh, that's Jimmy Younger, sir," Paul admitted.

"Jimmy? Is this a dinner party or an FBI operation? I'm confused."

"Sir, Jimmy was with us when—" Emily began.

"Listen, Stark, you're missing the point. Our window of opportunity is fleeting. We've got to move now," Paul said. "Thrasher, does this plan make sense to you?"

"Yep."

"Sever, are you keeping up, or am I being unclear? Is it me?" Paul asked.

"Well, I think I understand your point, Agent Stephens. The plan sounds strong but I also agree with Agent Stark. It would be nice to have additional information about our suspects: the size of the group, their motivations," Sever said.

Paul heard Thrasher grunt with displeasure, and he imagined Sever looking at Stark with the expression of a kid forced to choose between living with his father or mother. "Well then, I'm glad you're with us, Sever. Aren't personality, motivation, and behavior your specialties? What can you deduce about this Acacio Nicas guy and his organization?" Paul grinned as he could sense Sever squirming. "Sever? Are you there?"

"Yeah, I'm here." Sever paused. "We actually know a lot based on the behavioral evidence we found at the house. Nicas has already dispatched . . . I mean killed . . . what was likely one of his primary partners. He has a small inner group but doesn't trust them. This Scud guy who is still on the loose around Jameson may be the other member of his inner circle and will eventually face the same fate as the hacked-up corpse in the house. The drivers and other gunmen are likely just hired hands. No real ideology. No loyalties other than a paycheck."

"Okay, good. Now we're getting somewhere. We know Ace doesn't want anyone talking, and he doesn't hesitate to kill anyone who becomes a liability. They hit the thugs in our transport within an hour of being taken into our custody. He's bold," Paul said.

"Arrogant, and well informed," Emily added. "He doesn't fear us. Do we have an ID on the body yet?"

"No. We've got nothing. No fingers and no head make the ID process a little tricky. We're running a DNA search now, but it's slow." Stark sounded annoyed.

"Okay. Just asking," Emily said.

"So if Ace's people are only motivated by money, that may be his primary object as well," Sever said.

"Simple greed?" Stark asked. "But to what end? I don't buy it."

"Ah, Stark. You *are* keeping up!" Jimmy hollered from the backseat. "The guy wants to be rich. He wants *stuff* and the power it buys."

"Look, money drives this guy, but his resources are meager," Sever said.

"How do we know that?" Emily asked.

"If you saw the home where he based his operation, you wouldn't have to ask," Stark said.

"So our merry band of criminals is all hired thugs purchased on a shoestring budget?" Paul asked in confirmation. "So he'll only hire the essentials for his operation. Four guys are dead from the transport and four performed the hit."

"We found one dead at the house," Thrasher added.

Paul thought. "Four were driving the other two SUVs with the gold, and you said we've got them surrounded at a warehouse, right?"

"Yes."

"So they're not going anywhere. And we know we've got Ace and Scud."

"That's fifteen, and five of those are dead," Emily said. "How many more could there be?"

"A couple more. Maybe," Sever said.

"Well, Stark. It sounds like you've got your answers. We know the approximate size of group and motivation. Satisfied?" Paul asked.

Stark scoffed. "Not even close. Greed for the sake of being rich is a lazy explanation. Why is he willing to take such risks? For a new car or house? I don't think so. We still don't know what he's really after."

Paul leaned his ear closer to the phone Emily was holding. "Say again. I couldn't hear you correctly."

"You heard me fine," Stark said.

"No, what I heard is crazy talk. Of course we don't know everything, but we know enough to form an action plan. We can wrap this up. Let's do it," Paul urged.

"We're not proceeding until we have more actionable intelligence. We're not basing this operation on the guesses of a 'psychologist.' I've made my decision."

"But, Stark, we're close. We can finish this," Emily pleaded.

"We're done. Get back to the city, and we'll reevaluate. We need to formulate a real plan. We'll keep watching the warehouse and gold to gather more info."

"Come on, Stark, we're already here. We'll stay and keep watch. It's a no-brainer," Emily prodded.

Stark laughed with an exaggerated frivolity that seldom suited his personality and didn't match the situation. His laughter stopped as suddenly as it had started, and his voice deepened. "Mathews, I can't imagine you would ignore a direct order. Not today, with everything you have riding on this. I said get back here—NOW. Am I clear?"

"Yes, Agent Stark. You're clear."

Emily sat in the passenger seat and faced forward, a blank expression on her face. "I guess that's that," she said, hanging up.

Paul glanced at Emily and assessed her dour mood. "Yeah, I don't think so." He grabbed the phone from Emily's hand and held it up so he could see the display while still watching the road. He pressed a button and held the phone to his ear. He waited for the call to be answered and then spoke. "Can you talk? . . . Okay, call me back in two minutes." Paul set the phone on the console at his side. Turning in his seat, Paul stared at Emily while keeping one eye on the road. "What did Stark mean? 'Everything you have riding on this' today . . . What's he talking about?"

"Yeah, what's up?" Jimmy asked.

Emily rubbed the back of her neck, continuing to face forward. "I was going to tell you. The time just never seemed right."

"Tell me what?"

"Were you going to tell me too?" Jimmy asked.

"Yes, Jimmy, I was going to tell you too."

Paul looked at her and nodded, hoping to prod her into talking.

"You really want to know?"

"Yes," Jimmy and Paul said in unison with matching levels of eagerness.

Emily forced a grin and prepared to speak, but then she stopped as Paul's phone started ringing. Paul looked at the ringing phone and then at Emily and then back at the phone.

Paul's lips tightened with embarrassment. He hesitated, then reached for the ringing phone. "Sorry. I've got to take this. One minute," Paul said. He held the phone tight to his ear. His eyes narrowed as he ignored the others in the car and focused on the road. "Okay, Thrasher, are you ready for this?" Paul smiled when he heard Thrasher's usual grunt. "Good, I was hoping you'd say that. Here's my plan."

(55)

EMILY STARED STRAIGHT AHEAD, WATCHING out of the corner of her eye as Paul ended his call and set his phone down. "You know, Stark's not wrong," she said.

Jimmy leaned forward and winced in pain as he set his left arm near Paul's headrest. "That dude was born wrong."

Emily grinned. "Maybe, but he's not wrong about this. Ace isn't seeking the lifestyle of the rich and famous. He's seeking his fortune for another purpose."

Jimmy's eyes scrunched as he frowned. "So what's his purpose? It can't be good."

"Nope, it can't be good," Emily agreed.

Paul nodded. "I agree."

"Really, Paul? You agree? You just said . . ." Jimmy started and patted Emily on the shoulder. Emily responded with an amused smirk.

"Yes. Really," Paul said. "There's a purpose behind his actions, and we need to find out what it is. The best way to do that is to catch him."

"Well, yeah," Jimmy said.

"And until we can catch him, we may as well get someone close to him to use for intel and leverage." Paul rubbed his eyes and sighed. "Man, I'm tired." Everyone in the SUV remained silent as the group was hit by a contagious wave of exhaustion. "Are you going to be okay, Emily? Going against orders and all with 'everything you have riding' right now?"

Emily bit her lower lip. "It *was* a direct order," she reminded him.

"Yeah, but it's Stark. No one takes that guy seriously," Paul countered.

Jimmy cleared his throat and leaned closer to the front seat. He spoke in almost a whisper. "So, Emily, what *do* you have riding on this? And what is 'this' exactly."

Emily exhaled as she stared at the ceiling of the SUV. Her eyes felt like they were sinking into the quicksand of her brain. She frowned at the thought that she had caused damage to her relationship with Paul by trying to hide from those questions. She couldn't hide, and she couldn't avoid the discomfort of her answers. Emily reached back and tussled Jimmy's hair and then leaned over and kissed Paul on the cheek, eliciting an instant grin from her boyfriend. "I owe you both an apology. I should have told you earlier."

Paul cleared his throat and reached his hand behind his head toward Jimmy and waited. He cleared his throat again and Jimmy removed a packet of fruit snacks from his pocket. "I told you she'd come around." Jimmy hesitated but placed the fruit snacks in Paul's palm. "Mmm." Paul opened the packet and tossed an orange fruit snack in his mouth and chewed. He offered one to Emily, but not to Jimmy. He smiled at his girlfriend but then became serious. "You should have told us what, exactly?" Paul asked.

Emily looked at the ceiling again and then at her watch. "Forget Stark. Keep driving, and I'll tell you everything."

*****

Paul's jaw dropped and his eyes blinked in slow motion. His lips attempted to form words, but no sound came out. Paul looked in the rearview mirror to see Jimmy scratching the back of his head and slumping back in his seat. Paul turned toward Emily, the corners of his eyes glistening.

"I'm sorry, Paul. When I applied with the task force, I didn't think there was much chance I would get it. It just seemed like such a long shot I didn't want to make you worry." Paul sat in stunned silence. "When Stark told me today that the position was mine, pending his formal endorsement as my supervisor, I panicked . . . a little." Emily shook her head and then placed a hand on Paul's knee as she stared at the profile of his face. "All I needed was Stark's lousy endorsement, and he made it clear this morning that he wasn't going to give it. He said that everything I've accomplished here in Kansas City is because of you. He doesn't think I can stand on my own two feet. He told me I had to prove that I could succeed today without you."

Emily waited, but Paul's stone face showed no reaction.

"Say something."

Paul shook his head. His voice was mellow. "What do you expect me to say? That I'm surprised? That I'm disappointed? That I can't believe you didn't mention the possibility that you might leave? Are you expecting me to say that I'm going to miss you?"

Emily's lips quivered. "Yes."

A light scoff escaped from Paul's mouth. "You didn't even give me a chance to talk you out of it. And then today . . . I thought . . . I thought . . ."

"What?" Emily asked.

Paul's grip tightened on the steering wheel. "I thought the last year meant something. I thought *we* meant something." His voice lowered. "I thought this relationship was going somewhere." Jimmy sat in the backseat, uncharacteristically quiet. He stared out the shattered side window at the trees zipping by. Paul continued. "I thought you would confide in me before Stark." He shook his head at the thought. "You told Stark before me, really?"

"Paul, he's my supervisor. He had to know."

"And I'm only your boyfriend." Paul's eyebrows arched. "I thought I knew you." He glanced at Emily. "I had no idea I was so wrong." Paul saw a tear streak down her cheek. She didn't bother to wipe it away as the SUV raced toward Jameson in awkward silence.

(56)

Agent Thrasher pounded away on his keyboard and hit enter. He watched and waited, and then his chubby cheeks lifted. He eyed the tempting donut on his desk but picked up the phone and cleared his throat. Instead of speaking in his usual gruff grunts, Thrasher strung full sentences together with all the charm he could muster. He remembered someone telling him once that "a smile can be heard," so he did his best to grin at the female dispatcher as he spoke, though the forced cheerfulness was more demeaning than charming. He hung up the phone with a relieved sigh, then he stuffed a large bite of donut in his mouth and chewed slowly, savoring the creamy filling.

His cell phone rang. Thrasher finished chewing and removed the phone from his belt. "This is Agent Thrasher. How may I help you?" He listened for a response, but no one spoke. "Hello, may I help you?" he repeated.

"Thrasher? Is that *really* you?" Paul asked.

Thrasher frowned and then grunted. "That's what I said."

Paul chuckled. "Now that sounds like Thrasher. Sorry, it's just that you sounded . . . cheerful. Were you smiling?"

Thrasher moaned, sorry he had ever tried to be pleasant in buttering up the dispatcher. "I've made contact."

"Dispatch?"

"Yes," Thrasher said.

"Interoffice memo?"

"Got it."

"The media?" Paul asked.

"Yeah."

"All stations?"

Thrasher took another bite of donut. "*I said I got it.*"

"Okay, okay, I'm just asking."

"I spoofed news updates on the website and flashed a notice toward the four IP addresses I identified as possible matches to Nicas. If he's tracking the investigation the way we think he is, he'll see what we want him to see," Thrasher said before sticking the remainder of the donut in his mouth.

"The noose is tightening," Paul said.

Thrasher smiled. "Oh yeah."

*****

Paul turned on the radio as he turned east on Highway 6 toward Gallatin. The radio broke the persistent silence between the three friends. They listened to a few minutes of AM talk radio, but then the news bulletin brightened the atmosphere.

BREAKING NEWS

The manhunt that began last night in a small northern Missouri town has ended. Melvin Scudder has been taken into FBI custody for his alleged role in the abduction of an area teenager. He is also being questioned as a person of interest in the investigation of a dismembered body found at a Kansas City home late last night.

Local residents near Jameson, Missouri, are breathing a sigh of relief at the quick capture of Scudder, and as law enforcement clears out, the peaceful town is returning to its usual serene setting.

The hunt for Scudder's assistant, Acacio "Ace" Nicas, continues in the greater Kansas City area.

Paul licked his lips and tried to force a grin but his cheeks remained heavy. "Way to go, Thrasher."

"Perfect," Emily agreed.

Jimmy slapped the top of the seat. "Woo-hoo! Gotta love the news." He shook his head. "Yep . . . love the news." He looked at Paul and then Emily. His voice lowered. "I don't get it. When did we catch the Scud guy?"

Emily grinned at Paul. "We haven't . . . yet," she said. "But if we can't catch a bad guy to use as leverage on Nicas, why not *pretend* to?"

Jimmy smiled for a moment, but then his face drooped. His head shook. "Right . . ." A large grin covered his face as if he understood, but then his expression went blank. "Huh?"

Paul slowed as he drove through Altamont but then sped up again once he was out of the town limits.

"We know a few things about Ace. One, he's an organized offender, which means he likely is tracking progress on the investigation. Two, he doesn't hesitate to protect himself by killing his liabilities. Three, his whole plan revolves around the acquisition of gold from the Jameson area. His cronies didn't seem to be finished, so we think he wants to go back to finish the job," Paul said.

"Mm-hmm . . . Yep . . . Okay . . . Yeah, I think I kind of get it," Jimmy said.

Paul scowled in disbelief. "Seriously. It's not complicated. Um, a little help here, Emily."

Emily turned in her seat to face Jimmy. "It's simple. All we did is give Ace information to draw him out, to do what he naturally is inclined to do, so we can find and catch him," she said. "He'll think he's at risk with Scud being captured, so he'll be motivated to move quickly, but he'll also think the Jameson area is clear for him to resume his gold hunt. When he shows up, we'll be waiting."

"Oh. Why didn't you say so, Paul? Geez, that *is* simple." Jimmy's head bobbed. "I like it." He thought for a moment. "Why did they say Ace is Scud's assistant?"

Paul grinned. "Call it our 'tweak of the day.'" Paul smiled, wishing he could see Ace's reaction to being called "Scud's assistant." "Oh yeah, that's going to drive him nuts."

"Okay, I get all of that. Can I ask one more, teensy question?" Jimmy asked.

Paul sighed and his eyes sagged. "What is it?"

"Won't everyone be mad about the lie?"

Paul cringed, unwilling to consider Jimmy's implied point. "Define 'everyone.'"

"Okay. Local police who are still looking for Scud. Residents of Jameson who may now be in danger. The media outlets. Stark." Jimmy wasn't finished, but Paul cut him off.

"All right, I get the point."

Emily's eyebrows arched. "Do you?"

"Look, we can smooth it over with the sheriff's department. And neither the news media nor Stark will care if we catch Nicas."

"And the locals?" Jimmy asked. "Aren't you kind of setting them at the center of a possible gun battle?" Paul thought for a moment and looked at Emily, begging for her to answer the question.

"Not a problem, Jimmy. We've got a head start. We'll be to Jameson in a few minutes, and we'll make sure everyone is safe and out of the way," Emily said.

"How will you do that?"

Emily bit the side of her lip. "I'll let Paul explain. Paul . . ." Emily motioned to Paul with her upturned hand.

"Well . . . the first step is to get there fast." Paul stomped on the gas as he turned north on Highway 13 toward Jameson. "We'll figure the rest out when we get there."

(57)

POPULATION 122. THE BEDRAGGLED SUV rolled past the Jameson city limit sign.

Reverberations of gunshot blasts echoed from the same corridor of buildings at the center of town as the night before. Pajama-clad residents stepped onto their porches and peered through windows in the direction of the disquiet. Paul scanned the streets as the SUV crept along the edge of town.

"So much for figuring things out when we got here," Jimmy said. "Looks like they beat us."

"How in the—" Paul's molars ground as his jaw clenched. "Emily, call for back-up—now." He looked to his girlfriend, but she was already on her phone making the call. Paul's mind raced, struggling to conjure a plan. Jimmy was right—Paul had placed the entire town in danger, and for what? A chance to be the hero by getting the bad guys fast? At what cost?

"Forty minutes," Emily said as she hung up.

Paul's head lowered. "You're kidding, right?"

"Uh . . . no."

"We're not even supposed to be here," Jimmy reminded.

"What about local law?" Paul asked.

Emily tucked the phone in her pocket and pursed her lips. Her eyelashes fluttered. "Thrasher's contacting neighboring counties, but Daviess County law is either searching for Scud or were decimated last night on the highway attack. Stark and the SWAT team won't be here for forty minutes. We're on our own."

Paul shook his head, glancing at his watch and then staring out his side window at an old man standing on the sidewalk with a dog yipping at his heels. Paul considered rolling down his window, but it was mostly shattered anyway. The SUV slowed further, and Paul brushed the remnants of window away with his gun.

"Get back inside," Paul commanded in a whispered tone. He raised his gun so the man would take him seriously. The man frowned and then shuffled back to his house.

"Paul . . ." Jimmy began.

"Yeah."

"Paul . . ."

"Jimmy, what?"

Paul felt Emily's soft touch on his forearm. "Stop, Paul."

Paul stopped the vehicle and looked. Both Emily and Jimmy pointed out the right side of the vehicle toward an aqua-blue home one block over. Outside the home, a group of men huddled. Some wore cargo shorts with work boots while others were in pajama pants, T-shirts, and flannels. Each held a weapon. Paul threw the SUV into gear and turned right toward the gathering group.

"Paul . . . what are you doing?" Jimmy asked. "Aren't we supposed to stay away from the guys with guns?"

Paul's eyes narrowed as the SUV blockaded the street in front of the forming militia. "These aren't the bad guys, Jimmy. But if we don't stop them, it's going to be a bloodbath."

Paul hadn't finished his sentence when a rifle stuck through the window and directly at his head. He studied the man holding the weapon: shaved head, white tank, hairy arms, and a thick goatee that hid most of his ugly face. Paul smiled and raised his hands off the steering wheel. "Good morning, fellas."

The man trained his rifle on Paul while the others surrounded the vehicle. "Don't see much good about it," the man replied. "What's your business here?"

Emily leaned forward and looked around Paul at the leader. "May I?" she asked, her hand moving slowly toward her hip. A man on Emily's side of the vehicle cocked his weapon. "I'm just going to show you my badge. That's all," Emily said in a soothing tone. She reached in her pocket, removed her credentials, and held them up for everyone to see. "We're FBI. We're here to help."

Paul watched the man's eyes wander from the shattered windows to the heavy dents and scraped paint on the side-quarter panels to the bullet holes riddling the black gloss of the SUV.

"Oh good. I feel safer now," the man said. "Looks like you've been through a war zone . . . and lost."

Paul laughed, trying to lighten the mood. "We didn't lose, but we didn't win either—not yet. If you like what you see, I'll make you a great deal. 'As is,' of course."

The leader's eyes burned into Paul as he stared in silence. Crow's-feet at the man's eyes thinned and his lips remained flat. Then he lowered his weapon. The rest of the men followed their leader and lowered their weapons. An audible sigh of relief filled the air.

Paul's cheeks ballooned, and he blew through a thin slit. "Good. We're all friends." Paul's door creaked, and he stepped from the vehicle. Emily joined him, but Jimmy stayed inside, spying through the shattered rear window. Paul flashed his badge to provide additional evidence of his and Emily's authority. Paul's stare roved over the group of nine men, some of whom looked like boys. He saw one young man flinch as another round of gun blasts cracked through the center of town. "And what exactly are you men planning to do here?"

The men looked at each other, but no one dared to speak. Paul nodded to the leader with the shaved head. "Well?"

The man nodded. "I'm Josh." He paused for a long moment. "We're going to do what any man would do. Protect our families and homes."

"With shotguns and hunting rifles?" Emily asked. "You're going to get yourselves killed. Do you have any idea what you're up against?"

The man met Emily's gaze. "Does it matter?"

"Only if you're smart," Jimmy called from the window.

Josh's face became stern, and his grip on the rifle tightened. "We *will* defend ourselves. If a man came to your home and shot up the place, what would you do?"

Emily nodded. "He's got a point."

"Look, guys, I understand the sentiment, but we cannot allow you to put yourselves at risk. I suspect the shooters are heavily armed. Your shotguns and rifles will be no match for them. You *will* die," Paul said. He watched the crowd, but there was no evidence that his words had penetrated their thick skulls.

"Right now, they're shooting up the old main street. I don't know why they're doing it, but I don't much care," the man said. "We're not going to wait for them to move on and start shooting up the houses down the block, or up the street. We are going to make a stand." Another round of blasts echoed from the town center. "Besides, those are just shotgun blasts. We can take them."

Shattered glass fell to the ground at the rear of the SUV as one leg stuck out of the rear window. Then another boot kicked through and cleared the glass. Jimmy climbed out the back window holding an M4 assault rifle. "This is what they've got," Jimmy said, holding up the weapon.

"Where'd you get that?" a man asked.

"War zone," Paul replied.

"Do you really want to go against assault rifles with a couple of shotguns and some rifles you use for deer hunting?" Emily asked.

The leader remained silent as he looked at his men. Each man nodded in turn. "If need be, we'll do it."

"No, you won't. I won't allow it," Paul said.

"Men, turn in your weapons," Emily said.

The men grumbled and showed no sign of giving up their guns.

"No chance, lady," Josh said, turning to his men. "Let's go."

"It's for your own good. We'll take care of this. Give us your weapons and go back to your homes," Emily said. The men continued to murmur as they followed Josh.

Paul reached over and pulled the M4 away from Jimmy. He pointed at the men. "This isn't a request. Hand in your weapons *now*."

Josh turned back toward Paul and saw the M4 aimed at his head. "Yeah, right."

"Stop!" Paul held his weapon firm and watched the men walk away. He glanced over at Emily and then lowered the assault rifle. He sighed with exasperation. "Wait." Josh and his men kept walking. "If you refuse to follow our official request, we will not be responsible for your actions or injuries." Paul looked at Emily and accepted defeat. The men kept walking. "At least let us help you protect your town."

The men stopped. Their grumbles and frowns first turned to looks of confusion and then to stern looks of determination as they faced Paul. "We're listening."

"I'm really going to regret this," Paul mumbled to himself, his head shaking gently from side to side. He felt his stomach gurgle and his heart race with nervous anticipation.

Emily stepped forward. "We'll break into three groups. Agent Stephens will lead the first group to flank Main Street. I'll lead the second group to cover from this side. Jimmy will go with the third group."

"What's the third group do?" Jimmy asked.

"Go door to door and get the people to leave. If they don't have transportation, move them to the edge of town. If the gunmen decide to spread out, we want everyone clear of the danger," Emily said.

"Where will we meet?"

"The school," Josh said. "It's at the edge of town and big enough for everyone."

Paul nodded. "Okay. The school is our fallback location. You—little guy, you come with me."

"The rest of you, split into groups and get moving," Emily said. "Josh, you're with me." Emily strapped an assault rifle over her shoulder and gave one to Josh. She handed the last weapon to Jimmy. "Check your ammo. Know what you've got."

The group stood ready. "Be smart. Stay safe. Follow instructions. Let's go."

(58)

EACH OF THE THREE TEAMS huddled for a moment and then separated. Jimmy and his group spread out across three town blocks and began going door to door, urging people toward the east end of town. Emily's team fanned out and pressed ahead toward Main Street. Emily raised her weapon as she stepped in a sideways, crossover pattern, her head turning to keep an eye on the remainder of her teammates. She motioned with her head, and they spread further.

Paul closed his eyes and stood in silence. He listened to the rapid shotgun fire and then the dead quiet. A dog barked and the leaves rustled in the gentle breeze. The scent of gunpowder hovered in the air. Paul opened his eyes and stared at the three members of his team, who were staring back at him. "Ready?" They nodded and grunted. Paul took a deep breath. "Go."

Paul broke into an instant jog. He held his weapon in both hands across his chest as his head swiveled. His men followed closely behind, their steps falling into cadence. Paul led the men wide to the north side of the lane as they approached Main Street. They stopped at the corner of the building where Paul had parked his SUV the night before. Paul moved laterally across the street and then behind the cover of an adjacent building. He crept quietly with his men close behind.

Looking onto Main Street, Paul saw the remnants of Jimmy's borrowed Dodge Charger wrapped in yellow police tape. Law enforcement had been too consumed with transporting prisoners and searching for Scud that the vehicle's carcass remained on the street where it had been gunned down.

Paul could see five gunmen. Four men held assault rifles as they created a semicircle perimeter around the man holding a shotgun. The man pulled the stock against his shoulder and fired the shotgun at the abandoned storefront. He cleared the action and then fired in rapid succession as his aim shifted gradually to the left with each shot. Each spray of shot lanced the building façade. When all the shells were spent, the gunman reloaded while the other men stepped close to the building and stared at the wall, brushing their hands softly over the brick. After a moment of staring and inching farther down the building, the men returned to their positions behind the shooter.

"We've got to do better than that," the shooter called and then continued to spray the building in a grid pattern. "Mr. Nicas will be here soon. He expects results."

"What are they doing?" one of Paul's men asked.

Paul shook his head. "They're desperate to find something, and they're afraid to fail." Paul grinned. "They know time is running out. This can work to our benefit," Paul whispered to his huddled group.

Paul motioned with his fingers, and the men followed him through a cluster of trees, behind a parked car, and then behind another building on the south side of the street. With one motion of his hand, the men spread out and took up positions between buildings along the backside of the street—close enough to see what was happening but far enough away to provide adequate cover. Paul pressed a button on his phone and waited. "Is your team in position?"

"Yes," Emily replied.

Paul examined his watch. "Where's our help?"

"Twenty-five minutes, give or take. Be patient. No one's in danger. Hold your position. We can wait."

"Agreed." Paul hung up.

The shooter reloaded while his men examined the brick wall. "Hurry up!"

The gunmen studied the wall, until one man yelled, "I've got something!"

The shooter held his weapon down and stepped toward the wall. He looked and then smiled. "We may all get to keep our heads after all," he said with an uneasy chuckle. "Back away."

The men moved away from the wall and the shooter resumed his fire, concentrating on the area he had just examined. He lowered his weapon again, and the gunmen all moved forward to reexamine the brick. "What do you see?"

"I've got two bricks."

"That's not going to cut it. There's got to be more—a lot more. We've got fifteen minutes until locals show up. We move out in ten." The shooter reloaded. "Where's the freaking gold?" he screamed. He raised his weapon and turned it toward the brick buildings on the other side of the street. He fired five shots randomly at different buildings and crumbling walls as his fellow gunmen dropped to the ground to avoid his haphazard line of fire.

Paul motioned for his men to drop and remain silent. The men fell to their stomachs and covered their heads in silence. After another round of shooting, Paul lifted off the ground and peeked around the wall at the gunmen standing in the center of the street. He heard some muffled curses. Then one man jogged to a Yukon at the end of the street and removed a small battering ram from the back. He held it over his shoulder and raced back to the man with the shotgun. The other men stood in various positions near the walls, searching the brick. They each shook their head in failure.

The gunman exchanged his weapon for the ram and walked to the brick wall. He traced a small area of shining gold with his finger, then he gripped the handles on the battering ram and swung the stubby metal pole against the brick. Bricks crumbled and fell to the ground. He swung again, causing more bricks to tumble. The man held the ram and beat it against one brick at chest level until it fell to the ground with a metallic thud. He bent down and picked it up. "There are more of these. Find them."

Two men remained on the east side of the street, and the other three searched the brick buildings on the west. "Got one!" The man utilized the ram to extricate the desired brick while the others continued searching.

Paul looked at his men who remained on the ground. Their desperate expressions signaled their desire to do something, anything before the thugs dismantled their town brick by brick. Paul wagged his head and motioned to the ground, urging them to remain still, when out of the corner of his eye, he noticed movement. His head jerked to the left in time to see one of his men hop to his feet and scurry around the corner of the last building.

Paul crawled to the front of the alley and peeked toward the end of the street. The smallest man in his group slunk around the bumper of the first Yukon. Paul caught himself mouthing words of warning. He watched as his teammate slid down the side of the Yukon. As the driver's side door slowly opened, the man looked inside and then pulled himself into the cab. The door closed with a gentle wisp. Paul couldn't tell if he had heard a sound or if it was merely his imagination meeting his expectation.

Paul's gaze transferred from the Yukon to a man on the opposite side of the street. The gunman turned toward the Yukon and raised his assault rifle. He heard. Paul glanced to the other two men on his team and motioned upward. The first man took the hint and jumped to his feet. He searched for a spot and then climbed up the back of the building by gripping the thick electrical conduit line leading to the roof. Paul motioned for the other man to take position around the side of the building near the Yukon. The man hesitated but obeyed.

Paul looked back to the Yukon. The gunman held his weapon ready as he approached. He moved forward, looking through the side rear windows until he approached the front passenger door.

Paul pressed a button on his phone and mumbled, "Hold your position. Cover me." He clicked his phone off and hoped Emily was listening.

The gunman scooted alongside the Yukon, peering through the windows, but before he could look inside the front window, Paul placed his weapon on the ground and stepped out of the shadows onto the street.

(59)

"Hey, hey, hey. What do you guys think you're doing?" Paul mumbled as he staggered out of the shadows onto the street.

The gunman at the Yukon halted and turned to Paul, his back against the window. He took aim.

Paul grinned despite the flurry of weapons aimed at him. He slurred his words. "Thiss iss *my* town." He took a clumsy step and stumbled but caught himself before falling. "Ya'll acting crazy and such. People is trying to sleep 'round here, don't ya know?"

The gunmen remained still, their eyes a blur of confusion. "Beat it!" one gunman yelled.

Paul stepped closer and stumbled again, this time falling at one of the men's feet. "Beat it? Me?" he asked, looking up at the barrel of the weapon. He raised his hand as if looking for someone to pull him up. The gunman ignored him, so Paul attempted to stand but fell again. He stared at the man's feet and took a deep breath as he considered his next move. Then, swiping his arm around the gunman's ankle, Paul pulled the gunman's feet out from under him. The man fell backward and a spray of bullets exploded into the air as his finger pinched the trigger. The gunman crashed to the ground and cracked his head on the pavement. Paul grabbed the dormant M4 as the other gunmen hurried to place him in their sights. Then the street erupted in gunfire.

The gunman closest to the north wall squeezed off two rounds, and Paul dove and rolled toward the gutter. The shots ricocheted off the pavement, missing their mark. Paul scurried to his feet and took the only cover he could find. His heart and breathing raced.

A gunman near the crumbling building aimed again, but three tight rounds whizzed by his ear, exploding brick dust into his face. The gunman turned as his frantic eyes searched for a target. He gritted his teeth and then lowered his weapon as the glare from a sniper's scope shined across his eyes. He growled, placed the weapon on the ground, and raised his hands in submission.

The gunman near the SUV took aim at Paul, who crouched behind a thick fire hydrant. Before the gunman could shoot, the passenger side door of the Yukon flew open and hit the man, causing him to sprawl onto the ground with his arms outstretched. One of the Jameson team members rushed from the corner of the building with his deer rifle held at his waist like an Old West gunslinger. He placed a knee into the back of the gunman lying on the ground. He pressed the barrel of his rifle into the man's head. "Push the gun away," he yelled in a high-pitched, shaky voice. The gunman complied.

The small man inside the Yukon grabbed the door and slammed it shut. He flipped down the visor and then rifled through the glove box but found nothing. Then he searched the center console and found a single key set on the bottom. He fired up the Yukon and pressed the gas, jumping the vehicle onto the sidewalk toward a gunman who was exchanging fire with Emily's team. The gunman turned to face the roaring SUV as a bullet crashed into the wall behind him. His eyes darted back to his armed target and then again at the SUV.

Josh emerged from the shadows of the building alley with his weapon raised. "Drop it now!" Josh screamed.

The gunman glanced back at the distracting SUV, which skidded to a stop. He refused to lower his weapon.

"Don't do it!" Josh yelled, but the gunman didn't listen. The gunman swung toward Josh and pulled the trigger. Josh dropped him with a shot to the chest. Josh's eyes widened as he watched the man collapse to the ground. Josh grabbed his leg and then limped closer to examine his enemy.

Blood pooled on the sidewalk, and the gunman remained still. Josh stood over his kill and winced as he bent over to examine the bloody hole in his thigh. He picked up the dead man's gun and strapped it around his shoulder. He tried to turn but fell to one knee. He spun in place and searched for another target.

Paul remained crouched behind the peeling silver hydrant. He extended his weapon around the hydrant and watched the remaining team members emerge from their protected hiding places between and on top of buildings. He caught Emily's eye as she stepped from behind a crumbling wall with her weapon aimed at the fifth man. The man held only his battering ram and backed away from Emily. He appeared to be unarmed. Emily's brisk stride brought her to within ten yards of the man when he turned his back to her. He dropped the metal ram and took a crisp step forward. "Stop! FBI. Don't even think about running!" she yelled. As she finished her warning, he started to run. Emily took aim. Her finger tickled the trigger, but then she lowered her weapon. She looked back at Paul. "Are you okay?"

Paul nodded. "You?"

"Why do they always have to run?" Gripping her M4, Emily gave chase.

Surveying the scene, Paul saw his cadre of men standing above the three prisoners and one dead gunman. Their smiles and hoots seemed to brighten the early summer morning, not because of what they had done, but because of what they had protected.

Paul signaled his approval with a simple thumbs-up and then looked back at Emily chasing after the runner. Paul reached into his back pocket and then held up zip ties for the men to see. "Zip 'em and load 'em. Meet back at the school."

Josh waved him on.

"Josh, you're in charge," Paul said, nodding his gratitude to the town leader. He tossed the zip ties to the ground and then turned to give chase.

(60)

JIMMY HELD THE DOOR AT the main entrance to the school. An old woman and a mother with five crying children were the last to enter on their way to the gymnasium. Jimmy released the door and stood outside as he watched cars drive past the school and out of town. He felt proud for warning the town and relieved that only a small number of residents chose to gather to the school for safety. Much of his burden had been lifted, but Jimmy stood as sentry in front of the glass door with his borrowed M4 resting across his arm.

The gunfire from the center of town had died down minutes earlier, and Jimmy assumed that was a good sign, though he couldn't be sure. He watched and waited, occasionally opening the door for a pajama-wearing straggler who wanted to enter. He paced to the side of the two-story brick school and waved at his teammates who kept watch at each corner.

"What now?" one man asked.

Jimmy shrugged his shoulders. "We wait . . . I guess."

Vehicles abandoned the town, and Jimmy's eyes followed them as they swept around a broad bend and out of sight. His shoulders loosened and the corners of his lips turned up with satisfaction, then his expression fell flat. He leaned forward and squinted, not believing what he saw. Two Yukons rounded the bend and drove *into* town. They slowed as they approached the school and then parked sideways in the middle of the street, parallel to each other, ten yards apart.

Doors swung open and men holding assault rifles emerged from the SUVs. The road was blocked with no access for vehicles to enter or exit the town, while five men bearing weapons looked desperate and seriously perturbed. The men spread out and stood ready like confederate soldiers, waiting for their general to order an attack.

Jimmy's chin dropped, and the weapon in his hands started to shake. "Oh crap."

*****

Cropland extended from the farming community at the outskirts of the small town. Paul and Emily stood together at the edge of a cornfield. The feed corn had tasseled but only reached as high as Emily's forehead. Emily rose onto her tiptoes as she attempted to look over the vast field for a sign of movement. "Do you see anything?"

Paul held a hand above his eyes to block the sun. His head swiveled from side to side. He could hear the harsh brushing of cornstalks but couldn't tell the direction from which the sound came. The runner had been fleeing eastward, so Paul focused his search along the same course when he spotted swaying stalks of corn. The line of bending stalks cut diagonally across the field. "There," Paul said, pointing.

Emily placed her hand on Paul's shoulder and lifted herself higher, but she still couldn't see. She followed Paul's finger past the cornfield and saw the school a short way in the distance. "Oh. That's not good."

"What do you think?" Paul asked.

Emily glanced at her watch. "I think we need help. And I think we don't want that guy anywhere near the school," Emily said. She exhaled, running her fingers through her blonde hair. "You go through, and I'll go around. Deal?"

Paul nodded. "Deal."

Without hesitation, Emily sprinted along the edge of the cornfield parallel with the road, still gripping her weapon. Paul brushed the first cornstalks to the side as he entered the field. Above the corn, his eyes locked on his subject, and he broke into a run, taking a tight angle toward the school in hopes of heading the assailant off in time.

*****

"Inside, everyone. NOW!" Jimmy yelled to his teammates.

They abandoned their posts around the building and raced toward the front entrance. "Who are those guys?" one of the men asked as he pushed through the door.

Jimmy stared at the Yukons. "Those guys are the problem," Jimmy said. He followed the last man in and then chuckled nervously as he bolted the glass door. "Lot of good this is going to do," he mumbled.

Jimmy watched the men standing in the road, knowing he would be little match for them when they decided to breach his weak defense. He hoped they wouldn't bother. Jimmy tried to consider various defensive tactics he could use to hold them off, but the only thought that kept coming to mind was *run*. He wanted to run. His hands shook. His thoughts swirled, and he could hear the echoed sound of his own breathing.

Jimmy snapped from his thoughts as a teammate brushed him on the shoulder and spoke. Jimmy looked at the man, but the garbled words sounded like they were being spoken underwater. Jimmy nodded anyway, and the man jogged down the school hallway toward the gymnasium. Shaking his head, he tried to dislodge the cobwebs, but the shaking only made his head hurt.

Outside, the gunmen began to stir. They abandoned their positions in the middle of the street and took cover behind their vehicles. Jimmy pressed his cheek against the cool glass, hoping to see what was happening, when he noticed the approach of flashing lights. The glass prevented a thin grin from forming on the right side of his lips. He saw two Sheriff's cruisers stop fifty yards away, near the wide bend that led out of town. Jimmy pressed his entire body and face against the glass and watched the action unfolding on the street.

THWUMP!

The thud against the glass nearly made Jimmy fall onto the floor.

He took five steps back and stared at the door, his eyes the size of silver dollars. The sound of his heart mimicked the *thwump* on the glass and then seemed to stop. He blinked rapidly, his shoulders bouncing with each breath.

A man wearing boxer shorts and a T-shirt stood at the door. "LET ME IN." Jimmy stared at the man but didn't move. The man turned and glanced behind him and then at the two battle lines taking shape down the road. "LET ME IN," he repeated. Jimmy tried to swallow and then took a step toward the glass. "They're after me. AND THEY HAVE GUNS!" the man screamed.

Jimmy took a deep breath and then unlocked the dead bolt. The man entered and Jimmy fumbled to relock the door. "Everyone's in the gym. Down the hall," Jimmy said, pointing. The man nodded and ran to join the others. Jimmy watched him disappear through the doorway into the gym. He scratched his fingers nervously on his head as he thought about the people in the gym. They were all counting on him.

THWUMP! THWUMP! Jimmy gasped.

"Jimmy, open up." Jimmy grabbed his chest and nearly dropped his weapon. "Jimmy, hurry."

Jimmy looked to the door. "Paul?" He quickly unlocked the dead bolt. "What's going on?"

Paul turned to the left and then looked down the hallway to the right. "Did a man just come in here?" Jimmy nodded. "Where'd he go?"

Jimmy pointed. "Why?" he asked but was afraid to hear the answer.

Paul bent over and took a moment to regain his breath. Corn pollen that had settled in his dark hair fell to the ground as he shook his head. He looked at his friend and with one raised eyebrow told Jimmy everything he needed to know. Jimmy tried to breathe, but the entire school was suddenly devoid of oxygen. After a pause, a soft rasp of breath entered through his hanging mouth. "I . . . I didn't know. Paul, I swear I didn't know."

"It's okay, Jimmy."

"He looked like the other people. He was in his underwear."

Jimmy waited but then grabbed Paul by the shoulders. "He said he was running from people with guns."

"Yeah, Jimmy, I know. He was running from me."

Jimmy bent over as he hyperventilated. If he'd had any food in his stomach, he would have vomited. "Paul, I . . . I . . . I didn't . . ."

"That way?" Paul asked, pointing down the hallway. Jimmy nodded. "Okay, Emily's right behind me." Paul pounded Jimmy on the back and squeezed the uninjured shoulder. "Don't go having a heart attack when she knocks on the door, okay?" He smiled, and Jimmy tried to reciprocate. "Just let her in and point her in my direction. Got it?"

Jimmy stood tall and took two deep breaths. He met Paul's stare. "Yeah, I got it."

(61)

EMILY PLACED AN ARM ACROSS Jimmy's chest as they stopped near the gym doors. "In there?" she asked. Jimmy nodded. "Wait here." Her eyes locked on to his. "I mean it." Emily stepped to the side of the metal gym door and peeked around the corner. "Everything okay in there, Paul?" she called.

Paul stood beneath the basketball rim with his automatic weapon held tight against his shoulder and his eye peering through the sight. "Not really."

Emily stepped inside and gulped. Three men with rifles joined Paul from various points around the gym. Each aimed at the center of the basketball court, where a man shielded himself with his arm wrapped tight around a teenage girl's shoulders. The man stood in his boxers and a T-shirt and held something near the girl's throat. Emily stepped to the side of Paul and entered farther into the gym for a better view.

"You don't want to do that," Emily said as she saw the serrated hunting knife at the girl's throat.

The man adjusted the knife and pressed harder. The girl cried out as the tip of the knife released a bead of blood from her neck. "Put your weapons down and back away. I'm not kidding," the man yelled. "Back away or I'll cut her."

Cries and groans filled the gym as the town residents watched.

"That's not going to happen," Emily said. She turned to Paul and whispered. "Do you have a shot?"

"No."

"I said drop your weapons or she's *dead*."

Emily looked into the eyes of the teenage girl. The teenager's eyes and lips were reddened by the steady stream of tears.

"Okay. Everything's going to be fine," Emily said to the girl. She turned her eyes on the man. "You're scaring her. That's not going to get you what you want. Killing her will definitely not get you what you want . . . unless you're hoping for a shot between the eyes. I'd be happy to oblige you on that one by the way." Emily glared at the man with determination and continued to speak softly. "Let her go and we can talk. No one needs to get hurt."

The man adjusted the knife again, and the girl's sob echoed off the wood floor and cinderblock walls. "Stay away."

"Okay. Easy there," Emily told the man, lowering her weapon. "Take the shot as soon as you have it," she whispered to Paul as she set her assault rifle on the floor. She stood up with her hands open in front of her. "See, it's okay. We don't want to hurt you, but we need to understand what you're doing. Why did you come in here? What do you want?"

"If I don't find the gold, I'm dead anyway. I don't care what you do to me!" the man screamed. "And it won't bother me one bit to take a couple of you with me."

"Now you see, that's just not very nice," Jimmy said, peeking his head into the gym.

"SHUT UP!"

Emily looked at Jimmy and Paul and then again at the man with the knife. She took one deliberate step in front of Paul, her left shoulder just below the barrel of his M4. She stepped slowly toward the man at the center of the gym. "Just help me understand. What do you hope to accomplish here?" Emily asked.

"Don't play dumb. You know what I want."

"No. I really don't."

"I want the artifacts. Someone has them or knows where they are. I WANT THEM! I NEED THE GOLD."

Emily shook her head. She scanned the rest of the room as people from the town backed up toward the bleachers. The adults held the crying children close, shielding their eyes from the pending tragedy.

Emily looked back at the man. "I'm not playing dumb. I have no idea what you're talking about. I'm not being difficult. That's just a fact." She took another slow step forward. "You're standing in your underwear, rambling about gold and artifacts. You're acting like a total loon."

The man pushed the knife tighter into the girl's neck. He seethed through clenched teeth. "Scud said he had the artifacts, but he missed the meet. I know you have Scud. That means you have the artifacts," the man said. "I WANT THEM."

Emily grinned, somewhat amused that the man possessed some clarity of thought. "Okay. I'm following you now. Scud . . . Artifacts . . . Gold. Somehow the artifacts lead to the gold. Interesting."

The man nodded. "That's what I said."

"And I bet your boss really wants that gold, doesn't he? What's his game? Maybe help his Uncle Alex reclaim control of the Kansas City organized crime syndicate?" The man scoffed. Emily stepped forward slowly. "See, I thought you were acting crazy, but really you're just desperate. You stripped down to make it look like you were a member of the town fleeing the bad guys. Okay—kind of smart. You say you snuck in here looking for the artifacts, but I'm thinking you really came in here for security. You're hiding from your boss, aren't you? You know what he'll do to you if he finds you." The man didn't respond. "You see, I've heard about what your boss does to people who fail him. And you have certainly failed him." Emily shuddered as she shook her head. "It's not pretty. You don't want to end up like the guy in Kansas City. Oh yeah, I understand perfectly."

The man nodded as he dug the tip of the blade deeper into the girl's throat. She squealed in pain. Emily looked at each man holding a rifle and then back at the girl. "The problem is we don't have the artifacts, and we're not going to protect you. We won't even kill you." She paused for a moment while she thought. "But we may send you back outside to join the rest of your group. They're fighting in the street. Why aren't you with them?" Emily paused and bit on her lower lip. "I'm sure they'll be happy to see you. I know Ace Nicas will be.

"Men, lower your weapons," Emily commanded. The armed townspeople looked at each other and then at Paul. "It's okay. Trust me. Lower your weapons," Emily repeated as she took another step toward the girl. She locked eyes with the girl and mouthed, "I got you."

"Emily!" Paul whispered.

Emily ignored his call and took another slow step forward. "Everything is going to be just fine." Her outstretched hands gestured downward in a calming motion.

"What are you doing?" the man yelled. "Stay away. Don't move."

"Nope. Sorry." She took another step closer. "I can't give you what you want. Instead, I'm going to give you what you fear most."

"Emily, what are you doing?" Paul hissed.

"Holding on to that girl is only going to make it easier for me to take you down. Have you ever tried fighting while holding on to a prisoner?" Emily asked. "I have, and it's not easy." Emily glanced behind her and noticed Paul still holding his weapon. "Paul, it's okay. Put it down."

Paul grumbled under his breath, bent down, and set his weapon on the wood floor. He nodded to the other men, and they followed his lead.

Emily took another step closer. "I've got to warn you, I'm tougher than I look." She stepped again and then bent down on one knee. She lifted the leg of her jeans to expose a small Velcro holster strapped to her ankle. She removed a thin knife. "You really only have one choice. Face your boss, or drop that ridiculously huge knife and let the girl go." She smiled at the man for reassurance. "It's going to be fine. Trust me. Answer our questions and we'll protect you."

Emily stood face to face, five feet from the girl.

"Stop. I'm warning you. Stay away." The man held his grip around the girl's shoulders and pressed the knife underneath her chin, eliciting a yelp from a woman in the crowd.

"She can't help you," Emily said, looking past the girl to the man with the knife. "Let her go."

The man looked around the gym and then stopped his gaze at Emily and studied her. Emily approached the man, gripping her knife. The man's shoulders rose, and he breathed heavily; then, in one harsh motion, he released his grip on the girl and shoved her toward Emily.

Emily opened her arms and grabbed the girl, stopping her momentum. "You okay?" The girl's head bobbed. Emily released her. "Go." The girl ran past Emily toward the bleachers and buried her head in a woman's shoulder.

The man stood in front of Emily, his knife still in hand. His shoulder's rose and his eyes widened as each of the men picked up their guns and placed him in their sights. "You'll protect me?"

Emily nodded. "Yeah. Give us your boss, and we'll protect you. Didn't you know you're my new best friend?"

The man held the hunting knife between his thumb and forefinger and then dropped it. As the blade stuck in the wood flooring, the deafening crack of a single gunshot echoed through the gym. The man fell to the ground beside his knife. Blood oozed from the center of his chest and pooled around the blade.

(62)

THE METAL DOOR AT THE opposite side of the gym slammed closed. Emily bent over and examined the man lying in his blood but quickly abandoned hope. She shook her head and looked up to see Paul sprinting across the gym.

Two other men joined Paul as he pressed the bar on the door. The door swung open, flooding the gym with morning sunshine. Paul squinted into the sun and stepped out of the school, his gun raised. The instant impact of automatic-weapon fire exploded all around him. One of the men yanked Paul back inside and pulled the door closed.

Paul gripped his weapon, backed up against the gym wall, and looked at the ceiling as he tried to control his breathing. He struggled to slow his rapid breaths into steady streams—in and out, but the tighter he held his weapon, the more it shook.

Racing to the group of men, Emily stopped in front of Paul and placed a hand on his heaving chest. "Paul, are you all right?"

He swallowed and then nodded, but Emily knew better. She stared into Paul's wandering eyes, placed her hands on his cheeks, and forced him to look at her. She pulled his face close to hers and then planted a forceful kiss on his trembling lips. She looked at the other men standing near and instantly became cold. "That was stupid, Paul. Be careful," she said, hitting his chest with the side of her fist.

Paul's brow furrowed. He pulled Emily in for a tight hug and then kissed her again. He took another deep breath and then released her. "Yes, boss," he said with an uneasy smile.

Emily stared into Paul's eyes. Satisfied with his recovery, Emily turned her attention to the other two men. "Okay. You, go back to the front of the school. Don't let anyone in here unless they've got a badge. If anything looks wrong, shoot first, ask questions later," she said to one of the men as she handed over her assault rifle. "And you," she said, pointing to the other, "you stay in here with the people. Gather everyone into a corner and watch. Same instructions—shoot first."

Both men nodded.

"But first, we've got to get out there." Emily motioned to the door. "We'll go right. Cover us," she instructed.

Paul and Emily took their positions at the side of the door as the man crouched in front. He looked at the agents and nodded, then pushed the door open. Emily and Paul burst from the gym into the school playground and ran to the right side as their ally laid down cover fire with the M4. No other shots were heard.

The man closed the door and then gathered the townspeople into a defensible corner as his partner raced out of the gym to guard the front entrance of the school.

*****

Jimmy followed his teammate and strained to look through the glass door at the battle lines between the Yukon gunmen and the two sheriff's deputies. The deputies occasionally yelled some commands to the gunmen, which seemed to have little impact, but there was no gunfire. Jimmy was thankful, but surprised.

He watched as two men left their positions behind the first Yukon. They scuttled back to the second and climbed in. "Not much of a fight is it?" Jimmy said to his partner.

"They're just sitting there. They're not doing anything. What's up with that?"

Jimmy thought for a moment. He looked at the scratch on

his shoulder that he preferred calling a "flesh wound" and picked the blood-dried cloth away from his skin. He gazed back out the window. Even though the deputies hadn't resolved the situation, it hadn't gotten worse either. Jimmy felt a wave of relief just knowing they were there.

"Look."

The other gunmen left their positions and climbed into the back of the second SUV, leaving only one gunman guarding the front line. "They're getting ready to run," Jimmy said. "Is there another way out of town?"

"North side . . . leads back to Highway 13."

Unlocking the glass door, Jimmy poked his head through a crack and then slithered his way out of the building.

"Get back here! What are you doing?" his partner called.

Jimmy ignored the man as he slowly backed his way along the school wall. He gulped as he heard the door lock behind him and watched as the back door to the second SUV opened. No one got in or out. Then the Yukon engine turned over and revved with the door still hanging open.

The lone gunman at the front SUV looked back with a surprised expression when the engine roared, but he quickly returned his attention to the sheriff's deputies. Jimmy watched him as he pulled a cell phone from his pocket and held it to his ear. His lips never moved; he only listened and then hung up. He resumed his position, weapon raised over the hood of the Yukon.

Jimmy inched his way farther along the shadow of the exterior wall toward the action. He placed each step carefully. His eyes darted from the deputies to the lone gunman at the front Yukon and then to the open door on the second Yukon.

"Stop!"

Jimmy swung around and looked back to the opposite end of the school to the source of the yell. Gunfire cracked, and a man in a gray suit sprinted from behind a cluster of trees toward the open Yukon door. Paul and Emily gave chase. The front passenger side window lowered, and an assault rifle extended as it fired on the chasing agents.

Emily and Paul dove to the ground and took aim at the Yukon. Sprawled on the grass, they fired defensively as the suited man plunged into the backseat and slammed the door closed.

The gunman at the front Yukon spun around and prepared to open fire on Emily and Paul. Jimmy placed his weapon against his shoulder and lined up his shot. He pulled the trigger and felt the kick from the weapon as it slammed into his shoulder. Jimmy watched the lone gunman crumple. The shot had entered his abdomen. Jimmy swallowed and then glanced at Paul and Emily lying flat on the ground. He held the weapon even tighter and joined them in spraying the SUV. The passenger window went up as the tires spun in reverse.

Jimmy stepped away from the wall as the Yukon sped away in reverse and then watched the deputies climbed in their cruisers to give chase.

(63)

Ace Nicas ripped off his suit jacket and then wiped the sweat from the side of his face. He rotated his jaw with an exaggerated motion.

"Sir, are you hit?" the driver yelled.

Ace examined his body and took mental inventory of every ache and pain. "No." He looked through the windshield as the FBI agents stood and as the police cruisers inched their way around the abandoned Yukon. "Do it now," he commanded. "Blow it!"

The front passenger removed what looked like a garage door opener from the glove box. He looked at Ace and then out the front windshield and pressed the button. The abandoned Yukon burst into a wall of flame. The hood blew twenty feet in the air and the windows exploded, spewing glass projectiles in every direction.

The whites of Ace's teeth shined as he massaged the brilliant light from his eyes. The police cruisers halted in place next to the burning wreckage and the agents sprawled on the ground, motionless.

"Did we get them all?" Ace asked amid the joyous bellowing inside the escaping Yukon. He looked closely at the police cruisers and then cursed as the doors opened and the officers stepped clear of the inferno. They had survived the blast but were stopped nonetheless. "It'll do," Ace said, and his men started to laugh.

Ace looked out the back window as the Yukon shifted into drive and turned onto a narrow side street. His eyes widened momentarily as he saw a man running at the vehicle and firing an assault rifle. "Time to cut our losses." Ace snarled. "I'll make my associates understand. Let's get out of here." The driver stepped on the gas, pulled farther away from the shooting man, and then drove toward the north end of town.

Ace scowled as he thought about the hazards of explaining his failure to deliver the promised gold to his new associates in the syndicate. He clenched his teeth and yelled. The other men in the Yukon silenced immediately. He shook his head and looked at his men, but none of them dared to make eye contact. "Losers," he mumbled.

Ace settled in his seat and clicked on his seat belt. His heavy breaths melted away his scowl, and then a smile covered his face. "I guess I'll have to make do with thirty bricks of gold." He paused for a moment. "Some guys just have all the bad luck," he said, glancing out his side window. He blinked slowly, and his clueless men laughed. Then he saw the massive grill of another Yukon crash into the side of his vehicle.

The smile on the face and the determination in the eyes of the other driver burned into Ace's brain as the vehicles collided. The escaping Yukon lurched sideways and the windows shattered inward. The screeching sound of crunching metal scraped across Ace's eardrums, and he fell sideways and hung in place by his seat belt. The Yukon slid across the pavement on its side, and Ace's head smashed against the car door. Then everything went black.

*****

Jimmy sat on the ground between Emily and Paul and placed his weapon across his lap. He nudged each friend in an attempt to wake them, but they didn't respond. Specks of blood covered their exposed skin where tiny shards of glass had penetrated. Not knowing the extent of their injuries, he didn't dare move them. Instead, he stared into the flames of the Yukon and the closest cruiser that had also caught fire. His eyes shifted farther down the road as one officer spoke into his radio and as the other aimed his weapon at an unconscious Ace Nicas.

Josh wobbled out of his seat, holding his head, and moved toward the Yukon that lay on its side. His steps were shaky, and he favored his right leg. Blood streamed down the side of his face into his goatee, but his giant smile told Jimmy he would be fine. The other men from town climbed out of the vehicle holding their rifles. They aimed their weapons at the Yukon, helping the deputies control Ace's men as they started to stir.

Jimmy leaned back into the prickly grass and closed his eyes. He reached over and touched Paul on the head, and then Emily, trying to assure himself that they would recover fully. His breathing slowed as the rising sun baked his face. Then he heard the familiar *thwat-thwat-thwat* of a helicopter overhead. He rose up on his elbows and blocked the sun with his hand. Then his head dropped back into the grass, and he smiled as the black chopper lowered into a nearby field.

(64)

PAUL AND JIMMY PICKED UP Emily from her apartment to take her to the Kansas City International Airport. They waited and watched as the security line in the Delta terminal boarding area evaporated. It was too early for most normal people to want to fly. The blackness outside confirmed it. Most passengers had already passed through the checkpoint and were waiting in a secure area for their boarding call. Jimmy, Paul, and Emily stood together, waiting awkwardly for the right moment to say their good-byes.

Paul knew he was fidgety but couldn't control the perpetual movement that took his mind off his discomfort. He held his hands behind his back and then clasped them in front as he shuffled his feet. He swallowed and then rubbed his finger in his ear as he tried listening to a PA announcement, but the tinny sound combined with the constant ringing he'd had in his ears since the explosion made it difficult to understand.

Paul tried looking into Emily's face, but his uneasy stare kept shifting to random points around the terminal. Then he mustered the courage to look back and gaze into the face he loved. He reached and outlined a small cut on her forehead that had mostly healed and then another on her cheek.

Emily traced a longer gash on Paul's arm.

Paul watched her finger softly touching his arm, and then his eyes wandered to her one small carry-on bag.

"Light packer," Paul noted.

Emily glanced at the TSA agent who was ready to wand her. She nodded. "Yep."

"Short trip?" Paul asked.

Emily closed her eyes for a moment and opened them as she reached for Paul's hands. She pulled him close. Her soft eyes looked into his. "No, Paul. I told you I'll be gone for at least six months, maybe a year. I just can't be sure."

Paul shifted again. "Of course. I just thought that maybe plans had changed. That's all. You know . . . it's a small bag."

"Nope, plan's the same. But I won't have much need for my stuff. It'll all be waiting for me when I get back," she said. Her eyes glistened. "I'm sorry. I'm going to miss you."

Paul nodded.

"I hope you'll still be waiting when I get back too."

Paul shrugged his shoulders. "We'll see." They each turned in opposite directions, looking anywhere except at each other. "I was kind of hoping you'd change your mind though," Paul finally said, facing Emily. "It's not too late, you know. You could transfer your assignment back to working with Stark, and Thrasher . . . and me." Paul shook his head. "A year's a really long time. Stay here. I promise I'll make it worth your while."

Emily stared at her feet as she grinned nervously. "I'm sorry, Paul. I can't. This is the biggest opportunity of my life. I have to . . . I want to go."

Jimmy moved closer to his two friends and put one hand on Paul's shoulder and the other on Emily's. "Dang, I was kind of hoping Stark would have demoted you, you know, for not following his orders and all. You did have a lot riding on that last case, and with all due respect, you kind of muffed it up."

Emily laughed. "I guess 'All's well that ends well'—or at least 'mostly well.' Besides, it's Stark. And . . ."

"No one ever listens to that guy," Paul and Emily said together in unison.

"Touché." Jimmy grabbed Emily by the shoulders and pulled her close for a hug. "I'm really going to miss you." He kissed her cheek.

"Be safe, and come home soon." Jimmy patted Paul on the arm and pointed to a distant spot near a food stand. "I'm just going to wait over there. Whenever you're ready."

"Thanks, Jimmy."

Jimmy saluted and then blew a final kiss to Emily. He turned and walked away.

"Wow. He's growing up," Emily said with a chuckle.

Paul lowered his head and smiled. "Yeah, gradually, but not too much." He raised his head and looked into Emily's eyes. "So I guess this is it." Extending his arms, Paul invited Emily into a firm embrace. He kissed the cut on her forehead and then her cheek.

Emily kissed him quickly on the lips and then let go. She reached down and grabbed the handle to her bag. "Good-bye, Paul. I'll see you in six months or so." She turned and strode to the security checkpoint.

Paul stood still and watched her until she disappeared from sight. He reached into the back pocket of his jeans and removed a black felt box. He opened it slowly and looked at the glistening engagement ring inside. His chest heaved and his head flopped back. He snapped the box closed and put it back in his pocket.

"We'll see."

(65)

JIMMY PULLED HIS VEHICLE INTO the roundabout at the Far West Temple site. He parked, climbed out of the car, and then moved to the passenger side to open the door for Nicki.

"Ahh . . . that's sweet," Liz said, glancing at Clay. Liz waited for a moment as Clay climbed out but then picked up her binder and opened her own door when Clay didn't make his move to mimic Jimmy's chivalry.

Nicki turned toward the west and looked out over a small pond and rolling green hills. She reached and grabbed Jimmy's hand, so he could share the view. "So this is where the trek would have ended."

"This is it. The refuge of Far West," Jimmy said. "Back in the day, Far West was the largest town in the county. Some estimates list the population at over ten thousand. Now there's nothing but hills, corn, and cows."

Nicki smiled and squeezed Jimmy's hand. "It's gorgeous out here. Peaceful."

"And hot," Clay added.

Jimmy scratched his head. "Looks a lot different in the light when I'm not driving ninety." His eyebrows rose. "Nice view."

"And its way better when you don't have to walk," Liz added.

Jimmy turned and pulled Nicki with him. They stepped through the black cast-iron gate that bordered the four temple cornerstones and then past the planters that overflowed with an assortment of bright wildflowers and elephant ears. They walked to the northwest corner and looked through the protective casing at the rough-hewn cornerstone peeking from the ground. They read the informational plaques, looked at each cornerstone, and then stood in front and read the inscriptions on three tall granite slabs. Clay and Liz followed closely behind.

"What happened to Paul?" Nicki asked. "I thought he was coming today."

Jimmy nodded. "We dropped Emily at the airport this morning. I don't think Paul was really in the mood for another adventure," he said. "He went to work instead. Besides, he's been tracking the FBI treasure hunt for the past couple of weeks. They haven't found anything, but he doesn't think they've tried very hard. He's a *teensy* bit frustrated with the whole thing."

"That's too bad," Clay muttered and then yawned. "Now, let's talk about this 'treasure hunt.' Why are we here again?"

Liz shook her head at the boy. "Because this is the end of the trek."

"I don't think so. The trek ends when we find our treasure," Clay said.

From the look on Clay's face, Jimmy could tell the words came out harsher than he intended. "Well, it ended here for the three men who died at Crooked River." Jimmy paused and shook his head. "Patrick O'Bannion, Gideon Carter, and David Patten are all buried at the Far West Cemetery with about two hundred others who once lived here."

Nicki and Liz glared at Clay.

Clay chuckled nervously. "What I mean is, if Ace and Scud and those guys found gold in Jameson, shouldn't we be looking there too?" Clay asked. "Oh, and if we find the *treasure*, how much do we get to keep?"

"I guess it all depends on what the treasure is you're looking for, Clay," Jimmy said, winking at Nicki. "One of the things I learned during the trek is that if our motives are pure, with God's help we will find what we truly need."

Clay rolled his eyes. "Dude, seriously. You didn't lure me out here with promises of adventure just to teach me a lesson, did you? You're not going to try to have a 'moment' are you?"

Jimmy laughed and held up his hands in a defensive posture. "Hey, I'm only pointing out the obvious. I found you guys, didn't I?" Jimmy cleared his throat and then flashed his winning smile. "Kind of saved your lives actually. Not too shabby if I do say so myself. Does anyone really think I could do that without an incredible amount of help?"

"Yeah, good point. Thanks, by the way," Clay said.

Liz bit on her lower lip as she looked at the ground. "I learned something too."

"Oh great. Here we go," Clay mumbled. Jimmy nudged him with a sharp elbow.

Liz looked up after a moment and saw everyone staring at her. She smiled. "Oh, I realized that we are who we are. Events and trials only enhance our true character," Liz said.

"Nice."

"Don't get me wrong. There are things I learned about myself that I don't really like. And I have all kinds of questions I need answers to, but that just means I should do something about it."

"Join the club, Liz." Jimmy nodded and then looked at Nicki. "What about you?"

"Hmm. Well, I didn't have the same kind of experience you guys did, but . . ." Nicki thought for a moment, "I was still reminded of the power and importance of good people working together: friends, leaders, neighbors, strangers. Together we can accomplish a lot, especially when we're unified in protecting our homes and families."

Jimmy scowled as he held his head in both hands. "Too many deep thoughts. My brain is going to EXPLODE." He stared at Clay.

Clay stared back. His head cocked.

"Ah, I'm just kidding, Clay. Don't worry. My head won't *really* explode . . . probably. But that would be seriously nasty if it did."

Clay grinned. "You are one weird dude."

"Thank you. Thank you very much," Jimmy said in an attempted Elvis impersonation.

Nicki winced. "That was awful."

Jimmy grinned as he cracked his knuckles, and then his eyes narrowed. "Well, let's get down to business. Liz, would you do the honors?"

Liz removed the thin binder from under her arm and placed it on the granite bench in front of the monument. She opened it.

"We'll follow wherever the clues lead us," Jimmy said.

Clay clapped his hands together with excitement. "Now we're talking."

"Don't get your hopes up too high, buddy. I'll be pretty surprised if we find anything. If the FBI hasn't found it yet, it's going to be tough. But the clues start here," Jimmy said.

Pictures of the seer stone Scud had stolen from Kingston and the rolled tin from Haun's Mill accompanied photocopies of the other recovered documents: journal pages, the parchment from Richmond Cemetery, and notes from the Barlow book.

"We got lousy copies?" Clay asked.

"You didn't think the FBI would let us hold on to the real thing, did you?" Liz asked. "They only let us have these because we recovered the originals."

"It's a little thing they like to call 'evidence,'" Jimmy said as he made quote marks with his fingers. "They tend to lock that stuff in vaults, not let goof-offs like us play with it."

"Okay, I get the point," Clay said with a smirk. He rubbed his Mohawk and bent over to look at the binder. "So do we know what any of this stuff means?"

Jimmy smiled. "Oh yeah."

*****

Jimmy extended his arm and held out the screen of his phone for everyone to see. "So if I figure right . . ." he pressed one last button, "there could be gold bricks out there adding up to fifteen *BILLION* dollars," he said with a giant grin.

Clay and Liz mumbled to each other and then snickered.

Jimmy scowled as he noticed the skeptical glances. Their faces didn't express the enthusiasm he expected. "Wait, hold on." Jimmy recalculated and pressed the final button. "Hehe. Sorry. What I meant to say is . . . fifteen *MILLION* dollars in gold."

"Forgot a decimal point, didn't you?" Nicki teased.

Clay raised both eyebrows. "Are you sure you didn't miss another decimal?"

Jimmy mumbled as he studied a scrap of paper from his pocket. "Thirty bricks—Average weight is twenty-seven Troy pounds—twelve Troy ounces per pound at $1,600 per ounce." He typed the numbers into his calculator app and then smiled. "$15,552,000—give or take . . . of course."

Nicki's jaw dropped. She grabbed Jimmy's wrist as her knees wobbled. "Seriously?"

"WOO-HOO, BABY! That's what I'm talking about!" Clay yelled and chest-bumped Jimmy and high-fived Liz.

Liz's eyes bulged, and they looked like they'd pop out of her head. Jimmy smiled as he watched the same look of awe fall over Nicki and Clay. A hush consumed the group, and Jimmy imagined the thoughts of grandeur running through each person's head. He knew the thoughts well.

"What now?" Clay asked quietly, as if ashamed of breaking the greedy reverence. "You said you know what the clues mean, right? Where do we start?"

"Well, I know what Scud told the FBI when he was captured, but he may just be playing with them." Jimmy said.

"The creep is hardly a reliable source," Liz reminded.

The group nodded in agreement. "Yes, but he *is* motivated to work out a deal," Jimmy said.

Liz shuddered.

"Let's look at the clues." Jimmy flipped to the first page of the binder and pointed at the picture of the seer stone. "Scud had heard stories about Mormon gold from Frank Barlow when he worked at the nursing home."

"But those stories must have sounded crazy. Scud actually believed the old guy?" Nicki asked.

"Over time, the old man got Scud curious enough that he stole the John Whitmer journal pages from the Community of Christ

Temple museum. When he recognized some of Clayton Barlow's notes in the margins of the journal, Scud thought he might be onto something. So he took his buddy Ace and stole the reference book from Barlow's house in Liberty."

Jimmy turned a couple of pages. "The journal pages and the book led them to the Richmond Cemetery." Jimmy pointed at a picture of the golden bar that had been stripped of its caked brick exterior. "In addition to the brick, there was also a parchment inside the casket. That parchment scroll led Scud to Haun's Mill, where he found a wooden box, inside a stone box, buried beneath a pile of stacked rocks on the east side of the stream."

"What was inside the box?" Liz asked.

Jimmy turned the page. "A rolled up strip of tin." He stared at the picture and shook his head.

"And?"

Jimmy rubbed the back of his neck. "There's a name and location scratched into the tin." Jimmy looked at the others, enjoying their anticipation. He flipped the page and pointed to the light engraving. *C. C. Rich. NE q.*

"C. C. Rich? That was you on the trek," Clay said.

Jimmy nodded. "That's right. It's also the homestead where we camped, remember?"

Nicki nodded. "That's why Scud was there. *NE q* must have referred to the NE quarter of C. C. Rich's cabin."

Clay licked his lips as he listened. "What did he find at the cabin?"

Jimmy looked into the eyes of each member of his group and then slowly turned the page to the next photocopy. "Property deeds and a length of rope."

Clay shook his head and frowned. He sat on the bench across from the book. "Oh."

"One deed is for a plot of land about a mile from here." Jimmy flipped the page. "These compass markings on the 'seer stone' indicate a northwest trajectory from the northwest cornerstone of the temple site." Jimmy pointed to the northwest and then flipped the page back to the deeds. "The other deed is for property near

Adam-ondi-Ahman, also known as Cravensville, which is now known as Jameson."

Jimmy smiled when he finally saw a couple of nodding heads.

"But I thought the gold belonged to the Confederate Army, not the Mormons," Clay said. "I'm confused."

Jimmy smiled. "Barlow mixed up the stories. He made notes in the Church history book and in the John Whitmer journal about where the gold was hidden. Those notes were correct. He placed clues for the Confederate gold in a place where no one would think to look. That's why the gold has never been found. The stories are jumbled and the clues contradict the timelines. Unless . . . you know what to believe, and what to ignore."

Jimmy pointed at some scribbles in the margin on a journal page. "See here, this notation refers to thirty bricks of gold that were transported from Cravensville and buried near the home of Hyrum Smith at Far West. The problem is, Hyrum left in 1838. The Confederate gold wasn't transported until after the skirmish in 1862."

"I think I'm following you now," Nicki said. She looked at Liz. "How about you?"

Liz shook her head. "No."

Jimmy smiled. "Clayton Barlow used Mormon clues to explain the whereabouts of Confederate gold, even though the Mormons had been gone from the area for almost twenty-five years. The two histories don't match . . . but the locations do."

Liz's face brightened. "Okay. Now I got you."

"So we should be looking for the Confederate gold on the land where Hyrum used to live, about a mile from here?" Nicki asked.

Jimmy's head bobbed with an exaggerated nod. "YES! Thank you."

"Dude, why didn't you just say so?"

Jimmy's shoulders slumped as he exhaled. He looked at Clay and tilted his head. "I just did, wise guy." Jimmy smirked and then motioned with his hand toward the vehicle. "Would you like to find Hyrum's property?"

Clay and Liz rushed ahead to the car, and Jimmy took his time, walking behind with Nicki. "Some days I really wonder."

"Wonder what?"

"Was I ever like that?" Jimmy said.

"To hear Paul tell it, you still are . . . some days." Nicki smiled and grabbed Jimmy's hand. "But that's not a bad thing." She tiptoed up to Jimmy and pecked him on the lips.

Jimmy pumped his arm at his side. "Yes."

The group climbed in the car and drove a half mile north. A log-cabin-styled bookstore sat on the east side of D Highway with a bronzed statue of Joseph Smith looking out over the land he once possessed. Jimmy turned west on Kerr Road. The tires kicked up a plume of dust, and then the vehicle stopped at the gravel intersection of Kerr and Winchester.

"We're here." Jimmy climbed out and pointed to the property to the south. The unimproved rolling hills looked like it may have appeared in 1838, minus the Hyrum Smith house. "This was Hyrum's land. Joseph F. Smith was born in the house that was likely up there somewhere," Jimmy said, pointing to the crest of a hill. "Don't know where for sure."

Clay walked to the edge of the property but stopped at the barbed wire. He looked around and then separated the two strands of wire as he climbed through.

"Clay, you're going to get in trouble." Liz called.

Clay ignored the warning, walked through the tall grass, and stood at the top of the hill where Jimmy had pointed."

"What do you see?" Jimmy asked.

"Grass. Trees. Bugs." Clay swatted his arm.

"Is there a sign that says 'the gold is here'?" Jimmy asked.

"Nope."

"Rats! Okay, on to plan B."

*****

Clay rejoined the group. They huddled and stared at the open binder on the hood of the car. Jimmy bit the side of his lip, flipped the pages, and finally settled on the copy of Hyrum's deed to the parcel that they now stood beside.

Clay glanced at Liz and then at Jimmy. "You didn't really think there would be a sign, did you?"

Jimmy smiled at Clay's question and then his lips straightened. "No, but it feels like we're missing something just as obvious."

"How can we find a place *near* Hyrum's home if we don't know where the house was?" Liz asked. "What does that even mean? 'Near' could be just about anything?"

"You're right," Nicki said, grabbing the book from Jimmy. "We need to figure out what 'near' means." She turned to the page with a picture of the length of rope found in the box at the C. C. Rich cabin. "Do we have any idea why the rope was included with the deeds?"

Jimmy shook his head. "What are you thinking?"

"I'm thinking it was put there for a reason." She studied the picture and then read a caption below. "The rope is exactly sixteen and a half feet long. And look here," Nicki said as she pointed to a scribble in the margin of the Hyrum Smith deed. *5chain DWP oak*."

Clay squinted, leaning close to look at the copy of the faded handwriting. "You can understand gibberish?"

"Of course. I'm a teacher," Nicki said as she turned to Jimmy. "Can I borrow your phone, please?" She closed her eyes as she concentrated and then typed in an Internet search: *measurement conversion calculator*. She studied the screen and then tapped on a link.

"Would you like to share?" Jimmy asked.

"I'll tell you if I'm right. If I'm wrong, well, it doesn't matter anyways." The web page loaded, and Nicki scrolled as Jimmy looked over her shoulder.

"There," Jimmy said, his voice raised an octave.

Nicki smiled and nodded. "I see it." She typed a number into a box and then stared. "One chain = four rods." She typed into a different box. "One rod = 5.029 meters." She typed again. "One meter = 3.2808 feet." She typed into the calculator app and then she smiled. "That translates into One rod = 16.5 feet. The length of our rope."

Jimmy's eyebrows rose and Clay's mouth dropped. "Are you kidding me?" Jimmy cheered. "You are AWESOME." He thought for a moment and his lips curled into a pouty expression. "But I feel stupider now. You is smart. I is dumb."

Nicki mimicked his expression and patted Jimmy on the back. "Math measurements can actually come in handy. Who would have thunk it?"

Jimmy rubbed his eyes and then stared at the hill Clay had climbed on Hyrum's land. He turned in place as he surveyed the surrounding area. "So five 'chains' would be approximately three-hundred and thirty feet, or a hundred yards." Jimmy grinned when he noticed Liz's surprised expression. "What? I know a little math too."

Clay grimaced. "So do we have to check everything within a one-hundred-yard radius of the hill?"

Jimmy shook his head. "Nope." He stared at Clay. "You want to know why?"

Liz brushed her bangs back behind her ears. "Because there's more to the scribbled note. DWP oak," she said. "What does it mean?"

"DWP—David W. Patten . . . maybe," Jimmy said.

"What does 'oak' mean?" Clay asked.

"It's a tree, Clay," Nicki said.

"Right. So we're looking for an oak tree that has something to do with David Patten within one hundred yards of Hyrum's property. Were Hyrum and Patten neighbors?" Clay asked.

Jimmy shook his head. "I don't think so. But Patten was buried at the Far West Cemetery." Jimmy scanned the area and studied the barren grass fields. "It's got to be around here somewhere."

"So let's look for headstones," Liz suggested.

Jimmy's head listed to the side. "No. I read about it. There's nothing left. The cemetery and all the graves are unmarked. The cemetery was tilled up and used for farmland. There are no tombstones," Jimmy said, his shoulders slumping.

"Where did you read about the cemetery?" Nicki asked.

"In a book," Jimmy said.

Nicki frowned. "Could you be a little more specific?"

Jimmy thought for a moment, and then his eyes brightened. "Yeah, I know the book."

Liz reached to her side and grabbed Clay's arm as she stared at Jimmy. "Do you have it with you?"

"No. But I know where we can get it. Wait here," Jimmy said, climbing into his car.

"Wait here? And do what exactly?" Nicki asked.

"Enjoy the ambiance of the country. I'll be five minutes." Jimmy turned the car around and raced one mile down Kerr road to the intersection of D Highway. He crossed the rural highway and then entered the Far West Country Book Store. Though he appreciated the rustic beauty of the cabin-styled store, he focused on his mission. He stepped to the counter and requested his book, paid, and then rushed out the door and climbed back into his car. The wheels of his car squealed as he raced back across the street and once again down the dirt road.

The car skidded to a stop on the gravel. He climbed out and waved his book over his head. *Sacred Places of Missouri*. "It's in here."

Jimmy flipped to the index and then turned to the page that referenced the Far West Cemetery. He read. Glancing up to the hill on Hyrum's land, he then turned to the plot across the street to the north. "It's there." A short way into the distance, a small, white farmhouse with green metal roofing stood beside a large wooden barn that had almost entirely crumbled to the ground. Jimmy's eyes shifted closer to the fence line running parallel to Kerr.

"Clay, grab the shovels out of the trunk," Jimmy said in an almost imperceptible whisper. He stepped across a narrow drainage ditch and grabbed onto the rusty barbed wire as he studied the landscape. Yellow butterflies fluttered amongst the grass and purple thistles. His eyes wandered to a small mound thirty feet east of the intersection along the fence line. Ten feet to the side of the bump, a thick white trunk mingled with the wire fencing.

Jimmy ran along the road and stopped at the fat stump that acted as a fence post for the barbed wire. He raised one hand and placed it on top of the stump and then climbed the wire like he was climbing a ladder. He jumped to the other side and stood at the bump of ground. He stepped fifteen paces as he circled the small mound. His heart pounded and his breathing quickened as he tried to swallow. He looked back at the others who were watching him with hopes of confirmation.

"What are you waiting for?" Jimmy yelled. "Come on!"

Clay tossed the shovels over the fence and then leapt over. He picked up one of the shovels and nodded toward the mound. "There?"

Jimmy confirmed with a nod of his own as Clay stepped to the apex of the mound and thrust his shovel into the dirt and frantically started tossing piles of grass and dirt off to the side. Jimmy took a position near Clay and started shoveling.

Nicki pulled up on the lowest line of wire while Liz crawled underneath and then followed while Liz held it for her. When they were both through, Liz picked up her shovel and hurried to the mound in a manner that more closely resembled a skip than a run. Within moments, all four frenzied treasure hunters were digging on the small mound, struggling to stay out of each other's way.

The afternoon sun beat down, and sweat poured from Jimmy's body, saturating his shirt. He took a moment to lean against his shovel. He watched Clay, who didn't show any signs of slowing. Standing up to his thigh in the hole he had dug, Clay raised his shovel and stabbed the dirt. The shovel clanked, and Clay's arms trembled at the impact.

The clank of metal on metal echoed through Jimmy's ears. He looked at the girls, who instantly stopped digging and focused on Clay's shovel, as if expecting to see gold bubble up from the ground like black crude oil.

Their eyes widened and they circled around Clay as he skimmed the dirt with his shovel. Jimmy helped pull dirt away from the hole as Clay tossed his shovel to the side and knelt. They pulled at the dirt and brushed it away with their hands like building a sand castle at the beach. Then, the first beautiful glimmer of gold caught a ray of afternoon sun.

Jimmy dug furiously as he ran his fingers over the creases between stacked bricks. He pried one gold brick from the ground and dusted off the dirt. He lifted the gold over his head like a trophy. "We did it!"

Clay leaned back into the dirt. His chest heaved from the exertion of digging as perspiration rolled down his cheek. He wiped the sweat with his wrist, smearing mud across his face.

Jimmy passed the brick to Clay, who cradled it in his hands and then kissed it. "Unbelievable," he muttered. He shifted the brick into one hand and hefted it above his head. "UNBELIEVABLE!" he repeated.

Clay passed the brick to Liz and then to Nicki. Each took a turn holding the twenty-seven pounds of delight.

Jimmy leaned into the grass beside Clay, and his breathing returned to a moderate speed. His entire body shivered as he looked at the gold in Nicki's hand. He slapped Clay's back. "We did it, young brother. We did it." Jimmy placed his dirty hands behind his head and closed his eyes. The sun beat down on his face. Sweat dripped from his temples, and a broad smile of accomplishment covered his face.

Jimmy pulled out his cell phone and pressed a button. With each ring, his smile grew as he anticipated Paul's reaction.

(Acknowledgments)

I first want to acknowledge the leaders and the youth of the Hamilton Branch who planned and carried out a youth trek similar to the one depicted in *Gold Clash*. I particularly want to thank David and Loretta Jensen, Dave McEwen, and Cheri Battrick for their planning and coordinating of the event and for the opportunity I had to play C. C. Rich as a youth leader. Even though this trek took place years ago, I still remember it vividly and with fondness. As the Far West Ward now stands where the Hamilton Branch once did, I too hope to create memories and testimonies for our youth and members.

I'd also like to thank the citizens of Caldwell County for being so welcoming and congenial to members of the Church in this special area of LDS Church history. It is wonderful to build strong and lasting friendships and apply important lessons we've learned from the mistakes of the past. Unfortunately, while many good and faithful Christians were among both the Missourians and the Mormons, many mistakes were made on both sides. One lesson of this Missouri era of Church history is that we must always live our Christian religion fully, regardless of denomination, with charity and humility.

I'd also like to thank my test readers for their time and critique of this novel. Their suggestions and comments were very helpful in turning out my final product. Thanks to my family readers—Mica, Lindsay, Teri, Chris, and Jon; my other test readers—Ginny, Reanna, Liz, Suzie; and all others who contributed.

Last, thanks to the CFI team, especially Shersta and Melissa for being so great to work with.

(About the Author)

Steve Westover served an LDS mission in Independence, Missouri, and graduated from Brigham Young University. He lives with his family at the center of many of the LDS Church historical sites spoken of in *Gold Clash*. Steve is active in his local business community and is the bishop of a local congregation for The Church of Jesus Christ of Latter-day Saints.

Gold Clash is the sequel to Steve's first novel, *Defensive Tactics*, which was released in 2010. In 2012 Steve also released *Crater Lake: Battle for Wizard Island*, the first book of his youth fantasy series. To learn more about Steve, read his blog, www.westoversleftovers.blogspot.com or visit his website, www.stevewestover.com.

0 26575 10971 9